The Haunting of Thores-Cross

A Yorkshire Ghost Story

D0890663

Karen Perkins

LionheART Publishing House

The Haunting of Thores-Cross

For Chris

Glossary of Yorkshire Terms

Addled	Confused, muddled
Ain't	Isn't, am not, hasn't, haven't
Anyroad	Anyway
Awd Carlin	Sharp old woman
Awd	Old
Barguest	Evil spirit in form of an animal
Besom	A broom made from heather or twigs tied round a stick
Canny	Astute
Ey up	Greeting
Frit	Frightened
Gimmer	Young female sheep
Hersen	Herself
Hissen	Himself
Ken	Know
Mesen	Myself
Mithering	Fussing, pestering
Nithered	Cold/frozen
Nowt	Nothing
Owt	Anything
Poddy Lamb	Orphaned lamb
Spain	Separate lambs and ewes
Stook	Sheaves of grain stood up in field
Summat	Something
Thee	You
Theesen	Yourself
Thine	Yours
Thy	Your
Tup	Breeding male sheep/ram
Wether	Castrated lamb
Whiskybae	Whisky
Witchpost	Carved wooden post used as protection against witchcraft.

Prologue

26th April 1988

'I dare you to go up to the haunted house.'

I glared at my sister in annoyance, then up at the house. I'd been there plenty of times with Alice and my friends, but never on my own. I did not want to go on my own now.

'Double dare you.'

'You little—!' I lunged at her, but she danced out of my way. She might have been small, but she was quick.

She laughed. 'Scaredy-cat, scaredy-cat, Emma's a scaredy-cat!'

I eyed the house again, then frowned at Alice. But a double dare was a double dare. And I was not a scaredy-cat. At ten years old, I could do this. I took a deep breath, ignored the butterflies in my stomach and started walking up the hill. I didn't rush.

I scrambled through the gap in the crumbling dry stone wall that separated the house from the field, using both hands to steady myself. Something caught my eye and I stopped to have a closer look. Curious, I reached into the jumble of stones, and pulled it from the dark recess in the wall.

A little pot. Made of stone, it was rich brown in colour, roughly an inch high and two inches round with a small neck and lip. An old inkpot. I shook my head. How did I know that?

'My story.'

I froze, then spun round to check behind me. *Who said that?* I looked back at the house. There was nobody here.

Although the stone walls still stood, there were no doors, windows, nor roof. Dark holes gaped in the walls and, I knew from earlier visits, it was knee deep in sheepshit inside. I must have imagined the voice. I glanced back at Alice, braced my shoulders and took a step towards the house.

'Write my story.'

My breath caught in my throat, then I sucked in a great lungful of air, turned and ran. Dashing past Alice, I didn't care that she was laughing at me, that I'd lost the dare. I was terrified, desperate to get away from that house, that voice. It was only when I'd stopped running that I realised I still clutched the inkpot.

Chapter 1 - Jennet

28th June 1776

Pa moaned and moved in his sleep. I groaned. I knew by now that meant he had shat himself again. I had only changed the heather and straw he lay on an hour ago – I would have to go through the whole thing again: wake him and force him to move so I could take the stinking bedding away and give him fresh. I cursed. Mam's body were laid out downstairs in the hall. She would be buried tomorrow, and instead of sitting over her, I were cleaning Pa's shite.

I sighed and got up to take care of the mess. I were being unfair. The bloody flux were because of his ducking in the sheep pit. But I had seen the bloody flux before, and it did not bring such a man to this so quickly, not in three days.

I were fifteen years old, had just lost my Mam, and Pa were leaving me too. It were his grief and guilt that had reduced him to this pitiful hulk. If he wanted to stay with me – take care of me – he would fight this. I heaved him over and recoiled from the stench of blood and shite; but gritted my teeth and gathered up the dirty bedding. Yet another stinking trip to the midden.

I picked up fresh from the dwindling pile downstairs – I would have to go out and pull more heather soon. I glanced over at Mam's body, then carried the bedding up and dumped it on the bed Pa had so recently shared with her. He rolled back over – without even a flicker of his eyes to show he were aware of what I were doing for him.

Tears dripped down my face. How could this have happened? I went back downstairs, took the pot of steaming water off the fire and poured some into the bowl of herbs. I had struggled to remember what Mam had used on Robert Grange at the Gate Inn when he had been struck down with this, and eventually recalled a tea of agrimony, peppermint and blackberry leaf, then as much crab apple, bilberry and raspberry mash as she could force down his neck.

The herbs needed to steep for a few minutes, and if he would not drink any of it, I would wash his face with the tea. At least the smell were fresh. I held my head over the bowl and breathed deeply, then carried it upstairs to Pa for him to breathe in the healing steam. He were too far gone for the mash.

Mam had taught me the cunning ways since I were old enough to walk and talk. She had showed me how to recognise the restorative plants and herbs, which ones helped fevers, which helped wounds, which helped women and childbirth – even preventing a child. I knew their names, where they grew, whether flowers, leaves or roots were best, and the best times to plant and pick them. I knew what she knew. Had known. But I were struggling to remember. My thoughts were as muddy as the sheep pit she had died in. I had racked my brains to think what to brew for Pa, and had had to take out Mam's journal to check. Even so, my remedies did not seem to be doing much good.

I dipped a clean cloth into the tea and wiped his brow. I did not know of any plant that healed grief. I only wish I did.

How could this happen? How could they leave me?

'Jennet?'

I started at the sound of my name being called and went downstairs to greet Mary Farmer.

'Thee's never alone here!'

I nodded, too worn out to respond with any enthusiasm.

'Ee, I thought that Susan Gill would be here with thee.'

'She were, she had to go help William with the sheep.'

'Oh aye, likely story, she's not a one for hard work, her. Happen the smell got to her.'

I glanced up at her, but she showed no embarrassment. I realised I had got used to all but the most pungent, and wondered how badly my home smelled.

'Go on, get out of here. Go get some fresh air, this is no job for a lass. Thee's done well, but let me stay with him for a bit. Go for a walk.'

I did not need telling twice. I grabbed my shawl and nodded my thanks. When I got to the door, Mary stopped me.

'Has thee put bees in mourning yet, lass?'

I shook my head.

'Well, do it now, if thee don't, they'll never do owt else for thee, thee knows that.'

I nodded and ran. I had never been so glad to get outside. The crisp June wind blew the fresh scent of heather into my face and hair, ridding me of the scent of sickness. Chickens scattering at my feet, I hurried to the beeboles in the wall bordering the garden to tell the bees of Mam's death, ensuring plenty of honey and beeswax to come, then walked up the track on to the moor and kept going – not in the direction of the sheep-ford, but the other way, uphill where there were just space. No walls, nowt constraining me; just wind and heather. I breathed deeply, trying to forget, but very aware I were now alone in the world.

Chapter 2 - Emma

4th August 2012

'Happy?'

I turned to my husband.

'Ecstatic.'

He wrapped his arms around me. 'It's finally finished. No more problems, no more arguments with builders. The movers have gone, it's just us and our dream home,' he said.

'Thank you.'

'What for?'

'The "our". This is my dream home, really. I was the one who wanted to build here, despite the problems with the planning permission. You'd have been happy anywhere.'

'It *is* my dream home, too, Emma. It's beautiful up here, we've done the designs ourselves, made all the decisions together: it's *our* home.' He kissed me, and I held him close in my excitement. This was our fresh start. 'Shall we go in?'

'Don't even think about carrying me over the threshold.' I laughed.

'I wouldn't dream of it.' He marched to the front door and left it open for me to follow him inside. I laughed again and followed him into our new home.

The downstairs was a huge open-plan living space with the front of the house mainly glass to make the most of the view. A large stone gothic fireplace on the north wall was the focal point for the three comfortable sofas.

Set out in a squat H, the kitchen-diner took up the south

wing, while the centre and north wing were lounge, with a cosy reading corner in front of the most north-western window. A wetroom/loo, utility and mudroom were hidden away in the eastern ends of the wings and a large entrance vestibule also served as the support for the staircase.

Upstairs, there was an office in the centre and four en suite bedrooms in the wings, ready for the family we didn't yet have – would maybe never have.

I loved it and had designed it myself. Admittedly, Dave had taken my designs, changed what wasn't possible or safe, then added some strange magic to make our dream home the showstopper it was. At times I had despaired that it would ever get built, and my encroaching on his expertise had led to the most serious fights we'd had yet, but it was worth it. Our marriage had survived and we both loved it. I hugged him and he squeezed me back. I hadn't been this happy for a very long time.

Dave let go of me and bent to take the bottle of champagne out of the cool box. He opened it, poured, then held out a full plastic "glass" to me – the real ones were still in a box somewhere. We touched our drinks together in a toast, both of us beaming.

'To us and our new life,' Dave said, and we drank. He led the way further into the lounge to the large windows in the opposite wall.

'Look at that view,' he said. 'We'll have that every day for the rest of our lives, if we want it.'

I stared out of the window at the expanse of water. The reservoir was half full, lined by a rocky shore and grassy banks. Pines hugged the rise of the hill until they gave way to the purple-blooming heather of moorland. From this side of the house we could not see another building and it seemed we were alone. I watched in delight as a flock of Canada Geese landed on the water. 'I know, we're lucky.'

'It's very isolated though. I'm worried about leaving you

on your own when I go up to Scotland. I need to spend a fair bit of time up there over the next few months – at this stage in the project I have to supervise things personally.'

'I'll be fine, you don't need to worry. There's so much to do to get the house straight, I'll barely notice you're gone.' I waved my arm at the boxes behind us. 'And anyway, I love the solitude; I'll get loads of writing done, and it's not like the old days – I have a phone and a car and everything.' I laughed again.

'I know all that, but still . . . This is a big house, which makes it a target, and the thought of you being on your own concerns me.'

'I'm used to it, I lived alone for seven years before we met, and anyway, you went overboard on the security – no one will get through those windows or past all the locks.'

'Yes, but still . . .'

'Well then, don't go away so much!'

'You know I have to.'

'Yes, you have to get away regularly because you can't cope with me full time!'

He laughed at the old joke. 'Now Ems, you know that's not always true.'

'As long as you keep coming home.'

'You know I always will.' He smiled tenderly and refilled my glass. I took it, sipped, then surveyed the view again. I'd travelled extensively, but this was my favourite place in the world. I belonged here.

'The perfect place to raise a family,' Dave whispered in my ear.

'Please don't,' I said.

'I've seen you with your nieces and you'd be a wonderful mother.' He ignored my protest. 'I know you're scared after what's happened, but if we don't even try, we'll never have a family.'

'I'm not ready.'

'Em, it's been a year. You're the one who insisted on so

many bedrooms, I thought that meant you were ready to fill them.'

'Not yet, and I know exactly how long it's been, Dave. One year, three months and eleven days, to be exact.' My breath hitched in my throat and I fought to keep control. 'I can't go through that again, I won't! I can't lose another baby!' I was losing my battle against my sobs.

He hugged me. 'Hush,' he said, kissing my temple and brushing away my tears with his thumbs. 'I know you're still grieving, I am too, but look out there. This is a new start, a new beginning. The miscarriage was bad luck, that's all, food poisoning – a bad piece of chicken. There's no reason we can't have a baby, we just need to keep trying. And this would be a wonderful place to grow up.'

'I know Thruscross is a wonderful place to grow up, but I can't risk it. I'd started to believe we would have a family, and then, then . . . It's too much. We had her name picked out, the nursery was almost ready . . . and she died, before she even lived. I can't lose another baby. I can't risk it happening again – I just can't.' I took a deep breath to calm myself.

He nodded and stroked my hair, then cocked his head at the sound of a car. 'That'll be your sister with the beasts.'

'And the nieces,' I said with a small smile and wiped my face clear of tears. Alice and the girls had babysat our three dogs while we moved house.

'Our family's big enough for the moment,' I said. 'If we don't try for a baby, we can't lose another.'

Dave nodded. 'Have you thought any more about adoption?'

'No, I've been too busy with the build. Let me go and greet Alice.'

He brushed my cheek with his thumb before letting go of me. 'Will you think about it now?'

I didn't answer but went outside to my family.

Chapter 3 - Jennet

1st July 1776

Pa groaned, but did not open his eyes. I had told him we were burying Mam today, but he could not hear me. She were in her box now – a simple thing, but I had used every penny of Pa's savings to buy it. I wiped the sweat from his face. It were chilly in the house, but the fever had a tight grip on him.

The front door banged and I went downstairs. Mary and John Farmer stood by Mam's coffin.

'Jennet.' John nodded at me, cap in hand. He would stay with Pa while I buried Mam.

'Here, lass, thee's never going dressed like that!' Mary said at the top of her voice as usual. I looked down at myself. Bodice stiffened with wood and reed, petticoats, collar of linen, apron and white forehead cloth and coif to cover long hair the colour of cooked mutton – all were the best I owned.

Mary led the way upstairs, showed John into Pa's room then strode to the chest against the wall and rummaged inside it. 'Here,' she said. 'Wear this.' She held up a long black skirt and shawl. 'Come on, lass, hurry up, they'll be here soon.'

I recoiled. 'They're Mam's,' I said. I could not wear Mam's clothes to Mam's funeral.

'Well, she don't need them now, do she?' Mary answered, impatient. 'They're thine now, Jennet. Quick, go and get changed.' She pushed me out the door, and I stood for a moment, then went to my room. It were easier than arguing with Mary Farmer.

'There, that's more like it! Just in time too, they're here.'

I could not look down at myself. I could not bear the sight of Mam's clothes on me. Both skirt and shawl itched. I knew I would be aware of every thread of wool on my skin all day. More noise at the door, and I followed Mary downstairs. Digger and his son, Edward, had arrived with the cart to take Mam to the church. I let Mary Farmer organise them. It were Mary who urged their care. Mary who gave instructions to John over Pa. Mary who pushed me through the door and out into bright sunlight. It were Mam's funeral, how could the sun shine? I looked back at the house and, for a moment, pity for Pa mixed with my despair. How long before Digger's cart came for *him*?

'Come on, lass, no dawdling!'

I turned back to the cart and started the long walk behind it down the hill, Mary Farmer at my side. After a few steps I stopped hearing her endless chatter. It became just another sound of the country, like the birdsong. Ever present but meaningless. We passed the smithy and William Smith joined us, then the Gate Inn and Robert and Martha Grange.

One by one, the village turned out, dressed in their best, and fell in behind us. Mary Farmer greeted them all. I hardly noticed. I felt as if my insides had frozen. My heart, my lungs, belly, everything. With each step, they splintered further. I wondered if I would make it as far as the church at the other side of Thores-Cross or whether I would be left on the side of the lane, a heap of cracked and broken ice.

'Here.' Mary Farmer nudged me and held out a handkerchief. 'Thought this might come in useful. John won't miss it. Not today.'

I took it. I had not realised I were crying, but when I wiped my face and eyed the scrap of cloth, it were sopping wet. My eyes and nose must have been streaming since we left the house.

I scratched my shoulder. Remembered I were wearing Mam's clothes and lost myself in sobs. Mary Farmer tried to put an ample arm around me, but I shrugged her off. I wondered if I would ever stop crying. The cart reached the bridge and turned right. I followed, walking alongside the river, the same walk I used to make every other Sunday with Mam and Pa. We shared a curate with Fewston and would have to make *that* walk twice a month, unless Robert Grange were making the trip in his dray cart and we could ride the two miles over the moor. I realised with a start that I would not have to do that any more – not if I did not want to. Less than half the village made the trip to Fewston, claiming a variety of ills, and we only went because Mam insisted. I cried harder at the jolt of relief I felt.

'Here we are, lass. Thee stick with me, I'll get thee through this.' Mary Farmer clung to my arm and I peered at the church. Digger and Edward lifted Mam down from the cart, ready for various men from the village to carry it inside. Robert Grange, William Smith, Thomas Fuller and George Weaver. Our closest neighbours. I took a deep breath and followed them into the plain single-storey stone building with the steps so worn they were more like a ramp. It were cold inside, despite the July sun. Or maybe that were me. Still ice, still cracking, but still in one piece.

I sat on the front pew, Mary Farmer beside me – mercifully quiet now – and sniffed. I used the sopping rag that had been a handkerchief, but it were not much use now. I could not bear to wipe my face on Mam's shawl. Did everyone know I were wearing her clothes? And what did they think of me if they did? Mam were not even in her grave yet.

The curate – a young dark-haired lad who had grown up in Fewston – started the service. I tried to listen, but I could not tear my attention away from the box in front of me. Mam.

Then I heard what he were saying, and the cracks widened. 'Merciful God? Merciful God? What kind of merciful God would drown Mam in the sheep pit?'

Mary Farmer tried to pull me back down on to the pew, shushing me. I had not realised I were stood, but I could not stop.

'What kind of merciful God would inflict the bloody flux on her husband? What kind of God would take Mam and Pa away? What kind of God is that?'

My sobs pierced the shocked silence that followed, and Mary Farmer finally managed to sit me down.

'She's distraught, poor lass – don't take no notice, she's distraught,' she told the congregation. 'Carry on, Curate, carry on.'

We moved to the graveyard and Mam were sunk into a great hole. Then Mary Farmer led me away as she were covered up.

At home, the stench hit me as we walked through the door. Pa were the same. My sobs tore the cracks inside me further apart. John Farmer went home. Mary Farmer stayed.

The next morning I were alone. I do not know when Mary Farmer had left – she must have waited until I slept. I dragged myself out of bed and went to clean Pa. It were for the last time. The bloody flux were not always a killer, but to survive it you needed strength, and Pa's strength had drowned in the sheep pit with Mam. There would be another funeral this week.

Chapter 4 - Emma

4th August 2012

My eldest niece, Chloe, was already out of the car when I opened the front door, and she ran to give me a hug. I grabbed her, spun her round and gave her a kiss, then gave her sister Natalie, three years younger at seven, the same treatment. Five-year-old Sophie needed help from her mother to get down from the Range Rover, then she ran over to join the scrum.

'Uncle David!' They abandoned me in their rush to greet Dave, and I laughed as three blonde angelic-looking terrors mobbed him.

I went to join Alice at the car and gave her a hug.

'How are you?' she asked.

'Great,' I replied. 'We're going to love it here.'

'I hope so.' She opened the boot and three equally excited balls of fur jumped down, then leaped up at me with their own enthusiastic greetings. I ruffled their heads before they bounded away to explore their new home.

'Come on in, you haven't seen the place since we finished it.'

'How's the unpacking going?'

'A complete mess.' I laughed. 'But at least we found the kettle. Coffee?'

'Would love one.'

I linked arms with my sister and we walked to the house. I whistled for the dogs and they came running.

'Thank you so much for looking after the beasts; I wouldn't have coped with them as well as the movers and everything.'

'My pleasure,' Alice said. 'The girls loved having them, and we've plenty of space. They were no bother.'

I smiled and felt ashamed for asking it of her. Alice had two dogs of her own, as well as a couple of horses, a flock of chickens and even a couple of goats. I didn't quite believe my three were "no bother".

'I'm very grateful, Alice, I don't know what we'd have done without you, I couldn't bear the thought of putting them in kennels.'

'Oh no, you couldn't do that! Don't worry about it, Ems, it was fine, honestly, we were pleased to help. You've had a hell of a time the last year or so, it was the least we could do.'

'Thanks, Sis. I know they couldn't have been in better hands.'

'Wow!' We had entered the lounge. 'It looks so different with furniture. Trust you to have unpacked your books first!'

I felt ashamed. 'Dave was furious when I started filling the bookshelves and left all the kitchen stuff in boxes,' I said. 'I couldn't even wait till the movers left, I just had to get them on the shelves.' I shrugged and smiled.

Alice laughed. 'I doubt he expected anything else of you, Em. Come on, I'll help you unpack the kitchen – Dave can amuse the kids, they adore him.'

'I know, he's great with them isn't he?'

Alice turned to me. 'Have you had any more thoughts . . . ?'

I shook my head. I'd already been through this with Dave, I couldn't do this conversation again. 'Don't.'

She nodded and stroked my upper arm. I turned from the pity I saw in her face, and led the way into the kitchen.

'Teatime,' I announced a couple of hours later. 'We'd like to treat you at the Stone House, a little thank you for having the beasts.'

'You don't have to do that, Ems, a sandwich here would be fine.'

'We want to. Anyway,' I surveyed the kitchen, 'I think we deserve it after all our hard work.'

'You have a point there. All right, that would be lovely. Kids!'

I jumped as she shouted the last word. The girls, Dave and the dogs ran in from outside.

'Wash your hands, we're going to the pub for tea.'

I chuckled when Dave obeyed Alice's instruction as well, then grabbed my coat.

Ten minutes later, we pulled into the car park, Alice and the girls behind us.

'Auntie Emma, Mummy said there's a haunted house.'

'Yes there is, though people live in it now, so I don't think it's haunted any more.'

'Bet it is!' said Natalie, and ran after Sophie making woo-woo noises.

Chloe stayed behind, looking thoughtful. 'Are ghosts real, Uncle Dave?'

'No, of course not. No such thing, it's just a way of explaining funny noises in the night. Now come on, help me find us a good table.'

They walked hand in hand to the pub entrance. Alice and I glanced at each other and laughed.

'I hope he's right.'

'About what?' I asked.

'No such thing as ghosts.'

I shrugged. I believed they did exist.

'Are you going to be ok, living out here? I'd forgotten how isolated it is.' She looked around. There was only a scattering of houses to break up the rolling expanse of moorland. 'There's not even a shop; and what if something happens, how would you get help?'

I shrugged. 'We'll make sure we keep plenty of supplies in. And there's always this place.' I laughed.

'Yes, but what if there's an accident? It would take ages

for an ambulance or something to get here.'

'Not really, it's not like it used to be when we were kids. The doctors' surgery in one of the villages has a four-wheel drive, and there's always the air ambulance if something serious happens. We're not that cut off, you know, not the way it was,' I said.

'Yeah, ok, but what about winter? I can remember drifts up to our shoulders, and not being able to get to the sailing club.'

I shrugged again. 'I work from home and Dave is pretty flexible. This is still a farming community; I'm sure a local farmer will plough the lanes – he'd have to, to get to his livestock.' I nodded at the distant sheep and the field of Highland cattle nearby – only the hardiest breeds survived up here. 'And we'll make sure we have plenty of supplies,' I repeated. 'We'll be fine.'

'I hope so,' Alice replied. 'But I can't help worrying.'

I gave her a quick hug, then turned at a shout from Dave. 'Come on you two, the girls are hungry!'

I smiled and linked arms with Alice. 'Don't worry, Alice, please. I know it's isolated, but we have thought it through, and we'll prepare well for winter. Anyway, it'll be nice, the two of us snowed in, curled up in front of a roaring fire – romantic.'

She gave a small nod, and we followed Dave into the pub.

'Where's the menu?'

'Above the bar.'

We crowded round to read the blackboard.

'What does it say?' Sophie asked.

'Shepherd's pie with chips and peas, steak and ale pie with chips and peas, chicken pie with chips and peas.'

'Is there anything vegetarian?' Alice asked the barman.

'Aye,' he replied. 'Chips and peas.'

She stared at him and I burst out laughing at the expression on her face as she realised he was serious.

Chapter 5 - Jennet

9th July 1776

'Here, cut that pie up will thee, Jennet?' Mary Farmer called. I picked up the knife and sliced the large rabbit pie. The other women bustled around me, but for the most part they left me alone – apart from Mary Farmer.

It were the shearing. Two weeks after the sheep-washing and Mam's death, the whole village had gathered again. This were the last place I wanted to be the day after burying Pa. *How had I let Mary Farmer persuade me to come?*

I picked up the platter of pie slices and carried it into the shearing shed. The rest of the year it were Thomas Ramsgill's barn, but as the biggest in the valley (and Thomas having one of the largest flocks), everyone brought their animals here to be shorn each year. By pulling together like this, a thousand head of sheep could be bald by the end of the day. Somehow Thomas Ramsgill got his flock seen to without getting his own hands dirty, but it still worked out better like this than each farmer trying to deal with his own flock alone. Plus we had a party. Not that I felt much like partying this year.

The pie platter were cleared in five minutes flat and I went back for more. Thomas Ramsgill had taken the biggest slice and I scowled. It were supposed to be for the men and women doing the work – not only the clippers, but the wrappers, catchers and sharpeners, too.

The animals were sent in to the waiting clippers, who perched on their three-legged stools. The fastest clipper

could take a fleece off in three and a half minutes –
muscles bulging and sweat dripping as they worked the
hand shears impossibly fast. I watched the ewes and
wondered which one of them had killed Mam.

The clippers' wives and daughters chopped off the dirty
locks around the tail before wrapping the wool into tight
rolls. They had fleeces from up to twenty clippers each to
lap like this and it were exhausting work. The catchers at
the door dabbed the sheep with tar marks to distinguish
each man's property and sent them off to their fold – one
flock at a time. Add to that chaos William Smith
sharpening countless pairs of shears, the bleating of the
sheep, cursing of the clippers and wrappers, and the smell
of sweating farmers and distressed animals, it were
impossible to keep crying. I were soon swept up in the
sheer busyness of the day and ran back and forth with pie
and jugs of ale. I caught Mary Farmer watching me and
smiled. She had been right to bully me out of the quiet
empty house. It were good to be around people and forget
– even if only for a few minutes at a time.

'How is thee, Jennet?'

I started at the deep voice, and turned to see Thomas
and Richard Ramsgill. The Ramsgills were the most
important family in the valley – Thomas the Forest
Constable, Richard the wool merchant, Big Robert the
miller and Alexander just getting his own farm
established. There were three more brothers still working
their father's farm.

Richard lived close to us. To me. Just down the hill at
East Gate House, near the smithy and the Gate Inn. He
were a stern man and had never spoken to me before
today. Now he raised his eyebrows at my lack of response.

'Umm,' I said. It were the one question I never knew
how to answer; I had no idea what to say to Richard
Ramsgill.

'I remember thy Mam when she were a young lass,'

Richard Ramsgill carried on, ignoring my stammering. 'It's such a shame. If there's anything I can do for thee, thee only has to ask.'

Thomas laughed. 'Is thee gonna find her somewhere to live, then?'

'What does thee mean?' I said, panicked into forgetting my manners. *Were I being evicted?*

'Well, surely thee knew? Thee'll have to leave the farm, the tenure won't pass to a fifteen-year-old lass. Did thy pa write a will?'

'Umm, no, I don't think so,' I said.

Thomas Ramsgill seemed embarrassed.

'Don't worry theesen about it, lass,' his brother said. 'I'll look into it for thee, see if there's owt can be done. Thomas here is being a bit previous. Don't worry, thee won't have to leave farm.'

What to say to him? 'Umm.' I were dumbfounded.

'By the way, does thee know what the terms of thy folks' tenure of land was?'

'Umm.'

'Tell thee what, I realise this is probably a bit much for thee. Don't worry about a thing, lass, I'll pop round later this week. See thee again, lass.' He doffed his hat and they walked away.

I stared after him.

Mary Farmer joined me. 'Ey up, lass, what did *they* want? Thee take care round likes of them, thee mark me words. Careful, lass. Now, grab this jug of ale, I reckon them in barn are getting a thirst on.'

Chapter 6 - Emma

12th August 2012

I whistled again. The beasts would stay out all night and day if they could. Cassie the Irish Setter came first. She was the eldest at nine and I'd had her since she was a puppy. The other two, both German Shepherds, would follow given time.

It was getting chilly now the sun was going down, and I was splashed head to foot with mud. I turned towards the house and smiled as I always did, unable to help myself. It had taken nearly two years and a great deal of determination to build.

From the big upstairs office window I could see the dam to the left – innocuous from this side but terrifying from the other. It had a massive drop, like a black run with no snow – or a ski jump that kept going down. Functional and massive, it hid nothing of its purpose and had given me nightmares as a child sailing here. I'd been terrified of getting swept up to its lip and having to stare down that chasm, knowing it was the only place for me to go.

I shivered and whistled again. Running up the slope after Cassie, I could hear Delly and Rodney following, and was laughing at them when we burst into the mudroom – cold, filthy and exhilarated from the fresh air. I towelled the dogs off and took off my coat, then walked into the kitchen for a hot chocolate. Dave already had the kettle steaming and handed me a mug, smiling and shaking his head.

'You're like a child out there with those dogs, Emma, a carefree little girl.'

I bit, hearing a reprimand in his words. 'You can't be surprised, surely?'

'I'm not complaining, relax. It's great to see, I wish I could do it.'

'You can, if you try. Just let go and enjoy the moment. That's how I write and that's what's built this house.' I was on my guard, expecting another lecture on responsibility, which was hardly fair. I had met most of the building costs as Dave had invested so heavily in his building project in Scotland.

'Oh calm down! Why do you have to be so defensive? I know things are a bit tight at the moment, but once this Edinburgh project is finished, there'll be a massive return – there's plenty of interest in the flats already, even the penthouses. In a year or two I might even be able to semi-retire.'

Silence. Most of our conversations had ended like this since the miscarriage, and had got worse with the challenge of building this place. Dave had thrown himself into his work, and I had tried to do the same with my books, but I had struggled to write so had concentrated on the house. I worried that we'd put our whole selves into building the perfect home, and had nothing left over for each other – or a future family. I couldn't bear it if that were the case.

I sipped my hot chocolate and waited for the atmosphere to clear. The dogs had become expert at this and jumped at us both, tongues lolling, whenever they sensed tension starting to build.

'What's for dinner?' he asked, trying again for domestic harmony.

'I stuck a chicken in the oven before I took the dogs out.'

'That sounds lovely. I'm going through to the lounge – I've lit a fire. Join me?'

'No, I've got another couple of chapters to edit, then I'll be done for the evening.' It wasn't the friendliest reply, and I felt ashamed at the downcast expression on his face. We seemed to be constantly sniping at each other at the moment, and I wanted to ease the atmosphere between us. 'I quite fancy dinner in front of the fire though, is there anything good on telly?'

'Probably not. We'll see.' He'd cooled again. 'You can't hide from life in your books, Emma. You need to face things, and live. You told me earlier to live in the moment, but you're still living in the past!'

'No, I'm not.' I was aware of my voice rising, but couldn't seem to stop it. 'I'm trying to enjoy each day, because life is precious, that's why I wanted to move here and build this house!' I didn't understand how he could have got over the miscarriage already, and he didn't seem to understand why I was still grieving.

'Is it? Are you sure about that? You threw yourself into building this place – negotiating with Yorkshire Water for the land, getting planning permission, then sorting out the utility companies so we'd have mains electricity and water. And then after we'd lost the baby you were here almost every day keeping an eye on the builders, it became an obsession. I think you did it to avoid thinking about what had happened. And now the house is finished, you're obsessing over your books.'

'That's not true!'

'Isn't it? You didn't use to work this hard. When we first met, you told me you had to stay relaxed, or you couldn't write, that you couldn't force the words to come.'

'I'm not forcing anything. I'm not obsessing. I'm just writing and earning a living,' I shouted.

He sighed and shrugged. 'Whatever you say, Emma.'

I stared at him for a moment, but there was nothing more to add. I went upstairs.

I hesitated before I switched the light on, wanting to take in the view for a moment. I'd wrestled with the design of this room. The forty-foot long west wall was all glass to give an unspoilt view of the water, and there'd been a very real fear that it would distract rather than inspire me, and I had a lot of books still to write – I hoped.

I thought of Dave and our argument. I didn't know how to tell him that my latest book was not going well. I was struggling to plot it and keep my characters consistent, and had barely written anything worth keeping for over a year.

Reluctantly, I switched the light on, hiding the reservoir in the glare. I looked up at the ceiling for inspiration. It had been carpentered in the same way as the old ships had been many years ago and, with keelson and struts laid out along the length of the house, I could imagine myself in an upturned hull of a leviathan square rigger.

I had a sofa and coffee table positioned in front of the large glass wall and balcony, while my desk was pushed against the left wall under a large noticeboard. Book shelves took up most of the remaining wall space as they did downstairs in the lounge. You could never have enough books. Well, Dave could, but I couldn't, and he loved to complain that they were breeding. Maybe I should turn one of the guest rooms into a library. *Now there's an idea.*

I walked to the desk and settled down in front of the computer.

I jumped and stared at the dark window. A flash had lit up the reservoir, followed by a crash of thunder. I sighed in frustration and put down my pen – I could not focus on my pirates and the tropics when I faced, literally, the raging nature of the moors. I switched off the light and stared out of the window – hurricane-rated to withstand the weather here. Lit up by bright flashes of lightning and surrounded by battered pines, the reservoir was a seething mass of waves and mini-waterspouts from the needles of rain.

My mind flew back over twenty years to when I had learned to sail here as a child. I remembered a storm like this and everyone streaming into the clubhouse, glad to get out of it. The instructor decided it would be a good day to do our capsize drill and, surprising the seasoned sailors, he gathered his little band of aspiring mariners to the water's edge where his oldest boat awaited, still rigged with a wooden mast.

Apart from the sheer madness of it, the thing I remembered most was how warm the reservoir had been after the rain, and how much I had enjoyed my swim, despite the water I swallowed through all the laughter.

I got up and grabbed a coat from the bedroom, then went back into the office and opened the balcony door. I struggled outside against the wind and cursed when papers flew off my desk, then shut the door behind me. The balcony was fairly sheltered, and if I stood close to the windows, I could just about manage to stay clear of the rain.

I stepped forward and grabbed hold of the rail, then lifted my face to the full power of the storm. Another flash of lightning and crash of thunder. I laughed at the majesty of it, exhilarated by the force of nature, then hushed. *What was that?* After the thunder had reverberated away, I'd thought I'd heard . . . *No.* I shook my head, *I can't have.* I stepped back into the shelter of the house, ran my hands over my now sodden hair, and listened.

Yes, I hadn't imagined it. In the wake of the next thunderclap, bells – church bells. But there was no church for miles, certainly none close enough to be able to hear their bells. I stared at the water, thinking of the village that rested beneath. The only church close enough was—

'I thought I'd find you out here,' Dave said, and I jumped.

'It's beautiful.'

He put his arms around me and I snuggled into his

embrace to watch the rest of the storm, grateful and relieved that he'd made the first move to make up after our row.

'I'm sorry,' he said.

I stroked his arm. 'Me too, it's just . . .' I tailed off.

'I want a family so badly, but if you're not ready, you're not ready. There's no pressure.'

'I do want a family, you know that, I'm just scared.'

'I know, but we can adopt. You don't have to risk another pregnancy.'

'Yes, but if we adopt, we're giving up. And I want *our* baby – I'm not ready, not yet. And even if we do adopt, what if something happens? What if he or she gets ill or has an accident or something? There's so much that can go wrong – I can't lose another child.'

'Is it worth speaking to someone again?'

'What, like that counsellor? I don't know. How can talking help?'

'Isn't it worth trying? It helped me.'

'I did try! I spent three months talking to that grief counsellor. It was all right for you, but it didn't help me much, did it?'

'No, I don't suppose it did.' He squeezed and held me tighter. 'You're not on your own though, Em, remember that. You can always talk to me.'

'I know. I don't know what I'd have done without you.' I twisted to kiss him, then settled back into his embrace to watch the rest of the storm.

Chapter 7 - Jennet

15th July 1776

'Now then, Jennet, thee's got to eat, thee'll waste away.'

I sighed. Would Mary Farmer never leave me alone? I had been grateful for her help at first, but it were getting to be too much. She were here every day, fussing about me with non-stop advice and prattle. Even while she were forcing me to eat her soup, she stood at the table putting a large mutton pie together for later. I lifted the spoon to my mouth. The easiest thing were to do as she insisted. Maybe if she saw me eating, she'd leave me alone. Anyroad, I were hungry.

It had been a week since I'd buried Pa and I still felt as if made of ice. I did my chores, kept the house clean, fed the chickens – the sheep took care of themselves at this time of year and were loose on the moor behind the house. It were lambing season in February when they would need my attention, and I could not think that far ahead yet.

'By heck, summat smells good!'

I glanced up in surprise. Richard Ramsgill had walked through the open door unannounced. I stood in greeting.

'Mr Ramsgill! What's thee doing here?' Mary Farmer said at the top of her voice.

'Come to see young Jennet, Mary. Business.'

I smirked as Mary Farmer struggled to find words. He raised his eyebrows at her and glanced towards the door. Mary Farmer turned red as a rosehip and clapped the flour from her hands.

'Well . . . Well . . .' she muttered.

'Private business,' Mr Ramsgill stressed.

'Very well.'

I watched in amazement as Mary Farmer's nosiness battled against her deference to the man who controlled all our lives as the local wool merchant – and lost.

'It ain't seemly,' she muttered, just loud enough for us both to hear, as she picked up her shawl. 'Ain't seemly for a young lass to be alone with a grown man, not at all.'

Richard Ramsgill stared at her, waiting for her to leave, then closed the door. I shut my eyes for a moment in relief and opened them in surprise when he laughed.

'She can be a bit much, can't she?'

'She means well.' I leapt to her defence. 'She helped me all through Pa's illness, and every day since.'

'Oh, aye, I'm sure she has. Likes nowt else than to feel important, that one.'

I smirked at him. He pointed to the other stool in question and I nodded, embarrassed that I had not asked him to sit.

'Would thee like some soup?'

He shook his head. 'Not for me thanks, lass. A jug of posset wouldn't go amiss, though.'

I busied myself at the fire, pouring some of the curdled milk and ale that Mary Farmer had prepared earlier. 'There's not much spice in it I'm afraid, just some herbs from moor.'

He took a flask from his jacket and poured a little of the amber liquid into his jug, then took a sip. 'Mm, that hits the spot.'

I knew he were just being polite, but dipped my head at the compliment nonetheless. I sat back down in silence and studied my soup.

'I'll come straight to point,' Richard Ramsgill said after a short, awkward silence. 'I said at shearing that I'd look into thy situation for thee.'

I looked up at him. Would I be forced to leave the farm?

'Don't look so scared, lass.' He laughed and took another sip. 'I've been to London with our Thom since I last saw thee, to sort out enclosures.'

'Enclosures?'

'Aye, them new walls thee's seen going up? It's on King's orders, he's enclosing land and selling it. Our Thom's in charge of placing walls and allotting land, and me and me brothers are putting in to buy what we can. Anyroad, I had a word with land folk, and pleaded thy case. It took quite a bit of wrangling, but I finally got sight of papers and it seems farm belonged to thy mam – it were passed to her from thy grandpa and she had copyhold of inheritance on land.'

I did not react. What did that mean?

'It means thee can stay, lass. It means her tenure passed to thee on her death as her sole heir, even though neither of them made a will. And when these enclosures are done and land's awarded, it'll be thine for life.'

I sagged in relief. I had not realised until now how scared I had been that I would be turned out on to the moor – or on to Mary and John Farmer's hospitality. 'I can stay?'

'Aye, thee can stay, lass. Can thee manage farm does thee think?'

I thought of all the work involved in rearing the sheep, plus the haymaking and maintaining the farm. Pa had handled all that, with a little help from me and Mam. But the two of us had also been busy all year round with carding and spinning wool, gathering and drying our herbs, plus cutting peat and pulling heather, growing and gathering food and many more chores besides. How would I manage on my own? I were embarrassed anew to find tears in my eyes.

'Ey up, don't fret so, lass! Thee's not on thy own, thee knows. Mary Farmer's up road—' I cried harder '—and whole village'll pull together to see thee through first year till thee finds thy feet. And I'm sure one of young lads'll soon snap thee up – thee has thy own farm, lass, thee's quite a catch, thee knows, especially for a second son!'

'We struggled to manage with three of us, how can I do it all? I know village'll help, but they have their own farms and families to see to.' I sobbed harder. I ignored his comment about young men, I did not have my eye on anyone – although that Peter Stockdale always had a nice smile for me. Richard Ramsgill put down his posset and dragged his stool closer. He grasped my shoulder and I winced.

'Tell thee what, I'll let thee use one of me best tups in November, and send thee one of me best men for lambing. He'll see thee right, and he'll help thee with getting feed to them during winter, an'all.'

I cried harder at his kindness. It seemed my tears were unstoppable since Mam died. 'How can I ever thank thee?'

'Ahh, no need for thanks, lass. I told thee, thy Mam and me were great friends as nippers, it's least I can do.' He got up, poured more posset, then added a little of his own ingredient and passed the jug to me. I thanked him and sipped, gasping at the heat that slid down my throat into my stomach. I glanced up at him in surprise and he burst out laughing.

'Just a little whiskybae, lass, best thing for grief *and* tears in my experience!'

I took another sip, enjoying the heat now that I expected it, and smiled at him.

'See, that's better, lass. There's nowt wrong in't world that a little whiskybae don't put right.'

Chapter 8 - Emma

28th August 2012

There was only one problem writing about pirates in the Caribbean – I wanted to go sailing. Writing about the wind in my face and my ship slicing through the waves, the rigging singing, made me long to experience it myself. Trouble was, I didn't have a licence to sail on Thruscross and a white sail would hardly be inconspicuous – but what would they do? Charge me with trespass? What the hell.

Mind made up (let's face it, it didn't take much) I decided to go for it. After all the rain, Thruscross was full – a rarity in August – an hour drifting around free of the shore would do me good. I put my pirates away and went down to dig out my old wetsuit (a bit tight, but it still fitted) and lifejacket, then went to the garage to check the laser, *Guinevere*. A small singlehanded dinghy, it was pretty rugged and good fun in a blow, yet light enough that I could enjoy the meagre ten knots I estimated to be blowing out there. It was snug on its trailer and I hooked it up to the Discovery before driving down the old access road to the bottom. Just like old times.

It took some manoeuvring to separate the trolley and trailer, and more to get the mast up on my own, but a bit of frustration would be worth it. I felt guilty for a moment – I should be working really, but I consoled myself with the thought that I could justify this as research – what better way to plan a pirate attack than out on the water with the wind in my hair? Maybe this would cure my writer's block.

*

At last I was ready; *Guinevere* was in the water and I pushed off, then jumped in. It had been too long since I'd done this and I spent an age getting centre-board and rudder down, but at last I sheeted in, hooked my feet under the toe straps (a little optimistically) and made way.

Whilst I'd never left the water in my heart, I hadn't been in a dinghy for years. In my youth I'd sailed competitively, but life had got in the way. I'd never been able to bring myself to sell *Guinevere* though, and my return to a dinghy was long overdue. Perhaps alone wasn't the most sensible way of getting back into it, but hell, that had never stopped me before.

I felt my face stretch into a big grin, and relaxed. God, I'd missed this. Time to try a tack. Success. Gybe. Whoops, mainsheet caught round the transom. No problem, easily fixed. I unhooked it, sheeted in again and headed up towards the creek. How would my characters attack their rival? They needed to do something different, to take him by surprise. It wouldn't be easy, he'd been pirating for a long time. How would they get an advantage over him?

I was up at the creek already and running out of wind. It was shifty all over the reservoir – one of the reasons the sailing club had moved – and it had always been worse up here because of the high banks. I tried my hand at a roll tack – gently taking her through the wind whilst heeling sharply to help steer. Made it, not bad, apart from getting my arse wet, but that's sailing for you.

The wind was behind now and too light to run before, so I hardened up to a reach and practised gybing back and forth across the lake, heading southish towards the dam. I'd never been much of a light-weather sailor; I'd always preferred a blow, and now that the wind was dropping off I was getting bored. I turned my mind back to the Caribbean.

*

I grinned in triumph. I had my battle and knew how they'd fight. Now I had to get ashore and write it down before I forgot – I should have brought pen and paper out with me. Never mind, I'd remember next time. I had a brief image of me drifting around Thruscross, lying across the boat writing, then looked about me to get my bearings.

Oh no. Oh no. I looked wildly at the banks, but of course there were no transit poles to mark the danger – they'd gone with the sailing club. I looked at the dam again. It was far too close. I could see the water pouring over the outflow and hear it falling down the sheer drop on the other side. I pulled the sail in desperately, but there was even less wind than there had been earlier, and all I did was shake what little I had out of the sail in my panic. I knew in the depths of my mind that I had to stay calm and move carefully to get out of this, but calm was difficult to achieve this close to the dam.

I threw *Guinevere* into a tack, forgetting to roll her, and cursed when I got stuck. Head to wind and being pulled closer by the current of water flowing over the impossibly high dam, I had a flash memory of how the dam looked. On this side, a concrete wall with five overflows, blue sky shining through them. On the other, a concrete hell slide, one-hundred-and-twenty-feet long to a concrete sluice. Going over it would kill me.

I bit back my panic; I had to get the boat sailing. The closer I got, the harder it would be to get away. I remembered the nightmares I'd had as a child when I'd sailed on this reservoir every week, after I'd seen what was on the other side for the first time. They would not come true. They wouldn't. They couldn't.

I backed the mainsail across the wind so it could help the rudder turn me, and belatedly heeled the boat, but it wasn't enough. There was no wind, the water was glassy, and by the looks of it there were no gusts heading my way.

Why hadn't I paid more attention?

I examined the banks. I was too close to the dam and the shore was too far away to swim for. If I didn't get out of the current, I'd be swept over and killed for sure. If I swam, I'd still have to get out of the pull of the middle opening, then two more. Even if I managed it, then what?

Was that dead water beyond the overflows, or a swirling eddy that would keep the rocky shore beyond my reach and send me straight back into danger?

My best chance was in the boat; someone may see me and get help. There was a car park up there, people walked along the banks and they drove and walked across the dam itself, often pausing to peer over the sides. Surely someone would see I was in trouble and get help. Yes, my best chance was to stay in the boat.

I started shouting in the still afternoon, knowing I should wait and save my voice until I knew someone was there to hear me, but unable to stop.

How could I have been so stupid? I grew up here knowing the dangers. I'd heard stories as a child of a boat going over for a dare, although I'd decided it wasn't true – nobody could be that foolish. I'd seen a boat rescued from the lip of the overflow. Twice. But there was no rescue boat here today. I took a deep breath and tried to calm down, but all I could think was: *it's getting closer, it's getting closer*. I remembered my phone, safe in a pouch hanging from my neck and fiddled with my lifejacket and wetsuit to get it out. I powered it up and nothing. No signal. Not a single bar – I should have thought of that; of course there wouldn't be a signal on the water, I was lucky to get one on the bank.

I yanked on the sail in desperation and was rewarded with a little spurt of speed – of course! I could pump my way out of this! But the current had dragged my bow round towards the dam; I was facing the wrong way. I thrust the tiller across again to harden back up, but nothing – no steerage. I left the rudder hard over, stood, clambered forward to the mast, and shoved the boom against what little wind there was, whilst heeling her sharply. Finally, I was turning. Not much, but the bows *were* coming round. It wasn't enough though, and I realised I would have to make my own wind.

I stepped up on to the foredeck and grabbed the mast in both hands, using my splayed legs to rock the boat from side to side as hard as I could, trying to build up a rhythm and force my way to starboard. It was working.

I kept going.

I was side on now and still going. I steadied a little and smoothed the rocking motion to go forwards. If I kept trying to turn her, I'd lose time and get pulled backwards; I needed to go for speed and get to the shore.

Is it getting easier?

Yes. I was out of the pull of the middle and strongest overflow. Two more to go. I kept pumping. My leg muscles, especially the inside of my thighs, were starting to burn, but I knew my only chance was to keep up the rhythm. I had to get more speed up and keep it going when the next current caught me. Then no stopping until I got past the third.

I glanced to my right, I could see only sky. There was nothing through that deadly concrete hole but air. Then I realised I *could* see more than sky, the wooded cliff face was coming into view. I was looking through the last one! I was nearly safe.

I took a deep breath and kept pumping. So much for a nice, gentle sail! I was exhausted. My legs were beyond protest, my back cramped in agony every time I shifted my weight from one leg to the other, and my arms felt like they'd done a full weights training programme as they pulled the mast over. But I couldn't stop. I had to find more strength. I had to keep going.

The force of the current grabbed me again and threw me off balance. I tried to save myself, but my legs wouldn't respond. I was on my knees, mercifully still on the boat. I glanced round; my bow was being pulled back towards the dam.

'No!' I screeched. 'No! Not after all this! No fucking way! You're not getting me!'

I could almost see teeth around that square hole now; a concrete mouth waiting to chew me up and swallow me – although in this case it would swallow me then crush me. I was losing it. I had to pull myself together or I was dead. I pictured Dave; my sister and nieces; the dogs; my unfinished book.

I hauled myself back to my feet and hugged the mast, my legs shaking. I glanced over my right shoulder and my panic came back. *Good, it may save my life.*

I planted my feet as wide apart as I dared, gripped the mast hard and frenziedly rocked the boat. I was aware I was sobbing, but nothing would stop that now. *Left right, left right. Port starboard, port starboard.* What a time to start correcting my sailor speak. *Port starboard, port starboard.* I refused to look to my right, I didn't even let myself look behind for the shore, just stared at the sail and boom swinging across the boat and the uneven wake I was leaving – I could see the disturbed water being pulled towards the dam and over the drop. *Port, starboard. Port, starboard.* Can I look now? No not yet, keep going. *Port, starboard. Port, starboard.*

My sobs calmed in the monotony of the rhythm and I kept going. I thought running a marathon would be like this – *left right, left right, left right, port starboard, port starboard*, on and on and on. Forever and a day.

Aargh. Thrown off balance again, I fell, rolled off the deck and into the water. I put my feet down and felt rock. No wonder I'd fallen, I'd crashed into the bank! I sobbed again, this time in relief, and scrambled backwards, my shaking legs pushing against submerged rock. I'd made it! I was ok! I'd made it!

I collapsed on the rock, my hands gripping it tightly, breaking every fingernail in my desperation to grasp terra firma. I'd never been so pleased to crash ashore. I remembered *Guinevere* then, what had I broken on the rocks? Centre-board? Rudder? Hull? I turned back to the water to check for damage.

Horrified, I watched *Guinevere* drift towards the dam. I'd betrayed her – she'd got me to safety and I'd abandoned her. I had to watch her. I couldn't save her, but I wouldn't let her go all alone. I scrambled up the steps leading to the road, my legs still working, somehow, and staggered to the far side, realising that after the struggle with not a breath of breeze to help me, the wind was getting up.

Would she catch on the lip? No. Her mast was too short to save her, and I must have damaged her foils on the rocks: all they did was heel her over as she came sideways on, through the gaping jaws. I watched open-mouthed as she slid over the waterfall, the wind of her dive catching the sail and lifting her bows up as she surfed down the dam; then she heeled a little too far to starboard and capsized gracefully in mid-air, first her mast then her hull shattering on impact. No one would have survived that.

I sank to the ground, sobbing again, feeling as if I'd never stop, only now truly understanding how close death had come.

I stared at the wall, confused, how could I be in my bedroom? I switched on the bedside lamp, blinked a few times and, as my senses returned, realised it had been a dream. I sniffed and wiped tears from my face, then flinched. I'd scratched my cheek. I held my hands in front of me and examined them. Every fingernail was broken and dirty. I scraped the jagged remains of one nail under another, then held my finger up to the light. There was a small mound of peaty, brown dirt on my nail – the same colour as the mud of the reservoir's shoreline.

Chapter 9 - Jennet

19th August 1776

I opened my eyes and stared at the timbers above me, picturing scenes from my dreams – bright sunshine on the moors, heather in bloom . . . and Richard Ramsgill. Bathing in the beck . . . and Richard Ramsgill. I smiled, despite myself, and threw off the sheepskin I used as a blanket. Time to start the day.

'Ey up, lass, he's here again!'

I looked up from scrubbing the floor and stared at Mary Farmer standing at the open door. She had finished sweeping and had gone outside to knock the dust from the besom.

'Richard Ramsgill, he's only coming up lane again!'

I could not explain why my heart beat a little faster.

'Thee needs to watch him, lass. I don't trust him an inch. Just promise me thee'll take care with him.'

'Don't fret theesen, Mary, he's helping me sort tenure out so I can stay on here – for Mam's sake – they were friends when they were nippers.'

'Aye, I remember,' she said, paused, then turned back to me. 'Promise me thee'll take care. He offers a good bargain, but however much he gives with one hand, his other'll take back more. Whatever he's offering, he'll come out ahead on't bargain, thee mark me words!'

'Umm,' I said, threw my scrubbing brush into the bucket and stood, brushing off my skirts.

'I means it, lass, take care in thy dealings with him.'

I glanced up at her. She seemed serious. 'Aye, Mary, I'll take care.'

She watched me, then turned as Richard Ramsgill loomed behind her. 'Mr Ramsgill,' she said, in a completely different tone.

'Mary.' He nodded his greeting at her.

'What can we do for thee?'

'*Thee* can do nowt, Mary, though I'm heartened to see thee caring for Jennet like this.'

'Aye, well, her mam were a good friend, 'tis the least I can do.'

They stared at each other awhile, then Mary Farmer dropped her eyes. 'Aye, well, happen I'll be off now, John'll be wondering where I've got to.' She turned to stare at me. 'Think on what I said, Jennet.' She wrapped her shawl around her shoulders and hurried away.

I walked towards the fire, unsettled by Richard Ramsgill's company again so soon, and offered him a posset. He laughed and took out his hip flask. 'Don't forget secret ingredient, Jennet!'

I smiled and took the flask from him. I raised my eyes to his when he kept his grip on it.

'I meant what I said other day, Jennet, if thee needs any help – owt at all – thee can come to me.'

I dropped my eyes, shy, and thanked him. Why were he being so nice to me? He let go of the flask and I poured a measure into our jugs, then filled them with posset from the bubbling pot.

'By heck, lass, thee's got an heavy hand there!' He laughed and I joined in. I passed him his jug, took a sip of my own and choked – I had enjoyed the heat of the drink before, but had not seen how much whiskybae he had added. This must be three times as strong. I tried to apologise, but could not get the words out for spluttering.

Richard Ramsgill took my jug off me, picked another off the shelf and poured half the thick liquid into it, then topped mine back up from the pot. He handed the diluted drink back to me and sipped his own. I noticed he had only diluted mine. I sipped the posset, tentative now, and smiled my thanks. Better. I sat down at the table, wondering what to say to him, reddening as I remembered my dreams.

'I thought a lot of thy mam when she were a lass.' He sat next to me. 'Might even have married her if thy pa hadn't turned up.'

I looked up at him in surprise. Mam had never said owt like this – she'd hardly ever mentioned Richard Ramsgill.

He chuckled to himself. 'Aye. Swept her off her feet, he did, and never left valley again. Her pa, thy grandpa, weren't best pleased, he'd have much rather seen her married to a Ramsgill than a poor journeyman from Scotland. But one thing thee could say about thy mam were that she knew her own mind. Not even thy grandpa could turn her head from a path she were set on following.'

I grimaced – I knew that all too well.

'Aye. Hated thy pa for a bit, I'm ashamed to say.'

I glanced at him again, this time in disgust.

'Oh, sorry lass, but he were a lucky bugger to have the love of Alice; and me . . . I had to marry Elizabeth Cartwright. Oh, don't get me wrong, lass, lovely woman, Elizabeth, but she ain't Alice.'

He lapsed into silence and I stared at my posset, touched. He had loved Mam. I took a deep drink then turned my attention back to him. 'What were she like? As a lass I mean, before I were born?'

'Ahh, Jennet, she were a lot like thee – really bonny, loved the moors. Out there all hours, she were, just walking and digging up plants. Always laughing, she were, never had a bad word to say about anyone. But, by heck, she could talk a lad into trouble.' He paused and shook his head, laughing.

'What does thee mean? What trouble?'

'Well, I remember one time, she had me and our Thom sneaking into Pa's cellar – for a jug of this actually.' He picked up the hip flask then put it back on the table. 'Pa's best whiskybae – guarded it something fierce, he did. Daft thing were, if me and our Thom had worked together, we'd have done it, no sweat, but we didn't. Scrapping with each other to be the one to bring it to her, we were. When Pa came down to see what all noise were about, jug were broke on't flags with me and our Thom rolling around in his whiskybae like a couple of fox cubs. By heck, we got such a whipping!'

I laughed, trying to imagine Mam sending two Ramsgills to get whiskybae for her. I took another drink.

'Thee remind me so much of her, thee knows.' He put his hand on mine and I glanced up at him, startled. 'Thee has her laugh. And her eyes. The most beautiful eyes in Yorkshire I've always thought.' He tightened his grip on my hand and leaned towards me. I felt his rough skin against my face, his whiskers on my chin and my lips forced apart by his tongue.

I froze. His other hand stroked my hair, then my back. He took his face from mine, held me tightly for a moment, then pushed his stool back hard enough for it to clatter to the floor.

'Sorry, lass,' he mumbled and rushed out of the door.

I stared after him, flabbergasted, but also disappointed. It had been nice to be held. I picked up the other posset and drank deeply, my breath shuddering, tears running down my face, wishing I knew why I were crying. Because he had kissed me? Or because he had fled?

Chapter 10 - Emma

29th August 2012

I looked across at Dave, fast asleep and oblivious of my distress, and my breathing calmed. It had seemed so real – I still wasn't sure if it had been a dream or a memory. I studied my fingernails again and gasped when I realised they were clean. Was I still dreaming?

I got out of bed and walked to my office. I kept a kettle in there for when I was too wrapped up in my writing to make it downstairs to the kitchen. I needed camomile tea. Well, no, I needed brandy, but I'd make do with camomile tea while I wrote the dream out – it would help me let go of it and you never knew, it might turn into a good story.

I left the light off – there was more than enough moonlight to work the kettle – and stood at the window, watching the water. I loved it here, always had, and adored this room with its view over the reservoir. But I didn't understand why the same water that calmed me; that made this place home and was the source of countless happy childhood memories should also be the source of my nightmares.

The silver light reflected off the water had a shine more beautiful than diamonds, and I felt myself relax as the kettle came to the boil. I made my drink and took it out on to the balcony. The shore and trees were black – made darker by the bright beauty of the water, even the rocky, muddy shore of the half-full reservoir added to the beauty; the uneven shapes and hint of old roads giving the place character. I smiled and sipped my tea – too hot. I put the mug down and touched my burnt lip. And froze.

What the hell?

It couldn't be.

I turned back to the reservoir in disbelief. But there it was again. Church bells. Deep and . . . slow somehow, as if being rung underwater. I shook myself. I was being silly, my nightmare lingering. But no – I heard it again. Church bells, definitely.

'What are you doing?'

I screamed before realising the hand on my arm was Dave's.

'Sorry, Emma, I didn't mean to startle you.'

'No, it's all right – bad dream. And I thought I heard – there it is again! Did you hear that?'

'What?'

'Church bells! As clear as anything, didn't you hear them?'

He put his arm around me and hugged. 'No I didn't, and neither did you. You know as well as I do they took the bells away and knocked the church down before they flooded the village. They rebuilt the damn thing at Blubberhouses for God's sake! *You* told me that! You didn't hear any bells, it's just that writer's imagination of yours. Now bring your tea and come back to bed.'

I nodded in agreement. I *did* know there were no church bells ringing under that water. But I also knew what I'd heard, and it wasn't my imagination – that was Dave's rationalisation for anything I said that he didn't like. Nor was it the first time I'd heard the bells. I picked up my tea and followed him back inside; I'd lost the dream that had woken me – all I could remember was a sense of a black abyss and fear, and that could mean anything or nothing, I might as well try and go back to sleep.

I paused in the doorway and turned back to the view. Everything seemed peaceful out there, but I could have sworn I'd heard the bells again, just faintly, when I'd reached for the door.

I climbed into bed and curled up against my husband, grateful for his warmth.

'God, you're freezing, Emma, come here.' Dave pulled the covers up around my chin and pulled me closer to him. 'This has really got to you, hasn't it? It's just a bit of left over nightmare, that's all, nothing to worry about.'

'No, there were stories, as a kid. Hearing the bells meant something, something bad, but I can't remember what.'

'Shush, they were stories – you of all people know the power of those. The bells are in your imagination, they're not an omen. Nothing bad's going to happen, they were just stories.'

He stroked my face and I lifted it, ready for his kiss, but I couldn't shake the foreboding that gripped me. Dave's kisses grew more urgent and he moved on top of me, kissing my neck, then pushed my vest top up and kissed my breasts, my belly, then lower. I tangled my fingers in his hair, losing myself in the familiar sensations, in the feel of him, and gradually forgot my fears.

Later I lay in his arms listening to his gentle snores, but was still unable to settle myself. I thought back to the day I'd met him five years ago. I was still writing my first pirate novel and had been in my favourite coffee shop, scribbling away. I'd lost myself in those beautiful old sailing ships, and it had taken a while for me to realise someone was speaking to me.

When I looked up, I realised the coffee shop was full and this man wanted to sit at my table. I must have been ignoring him for some time because he seemed both embarrassed and cross, and I moved my bag and papers to give him room. I tried to get back to the Caribbean, but the spell had been broken. I smiled politely while inwardly cursing him for disturbing me.

'What are you writing about?'

'The *Zephyr*,' I answered. 'Pirates for girls.'

'What?'

'The *Zephyr* is my fictional pirate ship.'

'I see. Why the *Zephyr*?'

'It's named for Zephyrus, one of the Greek wind gods. Isn't it a wonderful word? I like how it looks on the page almost as much as how it sounds. Zephyr.'

He nodded. 'Pirates for girls? So – Johnny Depp?' He chuckled.

'No, not that kind of pirates for girls,' I answered, smiling back in spite of myself. 'Although they are in the Caribbean. I'm fascinated by those wonderful old sailing ships and the life they promised. Did you know the pirates of the Caribbean were the most democratic society of their time? And the cruellest – and greediest of course. There's a lesson in there,' I babbled, hardly aware of what I was saying.

'What, dictatorships are kinder?' he asked, his eyebrows raised.

'No, of course not, I just find it ironic, that's all. That the same men who prized freedom so highly wasted it so extravagantly.'

He smiled and held his right hand across the table. 'David Moorcroft,' he introduced himself.

'Emma Carter.' I shook his hand. He was quite good looking: dark hair, blue eyes, quite heavily built. He had a dimple on one side of his mouth – the right – a cleft chin and a slightly too heavy brow. He was clean shaven and wore a suit.

'What do you do?' I asked, nosey as ever – an essential attribute for a writer.

'Architect,' he replied. 'What do you do?'

I stared at him, then my manuscript in surprise. 'I'm a writer.' I laughed. 'Well, trying to be anyway – all I need is an agent and a publisher, and I'll have cracked it!'

He smiled. A year later I had a publishing deal and we were married.

Chapter 11 - Jennet

20th August 1776

I turned over on to my side, pulled the fleece tightly around me, and sighed in frustration. I had no idea what time it were, but I should have been asleep hours ago. I sighed again. Richard Ramsgill. I could not get him out of my head. Images of him pouring his whiskybae, holding my hand, the look on his face when he talked of Mam, the feel of his whiskers on my face . . .

I turned on to my other side and hugged the memory of his kiss close to me, my body warming as I stroked my cheek with my fingers. He were the only person who were happy to talk to me about Mam and Pa. Oh Mary Farmer tried, but she were more interested in keeping me busy so that I did *not* talk about them – or even think about them. But how could I not? The house had always been filled with them – Mam's cooking and the strange smells of the healing preparations she made all day long. The nights filled with Pa's snores and grunts and . . . other sounds.

Nobody in the village mentioned them – some would not look at me and even walked away when they saw me coming. Frightened my bad luck would rub off on them, no doubt. *Cowards.* I scowled.

But I were not completely alone. Richard Ramsgill looked at me, talked to me, touched me . . .

I turned over again, this time with a grin. He had loved Mam; he had only married Elizabeth because he could not have Mam. And now he loved me. So what if he were over forty and I were fifteen? I were a woman, of marriageable age – and a catch now with my own farm. A small one, aye, nowt like the size of the Ramsgills' holdings, and plenty of women my age married older, wealthy men. I frowned, remembering Elizabeth – *she* were not much older. Well, so what if he were already married? He must know what he were doing. Perhaps Elizabeth were ill and he were thinking of the future – a future with me?

Even if Elizabeth were well, Richard Ramsgill could do what he liked in this valley – the only men who could stand up to him were his father and his brother, Thomas, or "our Thom" as Richard called him. If Richard Ramsgill wanted me, there were nowt his wife could do about it. And I needed him, I needed a friend and I needed a friend's help. I could have lost this farm if he had not stood up to Thomas and found out the truth of the inheritable tenancy and the rights it gave me with the enclosures. *And* he had offered to send a man to help on the farm – I would not be able to manage the sheep without that. It had taken all three of us to gather enough winter fodder for them last year – I would not be able to do that on my own this time. No, I were lucky – lucky to have such a good friend, whatever Mary Farmer said about him.

I rolled over again, then sat up with a start at a noise outside. I sat as still as I could, then jumped when someone hammered on the door. I dared not move.

'Jennet! Jennet, is thee there, lass? Quick, let me in before some bugger sees me!'

Richard Ramsgill! I jumped out of bed and ran downstairs to the door. I smoothed my old linen shift and my hair as best I could, knowing I must look a right sight after all my tossing and turning.

He banged on the door again. Called my name. My heart leaping, I opened the door.

He swayed in the doorway, framed by the feeble pre-dawn light. I stepped aside to let him in and poked the fire back into life, excitement shivering through me as I thought of Mary Farmer watching from her window and seeing a Ramsgill at my door at dawn. How horrified she would be!

'Lass,' he said as he tried to run his fingers through my hair, then grabbed my shoulder as he nearly fell. I grunted, but kept my feet and put my hands on his chest to steady him.

'What's thee done to me, lass? Been at Gate all night, couldn't stop thinking 'bout thee. Bewitched me, thee has, bewitched me with Alice's eyes.' He kissed me. Roughly this time, his whiskers – the feel of which I had so enjoyed earlier – scratched my face. He stank and tasted of Robert Grange's strong beer. Smelled like Pa after he had celebrated the sale of the wethers or a good lambing.

'Shouldn't be here, lass, shouldn't be here. Can't be anywhere else, can't help mesen.' He kissed me again, and I felt warmth flood through my body at the insistent pressure of his mouth. His arms circled me – holding me tight. I never wanted him to let me go. I stumbled back with the weight of him and he came with me.

'Oh aye, lass, aye.' I could feel a hardness against my belly, which were fluttering like dragonflies darting over the marshes, and my breath grew harder and sharper. I moved my hands over his chest, copying the way he stroked my back, my waist, my backside.

I stepped back from him again to catch my breath, overwhelmed. Nowt like this had happened to me before. Oh, Arthur Weaver had stolen a kiss last Mayday, and it had been nice, but he were only a boy – he had not made my heart pound like this, my chest heave with the effort of drawing breath. He were not a man, not like Richard Ramsgill.

'What's up, lass? Thee knows I love thee, don't thee? Thee knows thee's bewitched me with her eyes, got me thinking 'bout nowt else? Bewitched me with her eyes,' he said again. 'But thee's not her, is thee lass? Thee's even more beautiful. Thy hair . . .' He paused, this time managing to run his hand through it, carrying on, stroking my back through my thin shift, my body shuddering at his touch. 'Thee wouldn't forsake me for a stranger, would thee, lass? Would thee?' he asked again, more forcefully.

'No,' I whispered, then said it again, louder. 'No, I won't forsake thee, Mr Ramsgill.'

He laughed. 'Mr Ramsgill, is it? I think we're beyond misters, lass. Call me Richard.' He pulled back. 'Only when we're alone, though. Only when we're alone. Ahh!' He had spotted his hip flask on the table. 'Thought I might have left that here.' He lurched over, grabbed it, uncorked it and took a deep draught. 'Here, thee too, lass. It's cold, thee's shivering, this'll warm thee up.'

I took the flask from him and sipped it, managing not to cough. I had drunk some earlier, trying to feel closer to him after he had left, and the fire of it did not shock me any more.

'Aye, that's right lass, getting a taste for it, ain't thee? Just like thy mam. Have some more, go on, there's plenty.' I took a longer drink, and this time did cough. He laughed and I joined in, passing the flask back to him. He drank deeply and looked around him.

He moved to the staircase, then up, and I hurried after him, my heart thumping and my mouth dry. What on earth were he doing? I followed him to my bedroom door which I had left open, my mattress visible in the dim light. He went in and stood by it, then turned to me. 'Come here, lass.'

My heart beat faster again, but I did not move. I suddenly felt scared. *What does he want me to do? I don't know what to do!*

'Come on, lass, there's nowt to be afeared of.' He held out his hand to me and my body moved towards him, almost of its own will. *Were I really going to do this? With Richard Ramsgill? Were Richard Ramsgill really going to do this with* me?

He grabbed my arm when I got close enough and fell backwards on to the mattress, pulling me with him. I cried out in surprise and we both laughed. 'Aye, that's right, lass. Nowt to be afeared of. Nowt at all.'

He kissed me again, not quite so roughly as before, and I hardly noticed the taste of the beer now – I could only taste whiskybae. One hand were behind my head holding my face to his, and the other were on my backside again. I felt a cold draught as my shift were pulled up, his hand gathering fold after fold as he exposed my skin to the cold air. I shivered.

'Thee cold, lass?'

'No. No, I'm not,' I whispered and he smiled, then rolled us over so I were lying on my back underneath him, my shift around my hips. He propped himself up on his arms and stared at me, his eyes drifting from my face, lingering on my chest, then further down to the tops of my legs now visible below the shift.

'Take it off,' he whispered, his voice hoarse. 'Take it off, I want to see thee.'

I did not move for a moment. *Do I dare? Do I really dare to do as he asks?* His eyes rose to my face and, as we stared into each other, I slipped two shaking hands between us and grabbed hold of my shift. I took a deep breath and slowly started to pull the old, thin linen up my body. I lifted my hips to free the material and it were bunched around my waist. Then I stopped. I could not lift it further without sitting up and I could not sit up when he were leaning so closely over me.

He realised my problem and reared up, kneeling astride my thighs and I pulled the shift further, raising my upper body as I did so. His eyes had left mine and I pulled my belly in tight as it came into his view, my breath coming in little gasps as I watched his eyes caress my exposed body. *Is he smiling? It's hard to tell in the gloom.*

I took a deep breath and pulled my shift higher, amazed

at my daring, my . . . my . . . *wantonness*. Aye, that were the word, my wantonness, and I realised I wanted this, I wanted to be with this man. I wanted never to be alone again. I drew a deep breath and pulled the shift over my breasts – I were almost sitting up now, then further until it were over my head and gone.

'Ahh, that's good, lass, oh aye, that's good.' I lay back down, naked, beneath him and he reached out to touch my breast – my left one first, his hand stroking it, circling the nipple, then cupping it and squeezing. Now both his hands kneaded my flesh and I gasped as he gripped too hard and pain shot through me.

'Aye, thee likes that don't thee, lass?'

'Mm,' I groaned and arched my back into his grip.

He stood suddenly and I looked at him in bewilderment. *What have I done wrong?* Then I realised he were fumbling with his clothes and they piled up around his feet. Jacket, shirt, breeches.

I stared at him. I had seen naked men before – it were impossible not to when families lived so closely together – but I had never seen a naked man like *this* before. He laughed and his hand closed around himself, moving rhythmically as I watched, then he moved and were once again astride me.

I reached out to touch his chest and he grabbed my hand to move it lower until I had hold of him. His hand closed around mine and he made the same movements. I tightened my grip and soon I were doing it on my own, his breathing hoarse and his hands on my breasts again. Then they were moving lower, over my belly and lower still.

I froze, my legs tight together and my hand still. He reached between his legs and started my hand moving again, then reached back to me.

'It's all right, lass, there's nowt to worry about. Relax.' He leaned down and kissed me, and I took a deep breath to calm myself. He pushed his hand between us.

'Oh.' I gasped as I felt his finger, slippery with a wetness I had not realised were there.

'Aye that's it, lass, move thy legs a bit.'

I did as he asked and his finger delved deeper and started moving.

'Oh!' I said again, surprised at the sensations this simple movement were causing. I parted my legs a little more. He moved his finger lower and probed, then smiled. 'Ahh, I'm the first. That's good, lass, that's good. Just relax.'

He leaned over me and took hold of himself. I pulled my hand away and rested it on his thigh. He moved closer, till he were almost lying on top of me. I could not see his face; he were looking down there, and I raised my head, trying to see what he were doing. Then I cried out in pain as he stabbed into me.

'Don't worry, lass, it's right. Won't hurt no more now.'

I stared at the roof. I had not expected pain. Mam had not sounded in pain at night with Pa.

He pulled away, then back in. It did not hurt as much this time and I started to calm. Again, again and again. Then he groaned and fell on top of me. I held him, not knowing what to do.

'Ahh, that were good, lass.'

I had no idea what to say, so stayed quiet. He were heavy and I struggled to breathe. Finally, he rolled off me and we lay side by side in silence.

Once his breathing slowed, he heaved himself off the bed and scrabbled for his clothes. My hand found my shift and I shrugged it on, feeling exposed. Fully dressed now, he leaned over and kissed me. 'Good, really good, but got to get back, work to be done.' He stroked my face. 'Beautiful,' he said. 'Beautiful, I'll see thee soon.'

When he had gone, I hugged myself. I were truly a woman now. And not just any woman – Richard Ramsgill's woman. I smiled.

Chapter 12 - Emma

31st August 2012

I woke once again sitting up in bed, heart pounding.

'What is it, not another one?'

'No, not a nightmare – a memory. Sorry to wake you, Dave.' I couldn't say any more and got out of bed. Dave followed me to the bathroom.

'What? What is it?'

'Nothing.' I stroked his face to reassure him and did my best to smile. 'Honestly, it's ok, just a scare from the haunted house I'd forgotten about.'

'The haunted house?'

'Yes, Mark and Kathy's place before they did it up. Just kids' fanciful stuff. It's nothing really.'

He said nothing for a while then, 'Tell me again, why did you want to build here? I thought this was a happy place for you.'

'Yes, so did I. It was. It is. I don't know what's going on – you're probably right, it's just my imagination working overtime – maybe it'll all make a good book!'

'Let's hope. Are you sure you're all right?' he asked again.

'Yes, nothing a hot shower won't fix,' I replied firmly. 'Now go downstairs and put the coffee on.'

Brushing my teeth, I looked out of the window and up the hill to the haunted house. For a moment I saw it as it had been when I was a child: decrepit, burnt and filthy with a fallen down animal shed and a low dry stone wall running up the side. There had been no high garden walls or security cameras then. Hell, there'd been no glass in the windows or a staircase, and it had only been inhabited by sheep and cows.

We'd played there often, although never alone. We'd pretended we weren't scared of it, that the only ghosts were in actuality the occasional tramp sheltering from the ravages of the Yorkshire weather. But still – there'd always been *something* about the place. I shuddered, finished in the bathroom, and went downstairs, following the scent of brewing coffee and burning toast to the large kitchen-diner below the guest bedrooms on the other side of the house.

Breakfast over, Dave left to go to his office in Harrogate, and I took the dogs for a walk. This was where my day usually started – apart from waking me up, walking alongside Thruscross somehow kick-started my creative centre and I came out here making soggy notes as the beasts ran and swam and played, rain or shine, two or three times a day – sometimes more, despite the fact we had enough land that I could just let the dogs out to amuse themselves.

Today, the walk did nothing for me. Tired and unfortunately uninspired, we walked slowly (yes, even the beasts now) back to the house. I looked up at Mark and Kathy's as we passed, remembering that Dave and I were invited for dinner tonight. Was that why I'd dreamed of the place?

Half an hour later, we were all in the office. Clean-ish dogs collapsed in a heap; notebooks; pot of coffee and a plate of biscuits – all the essentials – were close at hand, and I settled down to get the next chapter of my latest book down on paper.

I cursed. Hadn't there been something in my dream the other night? An idea for their next battle? I couldn't remember, but knew the harder I tried, the further away the idea would slip. I sighed in frustration and just started writing to see what came out of my pen.

I checked my watch and massaged my neck with a groan. It was only lunchtime, yet I felt mentally exhausted. I read over what I'd scribbled and frowned. This was usually the bit I enjoyed most, where I got completely lost in the story and was just as eager to find out what happened next as I hoped my readers would be. Unfortunately what I'd written today was crap and did nothing to move the story on.

I left the notebooks on the coffee table by the sofa and crossed to the desk. I had a series of large noticeboards on the only section of bookshelf-free wall, where I had laid out the overall plot for the book. Instead of studying my plans, I spotted the old inkpot hidden away on the shelf alongside. *How had I forgotten about that?* I took it down and put it on a sheaf of papers on the desk where I could see it, then went down to sort out some lunch. I'd try again later.

Chapter 13 - Jennet

16th September 1776

I put the posset on to warm through and sat down with a sigh; I were knackered. September were a busy month with the sheep and I had spent the entire week with Richard's man, Peter Stockdale, spaining the flock. We had to separate lamb from ewes until the gimmers – the young females – were weaned and could return to breed. The wethers – males – would be moved to the best pastures down by the river to fatten them up for meat for Pateley Bridge Market, but it were exhausting to chase lamb and ewe around the moors and drag the lamb away, bleating for its dam.

I giggled to myself, remembering Peter face down in the muck after a particularly stubborn gimmer had got away from him. I had laughed so hard I fell as well, and the pair of us had rolled in mud and sheepshit with the bemused ewes looking on for a good ten minutes until the last chuckles had died away. The job had taken twice as long as it should have.

Maybe the new enclosures that Thomas Ramsgill were forcing on the valley for the king were not such a bad idea. He had a team of men – including Peter Stockdale – building the dry stone walls. They might look ugly cutting their way across moor and pasture, but his sheep had been unable to escape. His massive flock had been spained in not much more time than it had taken me and Peter Stockdale to do my twenty five beasts. I dreaded to think how long it would have taken me on my own. A couple of the ewes were past wool production as well, and I had a lot of meat to butcher and hang in the chimney.

I got up from the table to stir the posset, adding a healthy glug of whiskybae from the flask Richard had left a couple of nights ago. It were Friday night, Richard would surely be going to the Gate and then he would come here. I smiled and got out the sheep's stomach and liver I had saved, then started chopping. I had energy again.

Meat done, I prepared vegetables, then went to the well to fetch water. I wanted my body and clothes as clean and fresh as possible, and I realised I were singing as I washed; the clear, icy water making my body shudder in anticipation of what were to come. I felt like a real woman, preparing for my man.

Richard had become a regular visitor over the past month. Although daylight visits were rare, he spent two or three nights a week in my bed. And it were more of a bed now – I did not make do with straw and heather any more, Peter Stockdale had arrived a week ago carrying a proper feather-filled mattress and bolster on his first day, then parcels containing brocades and blankets and even a cotton nightgown the next! The softest gown I had ever touched. I wondered if he knew what were in the packages. What had Richard told him he were delivering?

I had been ready a couple of hours when the door opened – he did not knock any more – and my impatience flew from me as I returned his greeting kiss. Richard had brought joy back into my life; I were not alone.

I dished up the meal, and he tucked in with relish. I picked at my own platter, enjoying the sight of him eating at my table.

'What's up, lass? Why's thee staring?'

I reddened and looked at my plate. 'Nowt.'

He put down his knife. 'No, come on, lass, what is it?'

'Well, it's just . . .' I paused, but he were still watching me. 'It's been so hard,' I continued in a rush. 'I don't know what I'd have done without thee – or without Peter.'

'Don't worry about it, Jennet, it's nowt. The least I could do.' He stretched out his hand and grasped mine briefly, then picked up his knife again and continued eating. 'We have to be more careful though, lass. Billy Gill made a crack in The Gate tonight about how well I'm looking after thee. He saw me t'other night, but Stockdale jumped in saying there were a problem with sheep. I think he took it – didn't say owt else, anyroad.'

I paled. *Does that mean he won't visit as often?*

'Don't look so worried, lass!' He laughed. 'It'll take more than Billy Gill to stop me coming here – he knows better than to put about rumour concerning me, or any Ramsgill for that matter!'

I smiled and looked up at him from below my lashes. *He's so important and powerful!*

He pushed the plate away. 'Enough of that, lass. Nice as it were, I've a hunger for summat else.' He took a swig of the whiskybae, ignoring my posset, stood, took my hand, and walked me upstairs to our richly covered bed.

Chapter 14 - Emma

1st September 2012

'Have you got the wine?'

'Yes! Both red and white,' Dave shouted back. 'Where's the torch?'

'In the mudroom, on top of the cupboard,' I called.

'Come on, Emma! We'll be late!' Dave *hated* being late.

'Hold your horses, I'm coming!'

Eyeliner, mascara, lipstick. I was ready and went downstairs to spoil the effect of my expensive linen wraparound top and black trousers with a heavy coat and wellies. Dave was still scratting about looking for the torch.

'Come on then, I'm waiting for you!' I called to Dave, laughing at his scowl.

Trudging up the lane, I was strangely nervous. I'd not been to the haunted house since it had been derelict, and Mark and Kathy Ramsgill had not been particularly keen on our build. Their invitation to dinner had been a surprise, and I hoped it was a genuine display of neighbourliness and perhaps friendship. We were very isolated out here, and I couldn't bear the thought of problem neighbours – especially since I worked from home. I hoped tonight would go well.

Wolf Farm was less than a hundred yards away over field and wall, but a couple of hundred by road, well, lane. We reached their gates only ten minutes late and pressed the intercom to gain entry. I remembered the place as open and perched on the hillside overlooking the reservoir, but now it resembled a prison with a high wall surrounding the house and garden, topped with cameras. The only way in was through heavy locked gates, and it struck me as a shame; the complete antithesis of the way of life that had built the sandstone farmhouse back in the 1600s.

'David and Emma Moorcroft,' Dave barked into the intercom and the gate slowly swung open. The front door shed a welcome rectangle of warm yellow light, beckoning us over the gravelled drive and yard.

'Welcome!' Mark Ramsgill greeted us. 'Come in, come in, just leave your boots by the door, let me take your coats. We're through here. Oh, thank you very much. Pinot Grigio and Merlot, Kathy will be pleased. Come through, come through.'

I had an impression of a friendly, cluttered, colourful hall littered with the detritus of family and dales living – lots of muddy boots, coats, umbrellas and hats – and then we were ushered into the front room, the one which no doubt looked over our house and the water. If either could be seen over that high garden wall, that is. I'd have to hope we were invited back in daylight to find out.

'Hello, hello, come in, ooh lovely.' Mark had passed the wine bottles to Kathy. 'It's nice to meet you properly at last, I'm so pleased you came. Would you like a drink? Wine or maybe gin and tonic?' she asked.

'Dry white for me, please,' I said.

'And G and T for me,' Dave added.

'I'll get them.' Mark bustled at the sideboard. 'Better not keep Kathy out of the kitchen too long. Please, sit down, make yourselves comfortable.'

'Can I give you a hand in the kitchen?' I asked.

'Oh no, no, ignore Mark, everything's under control. Roast dales beef – oh, I hope that's all right? You're not vegetarian are you?'

'No, that sounds lovely, thank you. It smells delicious,' I replied.

'Emma's what you'd call a selective vegetarian,' Dave joked. 'No red meat allowed at home, but she can't get enough of it when we eat out! I think she just doesn't like cooking it.'

'Trying to eat a balanced diet, Dave. Anyway, I wouldn't complain if you wanted to cook.'

'Yes, you would.' He laughed. 'It'd be inedible! How about you, Mark, can you find your way about in the kitchen?'

'Oh no, that's Kathy's domain.' He handed me a glass of wine and gave another to Kathy.

'Yes, the kitchen's mine. Mark can barely put beans on toast together!' Kathy sat next to me on the sofa, checking her watch.

'You have a lovely home,' I said to her with an embarrassed smile. The room was very much like the hall; colourful and full of an assortment of knick-knacks from around the world. It was a good size, painted cream to show off the paintings and textiles adorning the walls, with exposed beams and a lovely stone arched fireplace with blazing fire that took up most of one wall. They had a comfortable leather suite, an incongruous flatscreen at one end, and a rustic looking dining table and chairs standing in front of the fire. 'Do you do a lot of travelling?'

'No, not at all.' She laughed. 'I'm terrified of flying so I bring the world to me – mainly courtesy of car boot sales and TK Maxx. I love all the different cultures and types of art, I find them fascinating.'

I nodded and studied the knick-knacks. Buddhas nestled against Hindi deities and Egyptian and Chinese figurines. I spotted a boomerang, a couple of carved elephants, crystals and a collection of brass and copper plateware, including a beautiful Russian samovar.

'Are there any countries not represented?' I asked.

'Not many,' grumbled Mark.

'Oh, don't listen to him,' Kathy said. 'He picked half of

this stuff out, he just doesn't like to admit it.'

Which half? I wondered. Looking at Kathy, I guessed her choices were the representations of the East. She was shorter than I, with long, dark hair pulled back in a couple of combs, bright blue eyes and flushed cheeks, although that was probably the effects of cooking, and she wore a long, floaty red and gold skirt with a gold-coloured tunic. I'd put down money that the crystals were hers, too.

Mark was taller, also dark haired, although greying now, a little plump and dressed simply in jeans and checked shirt.

'Would you excuse me?' Kathy heaved herself off the sofa, checking her watch again. 'The stove calls for a moment.' She walked quickly into the kitchen, taking her wine with her.

'So how long have you been in now?' Mark asked with a broad Yorkshire dialect. 'Does it feel like home yet?'

'Oh yes, it's been about a month. We haven't finished unpacking yet, mind you. We love it here don't we, Dave? It was definitely worth all the hassle.'

'You were brave, doing a build from scratch. I remember all the problems converting this place,' Mark replied. 'Constant arguments with the architect and builders; I were glad to see the back of them. Never listened to a ruddy word I said!'

'Yes, they're like that.' I laughed, glancing at Dave. 'It's even worse when you're married to your architect! But we survived, didn't we, Dave?'

'Just about,' he muttered.

'You're an architect?' Mark asked, embarrassed. Dave nodded.

'So what do you do, Mark?' I asked to fill the awkward silence.

'I'm a teacher, over at Pateley Bridge. History and PE. It's where I met Kathy, actually.'

'Really?'

'Yeah, I were straight out of school myself and she were my star pupil! Oh, don't worry, we didn't get together until after she'd left, but twenty years and two kids later, we're still as happy.'

'How old are your kids?' I asked, not sure how to respond to that.

'Seventeen-year-old twins – Alex and Hannah. We're starting to think about university at the moment, which Kathy is finding difficult. But we hardly see them anyway, to tell you the truth. They're always out or staying at friends' houses.'

'So you're getting the house back to yourselves?'

'Yes. Do you have children?'

'No, no, just dogs, three of them.' Dave laughed. I sipped my drink to avoid reacting. 'And they're more than enough trouble!'

'Dinner is served!' Kathy came back in carrying bowls of soup. 'Hope you're hungry!'

'Oh, that smells delicious, Kathy.'

'Spiced pumpkin – home-grown.'

'Mark was just telling us how you met, Kathy.'

'Oh, ignore him. It wasn't anything like as sordid as he makes it sound; he likes to shock people and play devil's advocate. I'm hoping to go back to school myself once I've finished my training. I dread to think what he'll say to everyone.'

'Oh? What subjects do you teach?'

'No, not as a teacher, as school counsellor. I'm in my fourth year of training and should get my diploma in June.'

'Oh right. That sounds rewarding.'

'I ruddy well hope so,' Mark cut in. 'You wouldn't believe what it involves. I thought it would just be college once a week, but she has to volunteer as a counsellor. Volunteer! She don't get paid! Then she has to have counselling herself *and* a supervisor. It's costing us a ruddy fortune!'

'It'll be worth it, Mark, and in time I'll earn quite a bit in private practice. It'll take a while, that's all.'

'Where do you volunteer?' I asked.

'A local service that offers counselling in rural areas. It's a real lifeline to some of the more isolated, and you're right, very rewarding, even if I'm not getting paid for it yet.' She glared at Mark; it was obviously a sore spot.

'How's your beef, Dave?' Mark asked and I realised Dave hadn't said very much since the architect gaffe.

'Perfect,' he said. 'Tender and absolutely delicious. You should ask Kathy about those dreams you've been having, Emma. You never know, they might mean something.'

'Dreams?' Kathy asked.

'Yes.' I glared at Dave. They were mine to talk about, not for him to use as small talk at the dinner table. 'Nightmares really, but very real, very accurate somehow.'

Kathy and Mark glanced at each other. 'About the village?' she asked. Thruscross village dated back to the Vikings and had been flooded when the dam was built in the 1960s.

'No, just the reservoir. Why, do you dream of the village?' I asked.

Kathy nodded. 'I keep getting stuck in the mud, only it's not a foot deep like it is when the tide goes out. I sink further and further down and I know there's no end to it.'

Mark rolled his eyes. 'When the tide goes out,' he said in an exaggerated falsetto. 'It's not the seaside, eh Dave?'

'You know what I mean,' she said. 'They're always letting the water out to make sure the lower reservoirs stay full.'

'Maybe there's a book in the dreams somewhere,' I said, keen to change the subject.

'A book,' Kathy repeated. 'Are you a writer?'

I nodded. 'Yes, historical fiction, mainly.'

'Have you had any success?'

'Yes, some,' I said, modestly.

'I'm sorry, I've never heard of you,' Mark said.

'I write under my maiden name, Carter.'

'Oh! You're Emma Carter!' Kathy exclaimed. 'You write those pirate books. My daughter, Hannah, is a big fan. She loves all the description aboard the ships, says you must be a sailor.'

'Yes, I virtually grew up at the old sailing club here, actually.'

'You built your house where the old clubhouse were.'

'Yes. I loved it round here. I was very lucky to spend my childhood playing on and by the water, and couldn't imagine anywhere better to live.'

'You know, she calls this place the haunted house, don't you? Tell them about the inkpot,' Dave prompted.

'The haunted house? I'm not surprised,' Kathy said. 'There's something here. Not quite dormant; not quite finished. Waking. The dreams are only the start. Have you heard the bells yet? They say that means she walks again.'

'*The dreams are only the start. She walks again.*' Mark repeated his falsetto thing and I noticed Kathy grimace. My heart thumped. 'The start of what?' he asked. Do you think Jennet's coming back? Or is she still here after two hundred year?'

'Who's Jennet?' Dave asked.

'Jennet Scot,' Mark replied. 'This were her farm, or so my nan used to tell me.'

'Mark's family comes from the village, owned most of the land at one point,' Kathy added. 'His dad moved away as soon as he was old enough, but his nan only moved when the Leeds Corporation bought everything up and forced everyone to go so they could flood the valley.'

'Yeah, she were not impressed – tried to stop everyone drinking tap water! That didn't last long, though.'

'She sounds like quite a character,' Dave remarked.

'She were certainly that! Full of tales as well, and her favourite were Jennet. She were supposed to be a powerful witch, powerful enough to call up the Wild Hunt.'

'The Wild Hunt? What's that?'

'Oh, an old superstition – it goes back to when the Vikings settled here, when this were Thores-Cross, but Nan always said it were the devil riding the moors with his Gabriel hounds, collecting souls to take back to hell.'

'Charming,' said Dave.

'You're telling me. Apparently she foretold the flooding of the valley.'

'And supposedly put a curse on your ancestors – don't forget that!' Kathy added.

'Aye, my great-great-great-great-great-great-great-granddad or summat like that.'

'And now you live in her house. That's brave.'

'Oh, it's all a load of nonsense,' said Dave. 'Witches and devil hunts.'

'Wild hunts,' Mark corrected. 'And careful what you call nonsense round here, there's plenty of folk who still believe in fairies, hobgoblins and barguests and the like.'

'Barguests?' I asked. I had visions of ghosts perched on bar stools at the Stone House.

'Phantom animals – black dogs mainly. That's where the farm gets its name, Jennet were supposed to be able to turn herself into a wolf.'

'I thought it was big cats round here,' Dave joined in again. 'Wasn't one supposed to have been prowling around Harrogate a few years ago?'

'Aye, there's all sorts, especially on't moors, but it were a wolf that were supposed to have roamed in Jennet's day.'

'Did you say something about an inkpot?' Kathy asked.

'Oh yes tell them, Emma – maybe it belonged to Mark's witch!'

I glared at him. I wasn't sure if he was getting in the spirit of things or taking the piss, as he often did when the conversation turned to the supernatural. I carried on anyway.

'Yeah, I found it as a kid. I told you I more or less grew up at the sailing club. Well, we used to play up here a lot when the house was derelict. Did you know there's a natural spring in the next field? We used to collect frog spawn every year. Anyway,' I caught Dave's eye, 'I was climbing through the old dry stone wall out front – it was falling down already, honest! And I spotted a funny shaped stone, pulled it out and it was an inkpot! It wasn't just hidden, it was actually built into the structure of the wall.'

'Oh wow! Do you still have it? I'd love to see it.'

'Yes, I'll show you when you come to us for dinner. Not that it's anything special to look at, just rough stoneware. I searched online and apparently the walls were built around 1780, and the way it was built in, I reckon its original, which makes it about two hundred and thirty years old.'

'Maybe it *was* Jennet's! Perhaps she put it there so her story could be written one day.'

I did not react to that. I wasn't going to tell them about the voice I'd heard, not when Dave and Mark were so scornful of the idea of ghosts. 'Who knows?' I said. 'But I'd love to set a book up here, probably in the old village.'

'Oh, yes! Mark knows all the history and has loads of books about Thruscross. Did you see the map in the hall?'

'No, I didn't notice it, I'm afraid.'

'We'll have to get you a copy as a house-warming present. It's of the village and moors in 1851.'

'Oh, I'd love to study that, and perhaps pick your brains sometime, Mark?'

'No problem, especially if they're well-oiled! Any more wine anyone?'

'Well that wasn't too bad was it, Dave? Awkward at first, but they seem all right.'

'Hmmph. She's ok, but I dinnae know about him, did

you hear the way he spoke to her?'

'Oh, you're just annoyed because he doesn't like architects!'

'And what about all that witch stuff?'

'I know – fascinating. Who'd have thought it, a witch used to live in the haunted house!'

'Did you not hear about her before?'

'No, nothing. I always thought the haunting had to do with the village drowning, but maybe it's older. Maybe they're right, maybe she *will* be the plot of my Thruscross story.'

Chapter 15 - Jennet

30th September 1776

Where were he? I stared at the pottage on the fire, aware that it were already overcooked, and sighed. I stood up and moved the pot off the heat. I were not hungry any more. Another meal gone to waste to add to the others I had prepared for him over the last two weeks. Two weeks. I bit back a sob. I missed Richard so much – why had he not visited? I wiped the tears from my face. Anything could have happened. Maybe he were ill? Or somebody had seen him and he were being discreet. Maybe Elizabeth suspected something, or were he just too busy?

I walked to the door, then out into the garden, shivering in the white cotton nightgown he had given me, and tightened the thick, woollen shawl around my shoulders.

I had been out every night, staring down the lane, hoping for a glimpse of him striding towards the house as he used to. I had seen him once or twice, but he had not seen me, and he had not come. I had watched him turn right – going home after an evening at the Gate Inn.

I shivered again and stared over the moors, then lower down the valley towards the village. It were a full moon and the moors looked forbidding in the cold light.

Then – a movement. My eyes darted back to the path – he were there!

I rushed forward and he glanced up, startled. He stopped and stared at me a moment before putting his head down and turning right, his pace hurried. Going home. Again.

My heart sank and I sobbed, then turned and dashed back into the house, my hands clasped over my mouth to stifle the sound of my despair. He were not too busy. He did not want to see me.

I sat down heavily at the table, rested my head in my arms folded on the tabletop and let the sobs come – not caring if anyone heard me now. Not that they would – the nearest houses were too far away. I so wanted to see him, talk to him, touch him . . .

Why did he not want to talk to me any more? We used to spend hours talking and laughing until the dawn broke and he had to leave. Did I not touch him the way he wanted? Did he not like it? Were I no good? What were wrong with me?

Once my tears had run dry, I rose and went up to bed. He did not love me. He loved Mam. He had used me to ease his grief for her – his lost love. Tears flowed again as I thought of all the empty days, weeks, months ahead with no Richard. Years. How could he have made me love him, the selfish bastard!

My anger were refreshing – a relief from all the worry, disappointment and longing that had consumed me since I had last seen him a fortnight ago. He had got what he wanted. He had never cared. He had seen a vulnerable woman-child he could have his way with, and he had done just that. He had taken what he wanted, then thrown me aside when he were done.

God, I were so stupid! How could I have fallen for it? Mary Farmer had tried to warn me and we had laughed at her. *I* had laughed at her! In a fit of rage I pulled all the beautiful, expensive brocades off our bed. No, not our bed, not any more – only mine. I dragged my old, smelly fleece out, threw it on the mattress and crawled underneath it, sobbing once more.

I heard a noise outside and sat up, drying my face.

Richard? But there were nowt. Nobody. It were probably a fox. I lay back down feeling foolish and angry at the hope that had soaked my heart. It were no good. No matter how much I yearned for him, he were not coming. Would probably never come. I were alone again.

I could not even talk to Mary Farmer – I were so embarrassed at the way I had laughed at her warnings, how could I admit what I had done? I wished he had never spoken to me at the clipping, never visited – even if that would have meant losing the farm. Would Peter Stockdale stop coming too? Would I have to deal with the sheep by myself? I should have done that from the beginning – at least I would have known where I were.

Tears rolled down my face again. My cheeks were still wet when I woke the next morning.

Chapter 16 - Jennet

15th November 1776

It had been almost two months, and I still had not heard from him. I cried myself to sleep every night, but things had changed. If only I could find a way to tell him my news, then he would come back. He would leave Elizabeth and be with me. Me and our child.

I were sure of it. My courses had only been flowing a year, and were not yet reliable. When I had missed the first I had not worried, but now I had missed a second. As a cunning woman's daughter, I knew about these things – even if I had not thought to take any precautions against it. There were no doubt at all; I had been sick every morning for weeks and my breasts hurt summat terrible. I were carrying Richard's child. He had to talk to me now. He had to see me, and help me. Oh, I knew he had a wife and a family already, but Elizabeth had only given him one son and the rest were daughters. It were common knowledge that he were desperate for more boys – and I would give him one, followed by many more. Despite his abandonment of me, he were a good man. He had been grieving Mam too – he would stand by me, help me; this were not only our child, but Mam's grandchild. He would not turn his back on us.

He had only left me because of his wife, I knew that now. The hateful stares she threw my way at church or if we passed in the village proved it. She must have found out and threatened him with scandal if he did not stop seeing me. He had not stayed away out of choice. He still loved me, I knew it, he had told me he did often enough.

That night I dressed carefully and crept outside to the fork in the lane. Ahead were the Gate Inn, to my left the lane to East Gate House – Richard's house. I kept to the shadows, hiding in the trees – I did not want anyone but him to see me.

I imagined his face – the delight and love I would see there, banishing my fears and nightmares. How would he react? Would he shout? Cry? Laugh? Pick me up and spin me round? Declare everlasting love? I hugged myself in delighted anticipation. I hoped he would not be too long, the November night were cold, despite my woollens.

I caught my breath – someone were coming! I peered out from behind the tree. John Farmer and George Weaver. Damn! I stayed as still as possible, praying they would not see me. I need not have worried; they were drunk and could barely see their way home. I listened to their raucous singing until their voices faded, and breathed a sigh of relief. If John Farmer had seen me, he would tell Mary, and I did not want to have to explain to her what I were doing out here at midnight.

I peered out from my hiding place again – were those footsteps I heard? They were, and Richard strode into view a few seconds later. I took a moment to admire him, smiling to myself. How I had missed him! Tall, with a slight stoop, greying hair and magnificent whiskers – the best in the valley. He had nearly reached me, and I checked that nobody else were in the lane, then took a deep breath and stepped out.

'By heck, lass, thee scared living daylights outta me! What's thee up to skulking in't trees?'

I hesitated. He were not smiling. I had a whole speech worked out, but it started with him taking me in his arms, or at least pleased to see me. But he were not even smiling.

'I'm carrying thy child,' I blurted out.

Silence for a moment, then, 'Thee stupid little slut!' he

shouted, and before I could react, his fist connected with my face and I were lying in the dirt.

'But, Richard . . .' I gasped, unable to understand what had happened.

'Don't thee call me Richard, thee stupid little girl!' He kicked me in the belly. I curled into a ball to protect myself and the babby, bewildered and terrified by his reaction. 'I thought thee were a cunning woman, didn't thee think to take herbs for this kind of thing? Chant a damned spell or something?'

'I-I-I'd only just started my courses, I didn't think of it!'

'Whore!' He kicked me again. I felt a stabbing pain in my back, and screamed in pain and fear. 'Well, take something now and get rid of it!' He kicked out once more, but my senses were returning and I rolled out of his way.

'Damn whore!' he said again and spat, then strode off in the direction of East Gate House.

I stayed where I were, in the dirt, stunned, tears running down my face and unable to move. I could not believe he had hurt me – I were carrying his child. Damn him! He had called me a dirty whore and left me in the dirt! He had told me to get rid of our babby!

I sobbed and struggled to my feet, my whole body hurting, then staggered home. I knew the truth now – he did not love me. Elizabeth had not prevented him from seeing me – he had chosen not to come. He had abandoned me at the worst time of my life and now he had rejected me again. My hands clasped my belly. He did not want this child.

What would happen to me? He had called me 'whore', and everyone I knew would do the same when they found out.

I could not be alone, unmarried, with a child – the whole village would hate me. I had to do as he said. I sobbed again, my heart breaking, but I had no choice. I could not bear and bring up a child alone, not a bastard child unwanted by its pa and shunned by the whole village.

I reached the house and put on a pot of water, then fumbled in Mam's remedy chest, pulling out bottles and bunches of dried herbs by the light of my single candle. I found what I wanted, then shredded leaves and pounded roots before I put the mixture into a bowl and poured on the boiling water.

I drank it all down as soon as it were cool enough, but still burned my mouth. I did not care. I did not care about anything any more. I crumpled on to the floor, held my belly, and sobbed for the life I were killing.

Chapter 17 - Jennet

1st December 1776

'Thee ain't been to church in a while, lass.'

I glanced up. Mary Farmer stood at the open door. 'Thee can't hide away, thee knows. Folk understand thee's had terrible time losing thy mam and pa, but enough's enough. Thee ain't been to church since thy pa's sending off, there's talk of fining thee if thee don't go soon. Get changed and come along – it won't be so bad.'

I stared at her in silence a moment, then slowly got to my feet and moved away from the table. She were right. I could not put it off any longer. Mary Farmer came in and shut the door. I went upstairs, pulled off my old dirty homespun dress and reached for my Sunday best. I heard a gasp behind me. Mary Farmer had followed me.

'Jennet! Lass, what . . . what . . .' I heard a thump as Mary Farmer fell against the wall and I pulled my dress over my head. It were a bit tight round my belly.

'Lass, whatever . . . lass, thee looks . . .'

I stared at her and she took a deep breath. 'Who?' she asked.

'Richard Ramsgill.' I could not meet her eyes but stared at the floor. I had not wanted to tell her, but I knew she would not give up until she got the name out of me. 'I took red clover, raspberry, feverfew and horsetail, but it didn't work.'

'Ramsgill? But . . . but . . . that Damned bastard!'

I still could not look at her.

'Has thee told him?'

I nodded, aware that tears were rolling down my face.

'Nay need to ask how he took news.'

I shook my head, unable to tell her he had knocked me to the ground and kicked me.

'Well . . .' I looked up. I did not think I had ever known Mary Farmer lost for words before.

She stood up. 'Life goes on, lass. Thee needs church more than ever now. And it'd be better to be seen there an'all. Folk are already talking about thee not going, and thee hasn't been seen in't village neither. Best to face these things and get them over with 'fore thee gets any bigger. Come on, lass, thee's not on thy own, let's get this done.' She offered me her arm and I took it, grateful for her kindness.

It were awful. Even though I were barely showing, they all knew. I were aware of clusters of women glancing at me and gossiping. I got through the service and stood to leave the church in relief.

I walked out of the cool dark of the stone building into a bright winter's day and paused. The village were beautiful in the sunshine, the heavy frost now all but gone.

I grew aware of a silence around me, and Mary Farmer gripped my arm. Richard and Elizabeth Ramsgill stood on the path ahead of us, chatting to the curate and a couple more Ramsgills – Thomas's wife Hannah and Betsy Ward, a distant cousin. Richard saw me first. He glanced at my belly, then back at my face. I took a step back at the hate etched on his features as he glowered at me. I glanced away and saw the same expression on Elizabeth's face. So she knew. The others glanced at Richard and Elizabeth in surprise, then at me and back again. I saw realisation dawn in their faces.

'Well that's it, lass, that Betsy Ward has a tongue in her head as no one can control, least of all hersen. The whole valley'll ken afore sundown. Keep thy head up and say nowt.'

I raised my chin, aware my shame were visible in my cheeks, and we walked towards them. I kept my eyes on Richard, but his expression never wavered. I were aware that everyone watched us and my embarrassment grew sharper.

We reached them and they stepped aside at the last moment. They did not give us enough room and I had to walk on the grass to get past.

'Whore.'

I heard the quiet whisper, and was sure everyone else had heard Elizabeth Ramsgill's insult. I glared at her, then at Richard. His face now showed disdain, and my shame turned to anger.

'Lass!' Mary Farmer said, tugging on my arm. 'Thee'll only make it worse.'

I kept my mouth shut and carried on walking. Behind us, the silence broke into whispers and titters. I realised I would have to get used to that.

Chapter 18 - Emma

3rd September 2012

I studied the sky; maybe I shouldn't have come for such a long walk after all. I wasn't going to make it back before the storm broke, but I hadn't written a word worth keeping in days, and I needed to clear my head. I turned to call the dogs, but they were chasing rabbits – they must have run a marathon this afternoon.

'Damn it.' A rumble of thunder reverberated round the valley and echoed off the dam wall ahead.

I headed towards the trees as the first heavy drops of rain fell and lightning flashed. The bridge across the Washburn and to the path up the valley side was metal – there was no way I would cross it now. I was stuck here with what little shelter I could find until the storm passed.

It was only two o'clock in the afternoon, but it seemed like dusk already: dark, heavy clouds had moved in quickly over the moors and another flash of lightning lit up the valley, the thunder that came with it so loud I thought the dam had blown up. But no, it still stood.

I huddled in the tree line, trying to remember if this was safer than being out in the open. I decided I was less likely to be hit by lightning if there were other, taller, targets nearby. I screamed as another bolt of lightning exploded overhead, suddenly not so sure of my reasoning.

The dogs, although used to thunderstorms, went mad: circling and barking, then running up the hill before returning to circle around me again, and I realised they were ignoring the rabbits that streamed about us.

Something more than lightning was wrong.

I eyed the dam again. Had it been hit? Surely not, there'd be all sorts of precautions against lightning strike. It must have withstood hundreds of storms in the past fifty years. I watched it a moment longer. The amount of water coming down the overflow seemed to have increased. It couldn't all be rain, not so soon.

I glanced again at the rabbits and the odd behaviour of the dogs and jumped to my feet. Suddenly the decision whether to shelter in the trees or not seemed irrelevant. I wanted to be on higher ground – quickly, but realised I had a problem.

I was at the bottom edge of Hanging Wood, which covered the valley side, and it was *steep*. Almost sheer. I could only climb by using the trees as a ladder; hauling myself round to brace against a trunk then reach for another, but everything was soaked and slippery already; the trunks mossy, the ground a mush of wet pine needles.

I glanced at the dam again; there was definitely more water flowing over it. Too much. I realised that lightning must have struck the water behind it and maybe cracked the overflow.

'Shit!' I screamed in terror as I slid backwards, losing the precious few feet in height I'd gained, colliding with trees, striking my elbow, and scraping my legs. I looked up at the impossible slope – almost a wooded cliff – and nearly cried. There was no way I could get up there. I spotted Cassie, the Irish Setter, barking at me, and I shouted at her to get on. She did, and I cursed her for leaving me until I realised how she managed the slope. That was it – thank you, Cassie!

I got to my feet again and followed, this time following a diagonal line, and soon got a rhythm going. I could dig my feet sideways into the mush and brace them against the trees at the same time. That was better: six feet, twelve feet, fifteen, time for a rest. *Surely this is high enough?* I steadied myself astride a strong pine to catch my breath and study the dam.

The sky was lightening and I had made no mistake, there was far too much water pouring into the valley. Another horrific crack, but this time not from the sky; masonry fell from the top of the dam and crashed a hundred and twenty feet on to more concrete. As I watched, the new V-shaped split in the centre became a U as cascading water forced the restraining wall out of the way. Water thundered into the valley. I needed to get higher, and started to scramble upwards again.

Another rest. I must be twenty five feet up now and my legs were shaking. I wasn't sure I *could* climb any higher.

Cassie nosed up to me, whining, and I put my arms round her. She was terrified, poor thing, and I didn't blame her – I felt the same way, and completely helpless.

Suddenly, another explosion rent the air and I screamed again as a concrete boulder the size of a house fell to the valley floor. Cassie yelped and jumped, and I couldn't keep hold of her wet fur. I screeched her name as she slid down the wet slope, careening off tree trunks. Despite her efforts to stop, her claws were ineffective in the pine mush. She splashed into water and was gone.

I screamed her name again, but to thin air. I looked around for the two boys, but couldn't see them in the gloom beneath the trees. I didn't want to call them in case they tried to come to me and ended up swept away as well. I was on my own, clinging to the wet hillside above a torrent of certain death.

Tears poured down my face and I clung on to my tree and watched the destruction unfold in front of me.

Poor Cassie. Where would she end up? She was a good swimmer, but there was so much debris in the water, the valley would be scarred for generations. What would those trees do to Cassie? Would she manage to climb on to one of them or would they drown her? I sobbed at the image in my mind of her fighting for her life.

I gaped downstream after her, and imagined what was

happening out of sight. Not just to Cassie, but to everyone in the path of this torrent. The road at Blubberhouses was impassable at every snowfall; this would definitely close it – and for how long? Three million gallons would surely wash it away completely. Then what? There were three more reservoirs downstream, would they hold this water? No way, surely their dams would crumble in its path. I had a brief vision of the *Dambusters* film: dam after dam falling away.

Then what? Otley and the Wharfe. How much would survive? What about Ilkley, Wetherby? What about York? How many homes, towns, cities would be destroyed before this brown peaty dales water reached the sea? How many people would be swept out of their lives?

My initial panic dulled and a horrified dread took its place. How close had I come to being swept away myself?

I don't know how long I perched on that hillside, watching Thruscross empty into the Washburn Valley – thrusting what was left of the dam out of the way. I'd heard of being speechless, and been afflicted that way many times, but this was the first time I'd been struck thoughtless. I couldn't grasp the enormity of what I was seeing. This was an inland tidal wave. Except this was much more than a tsunami, because there'd be no trough, no ebbing of the waters, not until the reservoir was empty. And Otley would soon be facing four times what I'd seen.

I checked my phone. I had to ring someone, anyone, to warn the people living in ignorance downstream. Nothing.

I got back to my feet to climb to the top – I couldn't afford to rest any longer, I had to get to the road at the edge of the dam where I'd have a better chance of getting a signal.

I came out on to the rocks above the road, grateful to leave the claustrophobia of Hanging Wood, and was greeted enthusiastically by two big balls of wet fur with even wetter tongues. Delly and Roddy. I hugged the two German Shepherds in tears, thinking of Cassie swept away. Then pushed them off to fumble for my phone. Emergency only – enough. I dialled 999 with shaking fingers, but had no idea which service I wanted. What could the fire brigade or police do?

'Everyone!' I shouted at the operator, 'Thruscross Dam's burst! You have to warn everyone downstream before it's too late!'

'Which service do you require?'

'Didn't you hear me? The dam's burst, water's flooding downstream, get whoever you can to move people out of the way!'

'Where exactly are you?'

'I'm at the dam.'

'Where is the dam?'

'Thruscross!' I shouted. 'Blubberhouses! Oh my God, there's a car! Get people up here quickly!' I dropped my phone and scrambled down the rocks to stop the car before it drove off the end of the road. Luckily the sight of a mud-covered, raving woman half falling towards them was enough to make the driver hit his brakes.

'Stop, stop, stop – the dam! Stop!'

'Are you all right? What's happened to you?'

'The dam!' I waved wildly. 'The dam's gone!'

'Oh my God.' The driver had got out of the car and was staring, horror-stricken. 'I wouldn't have been able to stop in time. There's nothing there! We'd have gone over the edge!'

'Steve, look! Bloody hell!' The woman passenger had jumped out and pointed at a car coming from the opposite direction. But there was nothing we could do to warn them.

There was a sharp bend just before the dam, they wouldn't have seen the gap until they were on the dam itself. We watched helplessly as the car slewed across the road, aquaplaning on the wet tarmac, then it hit the wall and scraped along the concrete towards the drop.

There was a moment at the very edge when I thought the car had caught, but its momentum was too much. I blinked as the headlights blinded me for an instant, then it plunged into the abyss.

The driver, Steve, rang 112 again. There was nothing else we could do. We couldn't get over there to warn traffic. Neither of us had enough signal to ring anybody to get down to the road before another car drove over the edge, even if I had known any numbers to ring. I hoped no one else would appear around that corner. At least it was afternoon mid-week and the road should be fairly quiet.

I walked out a little way on to the remains of the dam and peered over the wall at what was left of the reservoir. There was plenty of water at this end, but further up where the floor of the valley rose, mud-shrouded lumps had emerged. The village was rising again.

It was an eerie sight – tumbledown houses and bridges resurfacing after fifty years underwater. I realised with a jolt that Jennet would be there somewhere. The bodies from the cemetery had been moved, but she wouldn't have been buried in consecrated ground. Nobody in the 1960s would have known the site of her grave. Her waterlogged bones would be drying out, somewhere in all that mud.

I knew I had to write her story.

I sat up with a jolt. It was pitch black and I was completely disorientated. I remembered needing to see the village, wanting a closer look at the water-worn stone, but why was it so dark? Then I realised, and got out of bed fighting a panic attack. Gasping for breath, I stumbled to the window and pulled the curtains. The reservoir appeared peaceful and beautiful in the moonlight. I grasped the windowsill and stepped back, then bent over with a sob. *What's happening to me? It was so real.*

'Another one?'

I went back to the bed and Dave, and he rubbed my arms. I turned and sank against him, sobbing hard.

'It was so real, Dave! It was her – Jennet! I feel like I'm losing my mind, I don't know which reality is the true one, I don't know if Jennet is real.' I sobbed.

He held me and stroked my hair. 'You know, I don't know which is more frightening: the thought of you having a breakdown or being befriended by an eighteenth century witch,' he said in a misguided effort to cheer me up.

'Nor me,' I whispered. I wasn't cheered. There was nothing remotely amusing about this.

Dave kissed the top of my head. 'They're only dreams, Emma, she's not real, she can't be.'

'Hmm.' Logically, I accepted he was right, but it didn't help. My heart still beat madly in my chest, and I was convinced something was very wrong. 'Go back to sleep,' I told Dave. 'No point in us both being awake.'

'You sure?'

'Yes.'

'Well, lie back down then, snuggle up.' He patted my pillow.

'Maybe later.' I got out of bed. I knew I wouldn't be able to get back to sleep and was afraid it would worry Dave even more if he could feel me shaking next to him in bed. I stroked his arm to reassure him, then went to the office to put the kettle on.

I left the lights off and sat on the sofa, staring out at the moonlight reflected on the water. I knew exactly what was underneath that mirror-like surface. I could picture all the muddy humps and bumps, and had a clear picture of the village as it had been in my mind.

I didn't hear the kettle boil. I was already writing.

Chapter 19 - Jennet

1st December 1776

The sheep scattered before me in the moonlight as I trod through the heather, and I watched them go. The new stone walls snaked over the fields and lower moors, and it would not be long before these sheep would have nowhere to run. I knew it would make the farming easier in some respects, but they would be restricted to the same patch of field or moor, unable to roam to find better grass, and I doubted I would be allotted prime grazing land.

The barriers would also make my nightly wanderings harder. A number of the plants I used were best picked under a full moon, and the work were tiring enough without having to clamber over piles of stones or detour to go through gates. I bent to pick a clump of mushrooms and straightened, my gaze on the village below and the church.

I paused for a moment, watching the site of my humiliation that morning. *How could he have treated me that way? How could he?* And why were all the sneers and gossip directed at me alone? I might be carrying the child, but he had planted it there; how could he and his wife get away with calling *me* whore? Why were people not sniggering, pointing and whispering at *him*?

I sighed, determined not to cry any more – I had been doing that all day and did not think there was a drop of water left inside me – and carried on my search for useful plants. They were hard to find at this time of year, but I had been doing this all my life and knew where to find the most sheltered spots and the treasures they hid. Some of Mam's old customers – Marjorie Wainwright, Susan Gill and Martha Grange amongst them – had on occasion knocked on my door over the last few months asking for cures for their ailments, and in return they had helped with the sheep or paid me in winter fodder. I had hoped that word would spread that my remedies were as effective as Mam's had been, but that seemed unlikely now. Would I lose even the few customers I had? Would they turn their backs on me and make the long walk to Peggy Lofthouse at Padside? She were the next closest cunning woman to Thores-Cross, but Mam had always said she were no good. How would I manage if Mam were wrong and Old Peg took all my custom?

I pulled my shawl tighter against the cold night and tried to concentrate on the ground in my search for the ingredients I needed. If I did not, what else would I do?

I walked off the moors and trudged through the more fecund fields just above the village, stopping and bending every so often. Hazelnuts, mushrooms, rosehips and more – my basket were nearly full by the time I reached the graveyard. I closed my mind to the memories of the day and crossed to Mam and Pa's graves, the bare earth stark in the moonlight – it would be spring before nature covered them with a carpet of green.

I knelt down and pulled away the few weeds that had taken root ahead of the grass.

'Oh Mam, what am I going to do? They all hate me – Richard hates me. He never loved me – did he ever love thee, I wonder? Or did he just want what thee wouldn't give him? Oh Mam, I'm so sorry, I've been such a fool. Mary Farmer is the only friendly face left – thee can imagine!' I smiled through my tears – I did have water in me, after all.

'What am I going to do? I'm struggling with the beasts already – what am I going to do with a babby as well?

Mary Farmer's getting on, she won't be much help.'

I had visions of tramping around the moors, chasing down sheep, with a child strapped to my back. I cried harder, then sat up as the wind caressed my cheek. It felt like fingers – Mam's fingers. I put my palm to my face. 'Mam,' I whispered. I sat in silence for a while longer, knowing Mam were near. I felt at peace for the first time since Richard had failed to visit.

Chapter 20 - Jennet

24th December 1776

I leaned on the garden wall and peered down at the village. A constellation of candle and lantern flames moved from house to house as the wasaillers endowed songs and blessings on their neighbours.

Every house but mine. They would not come here. They would not bless my home. The only one in the dale to be left out, and all because of an innocent child who had not yet been born. I caressed my belly. I shed no tears. The time for tears were past. I had no more upset, no more frustration, no more shame or pity in my soul.

All I had now were hate. Hate for Richard Ramsgill, hate for his wife and hate for every single villager who had pledged their condolences when Mam and Pa died, who had told me I could come to them if I needed anything. But when I needed a little compassion, a little human kindness, they all turned their backs and called me names.

Well, I did not need them. I did not need anyone. I had my wits, my home, my beasts, and I would soon have my child – only four months to go now. My first and last Christmas alone. Soon I would have everything I needed, and the whole village could go to Hell for all I cared.

The wasaillers walked up the lane. I watched their candle flames grow larger as they reached the Gate Inn. They were there a while, no doubt enjoying mince pies and spiced ale. Then the smithy. They did not spend so long there, despite the warmth of the forge. Closer now. I cursed my heart as it leaped in hope of them continuing straight up the hill to my own door, but no. They turned off, to East Gate House, home of Richard and Elizabeth Ramsgill.

Well bugger the lot of them! I did not need any of them, least of all Richard Bloody Ramsgill. I would soon have everyone I needed, once my babby were born. I already had every*thing* I needed – the moors always provided for one such as me, and the beasts had proved to be good at looking after themselves. I had meat, crops and the knowledge of a cunning woman.

They still came to me – oh aye they did. Not by day any more, no, but at night the villagers would creep up the hill, avoiding notice, coming for my cures, my restoratives and my preventatives. And they paid, by God they paid. They did not have money, nobody had actual coin to spare, except the bloody Ramsgills, but they gave me what I asked or left empty handed no matter how they pleaded.

Grain, hay, meat, cheese, even whiskybae. Only what *I* needed. Only what *I* wanted. The same women who called me whore, harlot, slut when my back were turned. But I knew, oh aye, I knew.

So when they came to me, they paid dearly. I even had Hannah Ramsgill up here, can thee imagine? *She* did not go home with the remedy to cure Thomas' inattention, oh no! She got something else entirely. But she cannot tell anyone! Not without admitting she cannot attract her husband any more – and she only thirty two! She runs away from me now if she sees me in the village. Hah! A Ramsgill running from me in shame – that were more like it! I laughed out loud at the memory.

The wasaillers emerged back on to the lane. They marched straight past my house. Not a single one even paused. I watched them reach Mary Farmer's house further up the hill and gather around her door. The sound of their singing and cheers drifted down to me, and I grabbed Pa's old sheepskin coat and walked away into the blessed silence of the moor.

It were not proper silent of course, but I could enjoy the whistling of the wind and the mournful cries of owl and curlew. This were where I belonged, on the moor with bird and rodent, not with the rats of that village. Here the air were pure, there were no whispers of scorn or delight in another's fall; no sneering laughter or vicious insult. Here, everything were as it should be. Heather, bracken, sheep, grouse, and of course the ever-present owl. Sometimes audible by its hoot, often surprising as it glided past on silent wings; then a thump and squeal of its prey and it were gone. Aye, I could learn a lot from the owls.

I headed south towards the fairy spring near the rocking stone. The wind were getting up and I were frozen, but did not care. I thought I would be cold for the rest of my life. I pulled the coat tighter around myself, bent my head to the wind and trudged on. At least I could not hear the wasaillers any longer.

I reached the spring and knelt. Mam had died not far from here, and I felt close to her now. I did not like going to the graveyard any more – the village were too close. Anyroad, her spirit were out here on the moors, and this spring were where I felt close to her. She used to come here regularly, dragging me along with her, even as a toddler. She would sit for hours with me on her knee, telling me stories of the fairy folk, the giants, all the beings who were here long before us and who we ignored at our peril. I used to love the sunlight dancing in the little splashes of water as it fell a few inches off a stone and she told me those glints of light were the fairies. That if I ever needed help or a friend I should come here and make my wishes known. They would always help me, no matter what. I hoped she were right.

*

I shivered again as the December wind cut through my thick woollens. I looked up in alarm at a familiar but dreaded sound. The rocking stone were moving. The grinding resonated in my heart and suddenly I could not bear to be out here any longer. I turned for home and ran as best I could through the heather.

Chapter 21 - Emma

4th September 2012

'Emma!'

I woke with a start, not sure where I was, then registered that Dave was bending over me with a mug of coffee. I'd fallen asleep on the sofa. I sat up with a groan and paper and pen slid to the floor.

'How are you feeling?' Dave sat down and passed me the mug.

'What time is it?' I groaned.

'Ten o'clock.'

'What?' I looked out of the window and realised he was right.

'Where are the dogs?' I couldn't believe they'd not woken me, they must be desperate for a walk.

'They're downstairs. I let them out earlier to do their business, but I thought you should sleep. Any more dreams?'

I shook my head. I'd take the beasts out later. I could do with a long walk myself to try and clear my head and make sense of the last few days, well, nights.

I bent down to pick up my notebook and flicked through it. 'I must have been writing for hours,' I said.

'Don't you remember?'

'Not really. I was in a bit of a daze to tell you the truth. I must have still been half asleep.'

'Well you *were* writing through the early hours.' Dave tried to reassure me.

'I suppose so.' I put the notebook on the table. 'I'll read it through later. It's probably crap.'

Dave laughed. 'That's what I like to hear – optimism. You never know, it could be your next bestseller.'

I pulled a face at him. 'What time do you have to leave?' Dave had yet another business trip to Edinburgh. I knew it was important, but still, I did miss him when he was away, despite my assurances that I was fine.

'This afternoon,' he replied. 'My first meeting is over dinner. If I leave at two, I should get there with an hour to spare. Time to settle in the hotel and have a shower.' He stopped and regarded me thoughtfully. 'I could cancel if you want me to stay with you.'

'Don't be silly.' I laughed. 'It's only a few bad dreams, I don't need a nursemaid, I'm not ill. I'll be fine.'

'I know, but . . . we're so isolated here, you're on your own when I go away, I worry about you.'

'I like being alone sometimes, you know that, and I love the peace and quiet here, you know that too.'

'Those dreams are far from peaceful.'

'It's just my writer's imagination,' I said. Part of me wanted to ask him to stay and I realised I felt vulnerable since the nightmares had started. I got a mental grip of myself. I was a grown woman, and had moved here out of choice. Dave's trips to Scotland were important, I could not ask him to stay because of a few dreams, nor would I give him cause to worry. 'If I do have a problem, Mark and Kathy are up the lane. What could you do if you were here, anyway? You can't control my dreams.'

He nodded. 'Fair enough, but if you do get another one and want to hear a friendly voice, ring me – it doesn't matter what time.'

'Of course I'll ring you – you know I don't mind waking you up!' We laughed.

'All right then, I'll go and pack. Do you want to go out for lunch?'

'Oh, that's a nice idea, let's go for chips and peas!'

*

I waved Dave off, then pulled my scarf tighter round my neck and whistled to the dogs. They came running, and I made a fuss of all three of them. Especially Cassie.

'How do!'

I glanced up at the shout and returned Mark's greeting, then made a fuss of his border collie, who had just cannoned into the mêlée at my feet.

'Delly, no!' I shouted as he went for Shep.

'Stand back,' Mark advised over the snarling. 'They're just sorting out who's boss, they'll settle down in a minute. Are you going out or coming back?'

'Setting off,' I replied, wincing at the snapping dogs, but none of them seemed to be bleeding. 'Are you sure they're ok?'

'Aye, they'll be right in a bit, can you cope with some company?'

I watched the dogs dubiously.

'They'll settle when we're off Delly's territory. Shep! Come!'

The collie ran to Mark, tongue lolling and chased by Delly; Rodney following behind.

'Delly, no!' I shouted, but he ignored me again.

Mark laughed. 'Come on, let's walk.'

I nodded and followed. All four dogs raced off down the lane towards the reservoir, Delly still snarling, but they seemed more playful now.

'I don't understand it,' I said, embarrassed at Delly's bad behaviour. 'He's the softest of dogs normally.'

'He's top dog,' Mark said. 'Mine came on to his territory, he showed him who were boss. He were protecting his pack, including you.'

'Really?' I said, pleased.

'It's what they do. See, Shep's got the message. See him licking Delly's snout? And now look, Shep's rolled on to his back, he's submitting. They'll be right enough.'

We walked down the hill after them, and they did seem

best of friends now. Although Shep was a little overfriendly towards Cassie, but she was more than capable of sending him packing, especially when Delly added his own encouragement. Then Roddy spotted a rabbit and all four of them were off. I laughed, relieved, and we followed much more slowly along the shore.

'There are some good walks around here,' Mark said.

'Yes, I took them up on to the moorland the other day. They were absolutely shattered running through the heather.'

Mark laughed. 'Yes they would be! Have you walked below the dam yet? It's beautiful.'

'*No!*'

Mark seemed taken aback at the force of my denial.

'Sorry. Another dream,' I explained.

'Sounds like a bad one.'

'Yes.' I shivered. 'I was walking down there in a thunderstorm, and the dam burst. Cassie was swept away, a car drove off the edge, and I woke up crying at all the people who must have been killed downstream.'

'Nasty,' Mark said.

'Yes. But the most profound part was watching the village resurface.'

'Hang on, I thought you were below the dam?'

'I climbed up the side of the valley.'

'Dreams.' Mark nodded. 'Anything's possible.'

'Anyway.' I was annoyed. I *had* climbed up the hill; it hadn't been the dream allowing the impossible. 'As the village reappeared, I kept thinking about that witch you and Kathy talked about.'

'Jennet.'

'Yes, and how her bones are still there, somewhere in all that mud.'

'It's unlikely she were buried in the village, Emma. She'll be under the moors somewhere, probably at some sort of crossroads to try to keep her spirit contained or confused or something.'

'No, she's closer than you think,' I said, suddenly sure of myself. 'I've started writing her story,' I explained, feeling shy. I was extremely self-conscious at the start of any writing project and could hardly believe I'd told this relative stranger what I was writing about when I'd only started last night. But then I realised why. 'Maybe you could tell me more about the legends?'

'I'd love to,' Mark said. 'What have you got so far?'

I frowned. 'I'm not sure really, I haven't read it through yet.'

'Don't you know?' Mark asked, incredulous.

I shrugged. 'I started in the early hours after my dream. I must still have been half asleep. I'll read it through when I get back.'

'Maybe that inkpot you found *were* hers, and *she's* writing the story through you. Oh God, listen to me, I sound like Kathy!' He stooped suddenly, picked up a large feather and presented it to me. 'Here, a goose wing feather to go with the inkpot – it's what Jennet would have used.'

'Would she have been able to write?' I asked, surprised.

'Aye, more than likely. She were a cunning woman, her mam would have taught her to write enchantments and recipes and the like.'

I pursed my lips and raised my eyebrows as I nodded, then took the feather and laughed. 'I know I'm old-fashioned using ink and paper, but I'm not quite that old-fashioned!'

'Research,' Mark said, laughing with me. 'Use it to get into your character's skin. Isn't that what you writers do?'

I shuddered, remembering my nightmare. It felt like Jennet was getting into *my* skin rather than the other way round, but I held on to the feather nonetheless. It was from one of the Canada Geese who visited the reservoir every year. I doubted they came in Jennet's time, although they would have kept geese. Surely it wouldn't hurt to have a play with the quill, and I suddenly quite fancied putting my old inkpot to its proper use again after all this time.

'Thank you,' I said, 'perhaps I will.' Our fingers touched and I glanced up at him, then took the feather and looked away, aware that my cheeks had flushed. *What was that all about? Have we just had a moment? I don't even find him attractive!*

I called to the dogs and threw a stick towards the water. They piled into the shallows – as far as my stick had made it – and sent water splashing everywhere. The moment, whatever it had been, was broken.

'So, has Dave gone anywhere nice?' Mark asked, breaking the awkward silence. I glanced up at him in question. 'I spotted the suit carrier as he drove past,' Mark continued.

'Edinburgh on business,' I said, not sure I wanted Mark to know I was home alone. 'He'll be back in a couple of days.'

'He's brave, leaving a woman like you on your own. Sorry, I don't know why I said that,' he added, colouring. 'I guess I'm a bit star-struck having a famous author on my doorstep.'

'You flatter me,' I said, uncomfortable with the way this conversation was going. I looked at him sideways. He wasn't bad-looking, really, although he walked with a bit of a stoop, but still, I loved my husband. I didn't understand why there was this atmosphere between us. I walked down to the water's edge and searched for a flat stone to skim.

'So how long has your family lived round here?' I asked Mark after he'd skimmed a stone of his own.

'Seven! Beat that!' he said. I sighed. Save me from competitive men.

'Six, ha!' he exclaimed.

I tried again, irritated. 'There, eight, your turn,' I said, the awkwardness gone now. He laughed and threw again, poorly this time.

'I've no idea how long the Ramsgills have been here – forever, as far as I know. Long before Jennet's time, anyway.'

'So your ancestors knew her?'

'Knew her? They probably hanged her!'

'Hanged her?'

'I don't know, it's all legend. Who knows what's true? Who knows if Jennet were real at all?'

'Oh she was real all right, I have no doubt about that!'

'Why not? How the hell do you know?'

I glanced up in surprise at the intensity of his words and shrugged, not wanting to tell him how deeply I felt a connection with her after my dream. 'Women's intuition?'

I cried out as Roddy barged past me into the water after the stones and nearly knocked me flying.

Mark laughed, his bad humour forgotten. 'No, seriously, the Ramsgills were prominent sheep farmers and wool merchants. They brought a lot of work and money to the area, they owned a great deal of land and one of them were even Forest Constable, so they had plenty of power. They still had to answer to the Duchy of Lancaster though, as did the rest of those who lived within the Forest of Knaresborough.'

'Forest of Knaresborough? We're a long way from Knaresborough here.'

'Only about twenty miles as the crow flies, we're right on the edge of what were the Forest. It's funny isn't it; thinking most of these fields were once woodland, full of deer and wolves and all sorts of other wildlife.'

'Wolves? Really? Are you sure about that?' I didn't think wolves were native to Yorkshire.

'So the tales go. Our house is called Wolf Farm, although that might be something to do with Jennet and barguests again.'

'It must have been pretty isolated,' I said, getting back to reality.

'Very. They'll have had a long trek to any markets, so the village were forced to be more or less self-sufficient. My ancestors were probably the only wool merchants for miles around; all the farmers, spinners and weavers would have had to stay on the right side of them.'

I looked around. I could see for miles, but only a couple of old stone properties were visible. 'I can't imagine living up here without a car,' I said. 'I like solitude, need it even, to write. But I like to be able to leave and find other people when I want to.'

'I know what you mean. But two hundred year ago, most of the villagers would never have left the moors. Only the few more successful farmers would have made the trek to the sheep fairs – probably the Ramsgills or their men – it would have taken days.' He paused and stared at me. 'You know, I have a couple of books on the history here at home, do you want to borrow them?'

'I'd love to, yes please.' We called to the dogs and started walking back up the hill.

'I'll bring them down with me tomorrow – same time?'

'Yes.' Then a thought struck me. 'Aren't you working?'

'Term starts next week.'

'Of course.'

'Happen you'll know what you've written so far by then.'

'I'm intrigued myself.' I laughed.

I was glad to get home again and relieved to get away from Mark, although I had agreed to meet him the following day. I towelled the dogs off and fed them, then headed upstairs to my office and settled on the sofa with the dogs flat out at my feet to read last night's folios.

25th June 1776

'Here, Jennet, put them pies out on't table, lass,' Mam said, thrusting a basket of cold mutton pastries at me. 'Get a move on, will thee, that pen's nearly empty, they'll be ready for a break in a minute.'

I sighed and were about to point out that we were only late because she had not been able to find the crab apple pickle, but spotted Mary Farmer walking purposefully towards us, and did as I were told. If I were already busy, she would not be able to give me more work to do. I took the basket from Mam and carried it to the tables, the coarse heather grabbing at my skirts.

The whole village had turned out for the sheepwashing. The flocks had been driven the mile to Thores-Ford early this morning, and everyone had been hard at work since daybreak. It would have been noted that we were late, but Mam were respected as the local cunning woman and she had helped at least one member of every family here at one time or another – she would be forgiven.

This were the start of our year – even though it were midsummer – when the sheep were washed ready for shearing in a fortnight. Their wool were our livelihood and, looking round, I saw shepherds, carders, fullers, spinners and weavers. And Richard Ramsgill, the wool merchant and most powerful man on the moor. I smiled at him, shy, and looked past him to my pa who were in the ford itself, along with William Gill, ducking the sheep in the now foul-smelling water, one at a time.

The ewe thrashed as she were held underwater then thrown out whilst the next one were dumped in. It were hard, dirty, noisy, smelly work, but essential if we were to get the best out of the fleeces, and the whole valley had gathered to get it done. Another half dozen to go, then they would be ready for a break before starting on the next flock.

The washing ford were a natural widening in the stream high up on the moors, by the rocking stone. I glanced over at it now; an enormous oval rock balanced on a plinth – put there by giants to amuse their young, the old tales said. There were not enough wind now to set it in motion, but in the most powerful gales, it would move, sending a noise throughout the valley that sounded like giants' grinding their teeth. But not this day.

'Jennet! Stop dallying, lass, they're nearly ready!'

I snapped back to myself and grinned at Mam, then got back to work.

'Whoa! Watch out there!'

I glanced up at the shout. The new flock being herded to the washing ford had broken loose and were stampeding towards us.

'The food! The tables!' Mary Farmer wailed. 'Stop them!'

Mam did as she were told – everyone did what they were told by Mary Farmer, it were easier that way – and ran at the approaching flock, trying to turn them back towards the ford, but to no avail. The first ewes ploughed into the trestles sending pies, pickles and ale flying. I put my hands to my mouth in merriment – I had never seen anything so funny and I would have given anything to have seen that look on Mary Farmer's face.

'Alice!'

I stopped laughing at the panic in Pa's voice and turned. One of the ewes had knocked Mam into the water. She could not swim.

I watched Pa jump in after her and wanted to help, but could not move. Everywhere were chaos. Sheep bumped my legs, but my feet were as rooted to the moor as the heather. I could only watch.

Pa surfaced, coughing, then disappeared. I could not see Mam – not even her skirts. I could feel the blood drain out of my face as I realised what were happening and finally moved my feet. I ran to the edge, screaming for me mam, and got there as Pa finally pulled her up. She did not move.

'Mam? Mam? Mam!'

Pa did not look at me and Mam had not shifted. He waded to the edge and handed her up to the men gathered there, and they hauled her on to dry land. No one would look at me.

I pushed my way through the men and fell to my knees. Her usually rosy face were white and streaked with mud and sheepshite. Her eyes were shut and her lips slightly parted. She had a dark red mark on her forehead and were not breathing.

'Jennet.' Pa's hands were on me shoulders and he tried to pull me back. 'She's gone, Jennet, she's gone. Come away.'

I did as I were bid. I did not seem to be able to decide for myself, I just did as Pa bid, and the ring of people closed around Mam.

I picked up my pen to write on and find out what happened next, how Jennet carried on; but no words came and I realised I was crying. After an hour, I threw the pen down in disgust and put the kettle on. I stood at the window with my steaming cup of coffee, but found no inspiration. Thruscross was shrouded in fog, just like my brain.

With a sigh, I turned to put my mug on the desk and picked up the inkpot. Then I saw the goose feather. *Why not?*

I fetched a knife from the kitchen, sharpened the shaft and poured ink into the inkpot. Feeling a bit of an idiot, I dipped in the quill, held it over the page, dropped a few blotches of ink, and started writing.

Chapter 22 - Jennet

27th February 1777

I sat back and watched the tiny lamb struggle to its feet and bleat at its dam. I rested on my heels in relief. I loved this time of year, and had not needed to give this ewe any help. At six years old she were strong and healthy and had already done this a few times.

I waited until the lamb started suckling, then got to my feet, picked up my lantern and looked around the dark moors.

I had driven my girls closer to the farm last month, where it were more sheltered with better grass – I would have to mark the new arrivals before they wandered again, to make sure everyone knew they were mine. I would give them a couple of months at least though, before I got the branding iron out and burned the initials of my great-great-great-great-grandpa on to the sides of their noses.

I stretched and glanced up at the tiny sliver of moon. I sighed, I could have done with a full one tonight. I held up my lantern and went in search of the last ewe I had marked as being likely to birth tonight.

She were the eldest of the flock, and in any year past she would have been mutton by now. But I only had one mouth to feed these days, and had decided to keep her for one more wool crop and, hopefully, another lamb.

I found her lying down, her birthing already started. I set the lantern down near her back-end and gave her face a rub before settling down to help her.

'Ey up lass, is thee all right?'

I jumped and peered at the shadowy figure behind the lantern. He held it higher, and I recognised Peter Stockdale.

'How do, Peter,' I said. 'What's thee doing here?'

'I've just finished up with Ramsgill's lambs for the night, saw thy lantern and wondered if thee needed an hand.'

'Oh,' I said, surprised. I could not remember the last time anybody but Mary Farmer had offered me aid. 'Um, she's the last one tonight, I reckon, but she's old and I think she's twinning.'

He crouched down next to the ewe and felt her belly. 'Aye, there's two in there all right.' He tugged on the ewe's ears. 'Thee's not on thy own, though, old girl.'

I glanced at him sharply. I wished he would say that to me and mean it.

Peter Stockdale caught my eye and smiled. I looked away embarrassed, back to the ewe's back-end.

'First one's coming,' I said.

'Let's have a look,' said Peter, pushing me out of the way.

'Hmm, it's taking too long, think we'd better give her an hand – give other twin a chance.'

I nodded and clasped my hands around my belly in fear. What if I had problems birthing my babby and there were no one to help?

He reached between the ewe's back legs, then pulled, emerging with the back legs of a tiny, limp lamb in his grasp.

'Dead,' he said, laid it on the ground and examined the ewe again. 'Next one's coming.'

I picked up the dead lamb, wiped the crud from its nose and mouth, then stood while holding its back legs and spun round. I had seen Pa do this successfully, but it did not work tonight.

I fell to the ground, dizzy, and sobbed.

'Never mind, lass, thee can't save them all. Here, look after this live 'un while I see to its dam.'

I took the newborn and wiped it down. It bleated at me and I grinned.

Peter Stockdale sat back on his haunches. 'Damn it,' he said.

'Oh no!'

'She's gone.'

I reached out and stroked the dead ewe's face.

'Don't fret, she were old. I'll help thee get her to farmhouse so's thee can butcher her.'

I nodded my thanks and hugged the poddy lamb.

'What'll thee do with that 'un?'

I shrugged. 'Hand-rear her, I suppose.'

'Does thee not have another ewe with a stillborn?'

I said nowt.

'Come on, lass, I knows thee's had hard time, and house must be terrible quiet, but let's give this little 'un a proper mam.'

I nodded, ashamed of my weakness, and led the way to another ewe who had lost her lamb. I rubbed the lamb on the ground around her, trying to pick up the smell of her afterbirth, then put it to the teat.

Now all we could do were wait for the milk to come through and the lamb to take it. We sat a little way back to watch.

'Thee'll not tell no one I were here, will thee, lass?'

I glanced up at him in surprise and disappointment.

'Sorry, lass.' He looked ashamed. 'But Mr Ramsgill wouldn't take kindly to this, and I can't afford to lose work.'

'Thy secret's safe with me, Peter,' I said. 'And I'm grateful for thy company.'

We sat in silence for a while and watched the lamb finish feeding and lie in the coarse grass.

'Did thee lose many?'

'Three lambs, but that one were only ewe.'

He nodded. 'That's not too bad, and at least thee'll have plenty of meat.'

'Mm.'

'How's thee faring?'

I shrugged and he nodded again. We sat in silence for a while, until the lamb had done its business.

The ewe sniffed the lamb's turds, then licked the tiny body.

'That's it, she's accepted it! I'll help thee get dead 'uns to house.'

'Thank thee,' I said as I stood. I realised I could see him properly now. He was my height, but twice as broad; with floppy, sandy hair and hazel eyes; his crooked smile revealed crooked teeth.

'Right then,' he said. 'Let's be off.'

Chapter 23 - Jennet

26th May 1777

'Come on, lass, keep pushing! Thee can do it!'

I swore; loudly and crudely. I had been pushing for hours already; if the little bugger did not come out soon, he could bloody well stay where he were.

'I can see head!' Mary Farmer exclaimed. She were the only one here, the only one who cared. But at least I were not on my own any more. I had been for the first six hours – I had had no way of summoning Mary, but she had got into the habit of checking on me twice a day. *Thank God.*

I had made myself up a bed downstairs where it were warmest, and had forced myself up to unbar the door for her when she had finally come knocking.

'Push, lass, push!' Mary sounded more urgent.

'What is it?'

'Just push, lass.'

'Tell me!'

'The cord's wrapped round neck. I can't get me fingers in, thee needs to push hard. Now!'

I screamed in agony at the ripping sensation as I forced the silent babby out into the world.

'Come on, Mary!' I screamed.

Nowt.

She held the babby up by its legs and I realised from the colour of him that he were dead. Mary smacked his arse.

Nowt.

She did it again with the same result and looked at me. My babby were dead. I sank back on to the filthy bedding, then screamed as another spasm of pain ripped through my body.

'Ruddy hell! There's another one! Come on, lass, don't give up now, he's been in there too long as it is, thee needs to get him out!'

I screamed obscenities at her and did my best, but I had been doing this for hours, my body felt mutilated beyond repair, and the makeshift bed were soaked in blood.

'Come on! Don't let him die too! Push, Jennet!'

I took a deep breath, gritted my teeth and heaved one last, desperate time.

'Aye!'

There were no noise. No cries. I lifted my head from the cushion of fleeces to see. 'Does he live?'

Mary were bent over the tiny body and I could not see. 'Aye, she does lass, but she's weak. See if she'll take milk.'

She handed me the tiny body she had wrapped in muslin, and I held my daughter to my breast. She moved her head slightly towards me, but did not take my nipple.

'Thee'll have to help her, lass.'

I looked at Mary. I did not like how sombre she sounded and my ravaged body flushed with panic. I took my breast, pulled the girl to me and forced my nipple into her mouth. I felt her lips close around it, but she were too weak to suckle. I looked at Mary in despair.

'I'll go to Gate for some goat's milk,' she said. 'Just keep trying.'

I nodded, and moved my breast against the tiny mouth, encouraging her to suck, but it were useless. I held the tiny body close, trying to keep her warm; trying to let her know she were wanted and loved. I realised I were muttering to her.

'Come on, Alice, come on, don't give up on me.' I had not known I had decided to call her for Mam until I heard the name pass my lips. I realised I could not feel her breath on my skin any more. I kept her in my arms, held against my heart. I did not look up when Mary Farmer returned.

'Oh lass,' she sighed. 'I'm so sorry.'

The sun were going down before I let Mary take the small bundle from me and place her on the table next to her brother. I had not cried. I did not want to cry. I stared at my only friend and all I felt were rage. It were so unfair. I had been used, berated and abandoned for these babbies, but I had wanted them and loved them, and neither had lived an hour.

'Suffer the little children,' I muttered.

'What?'

'That's what they'll say, ain't it? In that Damned church. "Suffer the little children." They'll say it's my fault, God's punishment for my actions and he . . . he gets off scot free!' My voice had risen to a shout. 'Well he won't, none of them will!'

I forced myself off the bed, staggered to the table and picked up my children. I stumbled towards the fire, hunched like an old crone, but with blood running down the inside of my thighs.

'I curse the Ramsgills! All of them! I curse them to die before adulthood!' I threw the boy on to the fire. Mary screamed and tried to grab me. I shook her off and she fell to the floor. 'Only one may live to carry the curse to the next generation, then they will suffer their losses!' My daughter joined my son.

'More peat, Mary, it needs to be hotter!' Mary backed away from me. She looked terrified. I managed to bend and knock more peat on to the pyre, then straightened as best I were able and watched my children burn. The room filled with the smell of roasting meat and the sound of the cracking of skin as it charred.

'I curse Thores-Cross! Let the Devil and his hounds be welcomed to hunt for souls here!'

I threw a handful of herbs on the flames to add potency to my words.

'They'll pay for this! The Ramsgills and Thores-Cross will pay for eternity!' I were screaming now. I turned to face Mary. She had reached the far wall, her face distorted with horror.

'Bear witness, Mary Farmer. They're all Damned now!'

Mary rushed to the door and ran. I watched her go.

Chapter 24 - Emma

5th September 2012

I sat back on the sofa, horrified at what I had written. *Where did that come from?* I put my notebook and quill on the table and massaged my right wrist. I realised tears poured down my face. Poor Jennet. Those poor babies. I propped my head in my hands and let the sobs out. I cried for Jennet, and I cried for my own lost child.

I jumped at the eruption of barking from the kitchen. Someone was at the door. I wiped my face and took a deep breath, then made my way downstairs to see who it was.

'Mark!'

I was surprised to see him, but stood aside to let him in.

'How do. I brought you those local history books I promised. Found something else you might like an'all, lass.'

I jumped at the 'lass' but managed a smile. 'That's great. I was about to make coffee, would you like a cup?'

'Aye, that'd be grand.'

I shut the door behind him and led the way to the kitchen as he greeted all three dogs jumping around us.

'Are you all right? You look upset.'

'I'm fine,' I said. 'I just got caught up in my story.'

'It must be a rum 'un if it's brought you to tears.'

'Umm, you could say that,' I replied, my voice shaking as I poured water into mugs. 'Milk? Sugar?'

'Yes to both.'

I nodded and finished the drinks, then passed a mug to Mark.

'So is it Jennet?'

'What?'

'Your story, is it Jennet's?'

I nodded, not trusting myself to speak.

'And does the quill work?'

I glanced at him in surprise.

'Your fingers.'

I looked down and managed a smile. My right hand was black with ink. 'Not the tidiest way to write! I wanted to try the inkpot and quill, I guess I got carried away.'

'Oh yes, the inkpot – you were going to show it to me.'

'Of course, it's in the office – would you bring the books up?' I led the way upstairs.

'Wow!' Mark stopped on the top tread and stared at the view. 'How can you possibly work in here? I'd be staring out the window all day!'

I nodded. 'It has been known, but these days I usually find it inspiring rather than distracting.'

I led the way to the sofa and coffee table where my notebook, quill and inkpot lay.

'Bloody hell, what a mess, Dave's going to kill me!'

Ink splotches covered the top of the wooden coffee table.

'An occupational hazard of being a writer,' Mark said and laughed.

'Hmm,' I said, horrified about the stains and concerned that I hadn't noticed them earlier. I sat down and put my coffee mug on the table. Mark joined me. He picked up the inkpot and examined it.

'You could be right, you know, about its date. If it were more ornate, I'd say it were later, but in 1700s Yorkshire, they didn't have time or inclination to make things pretty. Plain, useful and durable, that's the old Yorkshire way. This really could have belonged to Jennet.'

I glanced at my notebook. I had no doubt that it had.

'What have you brought me?' I asked.

He put the inkpot down, grimaced, showed me the fresh

stains on his fingers, then wiped them on his jeans.

I smiled to myself, thinking of Dave. He'd have never done that – a quick dash to a sink with soap and scrubbing brush was more his style. I missed him when he was away, but another couple of days and he'd be home.

Mark thumped three books on to the coffee table.

'These are the best local histories I have. *Life and Tradition in the Yorkshire Dales, A History of Nidderdale* & Richard Muir's *The Yorkshire Countryside*, but this is the real prize.' He pulled an old, leather-bound book out of the bag. 'Old Ma Ramsgill's journal – my great-grandmother.'

'Ooh, can I have a look? I love old journals!'

'Aye. All the family history's in here, and anything interesting about the neighbours too – a right gossip, she were.'

I smiled as he passed me the book. It was filled with tiny, cramped writing. My enthusiasm faltered a little – it would take me ages to go through it all, but who knew what gems were hidden in here?

I was aware of our knees pressed together and moved my leg away as I opened the back pages of the journal.

'Oh look, a family tree!'

'Oh aye, I'd forgotten about that. The Moores – my great-nan's side are on the right, but this one . . .' he leaned over and unfolded the large sheet of paper, '. . . is the Ramsgills.'

I pored over it, excited.

'Here, these'll be them that were around in Jennet's time,' he said, pointing.

'No. Here,' I corrected, indicating the name Richard, with Thomas, Richard, Robert and Alexander below it.

'How can you possibly know that, lass?'

I shrugged, a little uncomfortable. I stared at the names, realising how strange it was that the very names I had used for the Ramsgill brothers were here, together, on the

Ramsgill family tree. I shivered, then noticed something else that made my blood run cold.

'Mark – do you have any cousins?'

'Cousins? Nay. It's just me – I don't even have a brother or sister, they died when I were a nipper – meningitis.'

'I'm sorry. They?'

'Aye, twins. They run in the family, though you wouldn't know it, not many seem to survive.' He gave a small, strangled laugh.

'I thought twins only ran down the female line?'

'Aye, well, don't know about that, but there've been a lot in the Ramsgill family.'

I stared at the family tree, checking and subtracting dates. He was right – there were a lot of twins, and they had all died young.

'At first, I thought the tree was only tracing your line,' *straight back to Richard Ramsgill*, I thought but didn't say. 'But it isn't. Look. Only one Ramsgill survives to bear children. And always a man – carrying on the name.'

'Aye, we've never been lucky, us Ramsgills, but I never realised it were that bad. Let me have a look at that.'

I watched him, feeling numb. The ruddy colour drained from his cheeks as he studied the dates. I realised our legs were touching again.

'Mark, there's something I need to show you.' I felt nervous. I wasn't sure if this was the right thing to do, but he needed to know.

I picked up my notebook and found the passage, pointing to it with my finger.

I curse the Ramsgills! All of them! I curse them to die before adulthood!' I threw the boy on to the fire. Mary screamed and tried to grab me. I shook her off and she fell to the floor. 'Only one may live to carry the curse to the next generation, then they will suffer their losses!'

He glanced at me. 'That's just a bit of nonsense. You're a fiction writer – a storyteller, you've made that up, it means nowt.'

I thumbed through the notebook again and pointed out another passage.

The Ramsgills were the most important family in the valley – Thomas the Forest Constable, Richard the wool merchant, Big Robert the miller and Alexander just getting his own farm established. There were three more brothers still working their father's farm.

'Mark, how old are your twins?'

He glanced at me, jumped to his feet, and backed away.

'I don't know what you think you're doing, lass, but it ain't funny.' He turned and rushed downstairs. The dogs didn't follow, but watched him go. Cassie crossed to me and pressed herself against my legs. I stroked her absentmindedly, wondering what it all meant and thinking about the expression on Mark's face. I imagined it was very similar to the way people used to look at Jennet. But I was not Jennet.

'Why did you write that?'

'Mark, it's late . . .' And it was. I was in my dressing gown, ready to go to bed, but had somehow known who was banging on the door and had opened it.

He pushed past me and stood in the lounge.

'Why did you write that?' he asked again.

'I don't know,' I said. 'I'm not sure I did, I think . . . I think it might have been Jennet.'

'Bah!' he said, crossed to the sideboard with the whisky decanter and glasses displayed on its top, poured himself a drink, downed it and refilled his glass. I narrowed my eyes at the liberty he was taking, but nodded when he waved the decanter at me. He poured a couple of fingers into another glass.

'I don't believe in all that nonsense, Emma.'

'Neither do I, not really.' That wasn't strictly true, but I thought it the best response in the circumstances. 'Or I didn't anyway, but how else do you explain it?' I took the glass from him, my fingers brushing his. 'How did I know the names? Your family history?'

He didn't reply, but crossed to the window and stared out into the night. I followed and touched his shoulder.

'I'm sorry, Mark, I didn't mean to upset you.'

His shoulder relaxed under my touch and he turned. He caught hold of my waist and pulled me closer. We stared at each other a moment, then he kissed me. I stiffened, but didn't pull away. After a moment I returned his kiss.

I shrugged my dressing gown back on and held it tightly closed across my chest. I could not look at Mark. *Why on earth had I done that?*

'I-I-I need to get back to Kathy.' Mark looked at his watch and fastened his jeans. 'She thinks I'm at the Stone House, and it closed half an hour ago.'

I nodded, but said nothing.

'Look . . . Emma . . . I-I don't know what came over me.'

'Nor me,' I whispered, still struggling to find my voice.

'Let's just forget it happened.'

I nodded, though how on earth could I forget cheating on Dave? I hated myself. And Mark.

Chapter 25 – Jennet

28th May 1777

I lay in bed, sleep impossible to find, and flinched as lightning flashed.

'*One* drunk shepherd, *two* drunk shepherd, *three* drunk shepherd,' I counted, and thunder rolled. Three miles away.

My babbies had died – both of them. I remembered throwing them on the fire and Mary running from the house. Lightning flashed again – I counted – still three miles.

I rolled on to my side and swung my legs to the floor, then pushed myself up to stand. I stood for a moment, my legs trembling and, feeling dizzy, walked unsteadily to my clothing chest. Thunder crashed again.

Downstairs and feeling a little stronger, I stared at the fireplace. The fire had gone out long before.

I hunted around in the kitchen for some food and found a pot of cold pottage that Mary had left. I wolfed it down and paused to count. Two miles.

A gust of wind shrieked in the chimney and a puff of ash scattered in the room.

No!

I found a lidded basket and cleared the grate, shovelling the ash and small bits of bone into it. My babbies could not stay in this house and become nowt but dirt.

I pulled Pa's boots on to my feet and shrugged into his coat, picked up the basket and opened the door. The force of the wind and rain near took my breath away, and I watched the dark valley flash into being for a second. Only one drunk shepherd now.

I forced the door shut behind me and headed out on to the moors.

It took me an hour to reach the fairy spring – three times as long as usual – and I sank to my knees beside it.

'They're dead, Mam, my babbies are dead!' I sobbed. 'I cursed them, Mam, I cursed the Ramsgills, and I called up the Wild Hunt!'

I lifted my head to the sky and screamed my grief and pain at the raging heavens. 'And I don't care! I don't care if the Devil comes and claims every soul in this valley!'

Lightning flashed again and thunder roared with it. The storm were overhead. I struggled to my feet.

'Do you hear me?' I screamed at the storm. 'Do thy worst! Send thy hounds! Take this whole valley to Hell!'

I picked up the basket and removed the lid, then threw the contents to fly with the wind. 'Rest easy, my loves, rest easy on these moors – I'll avenge thee, don't thee fret!'

A new noise caught my attention – a rumbling, grating. The rocking stone. The spirits of the moors had acknowledged me; they would care for my babbies.

I turned to face the full force of the wind and raised my arms. I lifted my face and felt the power of this place. 'I'll avenge thee,' I said again, my words whipped away into the dark night.

I collapsed on to the heather, my rage spent. What had I done?

'I'm sorry, Mam,' I whispered. 'Take good care of my babbies for me.'

I got to my feet and started the walk home. My woollen clothes were saturated and heavy – it would take weeks to get them properly dry again – and my legs felt like lead. My whole body hurt and I thought I could feel blood dripping inside my skirts.

I finally made it, lit a new fire, stripped, wrapped a blanket around myself, and collapsed before it. I did not sleep, but lay for hours on the stone flags, staring into the flames, my mind and heart numb and still.

Chapter 26 - Emma

19th September 2012

I stared at the house on the hill above me and swapped the bag of books to my other hand. I didn't understand why I had started this stupid affair with Mark. I loved my husband. I loved Dave. I didn't want anyone else. So why had I responded to Mark? I didn't even find him attractive! But I was drawn to him for some reason.

And why was I going up there now? I didn't need to return the books today; they could wait for another time, and Dave was coming home tomorrow, so why was I trekking up the hill to see Mark?

I reached his gate and buzzed, then jumped as Kathy's voice said, 'Yes?' What was *she* doing here? It was her evening for counselling.

'It's Emma, returning Mark's books.'

The gate buzzed and I entered.

'Hi, Emma, how lovely to see you, would you like coffee? Or something stronger?'

'Uh, coffee would be great, thank you.' I wanted to dump the books and get out of there, but knew that would have seemed strange to Kathy. The last thing I wanted to do was socialise with Mark's wife. 'I can't stay long though, I need to get back to work.'

'Nonsense, you need a break – Mark says you're always working, even when you're walking the dogs you're planning your next chapters! And with Dave being away again, it'll do you good to have company for half an hour. When does he get home?'

'Tomorrow,' I said, uncomfortable. I would just have to make the best of it, and to be honest, company *would* be nice – for a little while. Apart from Mark's visits and Dave's phone calls, I hadn't seen or spoken to anyone for a week.

'Come on through, pop the books down in here and I'll put the kettle on.'

I put the bag of books on the coffee table and followed her into the pine-laden kitchen, feeling guilty at accepting her hospitality when I was being far too . . . hospitable to her husband.

'How's the book coming on? Mark says you're writing Jennet's story.'

'Um, yes. It's flowing well actually. Um, where is Mark? I have a couple of questions for him about his great-grandmother's journal.'

'Emergency at the school. Pipe's burst or something. It's all hands on deck to clear up the mess. A nuisance, though, I'm having to miss my course so that I'm home for the twins. And they're not even here! Milk, sugar?'

'Just milk please.'

Kathy put mugs, cafetière, jug of milk and plate of biscuits on a tray and led the way to the lounge.

'Oh, you *can* see the water!' I exclaimed without thinking. 'I was wondering, what with the wall—' I stopped, realising I was being rude, but Kathy smiled.

'Yes, we needed the place to be secure, especially with two kids, but I couldn't bear for the view to be completely hidden. Mark tells me the view from your office is spectacular – I'd love to see it sometime.'

'Of course, you must pop down whenever you're free,' I said, acutely aware of the number of times she was saying "Mark said".

'How are the twins?' I asked, my eyes darting to the journal I had put on the coffee table.

'They're fine. They're both leaning towards the

University of Leeds, which is a relief – couldn't be much closer!'

'That's good. Will they stay at home?'

'We're not sure yet. It'd be quite a trek for them, but certainly cheaper; we haven't worked the details out. They're both searching for jobs at the moment, anything to get some cash saved up.'

'Well if one of them has a green thumb, Dave and I could use a gardener—'

'Really? That's wonderful! Alex would love that – he's a real outdoorsman, I can't think why he's chosen business studies!'

'Oh, that's great. How about ten pounds an hour? It's quite a job to be honest, we haven't started yet, but it would be nice to have some home-grown veg and flowers – maybe some chickens too. And I'd love a herb garden: rosemary, sage, verbena and the like. Are you sure he'd be up for it?'

'Absolutely! I'm impressed, you really know your herbs. Did you have a garden at your old place?'

'No, not really, just a few pots.' I was mystified. 'I didn't know I knew all those herbs, actually. I must have paid more attention to my research than I thought.' I laughed, then realised I hadn't actually done any research – I'd little more than glanced at Mark's books, even the old journal, and had only brought them back in the hope of seeing him.

'Is that for Jennet?'

I nodded.

'Yes, she would have had a herb garden – quite an extensive one. How's the book coming on?' she asked again.

'Really well,' I replied. 'It's strange, normally I plan a book out – plot, characters, motivations, everything. But this one, this one's just flowing.'

'Mark said you're using her inkpot.'

'Mm. Though I don't know if it was actually hers.'

Kathy looked at me. 'And how are you sleeping? You look tired, are you still having nightmares?'

I started to feel uncomfortable with all her questions. 'No, actually, not since I started writing her story.' I stopped. I hadn't made that connection before.

'Maybe she just wants her story known,' Kathy said.

It didn't sound like a question, and I had no idea what to say in return. I decided to change the subject. 'Have you seen the family trees in the old journal? They're fascinating!'

'Not for a long time.' She was looking at me strangely.

'In fact it's really odd, the names I used for the Ramsgill brothers in my story are all there – as brothers! And at about the right time too.'

Kathy put her mug on the table and stared at me. 'Let me see,' she said.

A little unnerved, I opened the journal and unfolded the large sheet of paper with the Ramsgill family tree. Wordlessly, I pointed out Thomas, Richard, Robert and Alexander.

Kathy traced the line from Richard all the way down to Mark.

'An unlucky family,' she said.

I glanced at her, but said nothing.

'Have you told her the rest? The curse?'

We both looked up, startled. Mark had arrived home and stood in the doorway, watching us.

'The curse?' Kathy asked.

'That's not in the journal, it's in my story,' I said, quickly.

'The story that's mirroring history,' Kathy said, pointing at the brothers' names. 'What's the curse?'

'That only one Ramsgill child survives to sire the next generation,' I said, my voice soft.

Kathy nodded and Mark threw his coat and bag on to a chair. I glanced at him; he seemed angry. 'It's nothing,

Kathy – fiction. The brothers' names are coincidence, they're all traditional ones – they're pretty obvious choices! And as for the curse, *you* told her about the Ramsgill curse when her and David came for dinner!'

Kathy raised her eyebrows at me, then turned back to her husband. 'We didn't know there was a *real* curse. I'd always thought it was just a family story. How could Emma make up a curse that fits near a dozen generations of Ramsgill family history?'

'She had Old Ma Ramsgill's journal.'

'You didn't show that to me until *after* I'd written about the curse, Mark. Don't you remember? I showed it to you when you brought me the journal.'

He looked away, no doubt remembering what that had led to, and I felt ashamed. *What am I doing?*

'We don't actually know if this family tree is correct, there's nothing to worry about.' I backtracked, trying to reassure Kathy and wishing I hadn't said anything about the Ramsgill brothers and Jennet's curse.

'Aye, nowt to worry about.' Mark had poured himself a whisky and downed it in one.

'So why don't you check it?' Kathy asked him. 'You're the historian – even I know the Internet is full of these genealogy sites. Find out if these people really lived and . . . died as it's written here. Do some research.'

Mark glanced away and I realised he already had.

'Speaking of research, I must get back to mine,' I said, suddenly desperate to get out of there. 'Thanks for the coffee, Kathy, and send Alex down at the weekend when Dave's back, if you're sure he'll be interested?'

'Ten pounds an hour and no commute? Believe me, he'll be interested,' Kathy said. 'You don't need a cleaner as well do you – for Hannah?'

I laughed, pleased the mood had broken, although a glance at Mark showed he was still brooding.

'I'm not sure about that – I get distracted if anyone but

Dave is in the house, but I'll think about it,' I promised.

The door shut behind me and I breathed a sigh of relief. Then raised voices from inside reached me. I hesitated a moment before turning my back and walking home.

Chapter 27 - Jennet

20th July 1777

It had been nearly two months since my babbies had died, and past time I showed my face in the village. I smiled the odd greeting, but none were returned. Hopefully it were just because of the rain. Lizzie Thistlethwaite, Martha Grange and Susan Gill, huddled on Street Bridge passing the time of day, stopped talking when they saw me, glanced at each other and scuttled off up past the mill. They were aware that I knew not one of them lived up that way, but they did not care. They had turned away from me as if I were poison. It had nowt to do with weather. I did not know if Mary Farmer had gossiped or if it were just one more thing to add to my run of bad luck.

I pursed my lips and shifted the sack of grain to my other shoulder, wondering if I would have to get used to this treatment. Let them go; stupid, silly women, what did I care? I had my house, my beasts and the moors. I went to the fairy spring regularly, and Mam and my babbies were always there. I still had Mary Farmer, too, though she were a little more reserved since the babbies, and I still had my customers.

In they crept, usually at night, anxious that nobody saw them. And they paid what I asked: a dozen eggs for a nerve tonic; a sheaf of oats for a fever remedy; a round of cheese for a love potion.

They hated me and they feared me; but they needed me and they kept me. Aye, Mary Farmer must have gossiped. I would soon sort *her* out.

*

I reached the mill and thumped the sack down in relief – my back ached from carrying it the mile from my farm.

I glanced up at a cough. Big Robert Ramsgill, the Royal Miller, walked out from one of the mill's dark corners. He spoke, but I could not hear him over the rumbling and splashing of the waterwheel and the grinding of the great stones. I cupped my hand over my ear, and he came closer.

'What's thee doing here?' he repeated.

I stared at him in surprise and gestured at my sack of grain.

'I'd like it grinding into flour. I've brought thy wife's herbs – three months' worth – Mam taught me the recipe.'

Big Robert Ramsgill eyed the packet in my hand and the sack of oats, then shook his head.

'She wants nowt made by thy wanton hands.' He coughed again.

'What? But I've been making them for years! And it's thy brother thee should be insulting – not me!'

'Get out of here! I won't hear abuses against my family!'

I watched him bend double with the force of his cough. I took a deep breath; I could not afford to lose my temper.

'I could help thee with that cough an'all.'

'He said leave.'

I turned. His son – Little Rob – stood at the door and glared at me. As we stared at each other, his twin sister Jayne joined him – one either side of the doorway. They were a year older than I and we had never got on. As the son and daughter of the Royal Miller, and Ramsgills to boot, they looked down on me. Even now with my own farm, I did not engage their interest – my farm were not large enough.

I glanced back at Big Robert Ramsgill. He had recovered from his coughing fit and stood firm again, though was dwarfed by his son. I sighed and bent to heft my sack on to my shoulder.

I staggered through the door and felt hands on my back. They shoved and I fell. The sack split open when it landed, and my precious oats scattered in the muck of the street.

'No!' I cried and turned to remonstrate with the Ramsgill twins.

They stood and laughed. 'That's it, slut, thee lay down in dirt where thee belongs!'

'What's going on here?' I turned to see Thomas Ramsgill, and my heart sank.

'How do, *Constable*,' his nephew stressed the word. 'This one's disturbing smooth running of King's mill. She's been asked to leave but refused – we were helping her on her way.'

His father joined him at the door, and the brothers glanced at each other.

'Why thee!' It were all I could think of to say in my rage and surprise.

Little Rob smirked and his sister giggled behind her hand.

'Be off with thee now, Jennet, there's a good lass.' Thomas Ramsgill said. 'We don't want no trouble now, do we?'

I got to my feet and gathered the remnants of the sack around the grain I could save. I glared at Little Rob.

'I know what thee did, and I'll remember. Thee ain't heard the last of this, I promise thee that.'

He laughed. 'What kind of curse is that? Thee has to do better than that, witch!'

'What did you call me?' I stepped towards him and Thomas caught my shoulders.

'Home, Jennet. Now, or I'll have to put thee in stocks.'

I looked at him. '*Me*? He's the one pushed me in dirt!'

He stared back and I gave up. I could not win here; I would have to find another way to deal with Little Rob.

I bent to pick up my grain best I could, and turned away. I paused when I saw Margaret Ramsgill at the door of Mill

House. She would not meet my gaze and dropped her eyes.

I started the long trudge home – with only half a sack of grain left. I would have to grind it by hand.

I dumped the sack in the garden and went in to find the quern-stones. I poured myself a jug of ale, downed it in one, then carried the heavy, round stones outside. I were angry – I might as well use that anger in the grinding.

Ten minutes later, I paused and stretched. My back, shoulders and arms were agony, and I would have to grind for near an hour to get enough flour for a day's-worth of oatcakes.

I bent back to the grind, but knew I could not do this every day. I would have to find another way to get my daily bread.

Chapter 28 - Emma

22nd September 2012

'Emma!'

I jumped and stared at Dave.

'My God, Emma, I've been calling you for ages, didn't you hear me?'

I glanced at my notebook, then back at my husband, disorientated.

'Sorry, I was engrossed.'

'You're telling me! But you need to take a break. You've been writing since the early hours and it's nearly lunchtime. You've not eaten or washed, I'm getting worried about you.'

'I'm fine.'

'Are you? Have the dogs been out?'

I stared at him, he knew what my reaction would be if *he* hadn't taken them out. Then I sighed, feeling guilty. I was neglecting the dogs, neglecting my husband, maybe even myself, but I just – had – to – write.

I pulled my eyes away from Dave. His look of concern should have filled me with guilt, but I only felt irritation.

'Emma . . .'

'What?'

He hesitated.

'Dave, what is it?'

'Don't take this the wrong way, I know you've tried counselling before, but what do you think about talking to Kathy?'

'Talking to Kathy?' I froze, *does he know about Mark?*

'Yes. Well, she's a counsellor, isn't she? She knows how to listen. Not only that, she's a friend, she might be able to help.'

'I don't need help, I just need to write this book!'

'Emma, you're not sleeping, you're always irritable, and now you've forgotten to take the dogs out. I'm getting worried – this is beyond obsession!'

I threw the quill on to the coffee table and stood. 'Fine. I'll take the dogs for a walk.'

Dave said nothing, just stared at the mess of ink splotching the coffee table. He glanced up and nodded. 'Just think about it, please.'

My irritation dimmed; he must be worried not to complain about the ruination of a perfectly good (and fairly expensive) table.

'What the hell were you thinking the other day? Kathy's in a right state!'

I didn't turn. Shep had run past me to greet my three – I had known Mark wouldn't be far behind.

'You said *you* would be there – I was taken by surprise to be welcomed by your wife!'

'You're a writer – you make up stories for a living, couldn't you have found something better to talk about?'

'I'm consumed by *this* story, Mark!' Now I turned to face him. 'It's taking me over – every waking moment I'm either writing her or thinking about writing her – it's driving me mad!'

He grabbed my arms and shook me. 'Get a grip, woman! It's a story – a tale! She's been dead two hundred year! You sound like Kathy now, going on about how Jennet walks again. It's just a bloody tale, get it in perspective!'

'Let go of me!' If anything, his grip tightened. 'Let go!' I shouted, shaking my arms free. I stared at him, then nodded past him. 'Dave might see.'

He sighed and glanced to his right, then walked to the

trees. I hesitated a moment and followed.

The gloomy day was positively dark under the pines and I paused, unable to see Mark. Suddenly, he thrust my body against a tree and kissed me roughly. I pushed against him, then gave in and returned his kiss.

His hands scrabbled at my waist and he shoved my jeans down past my hips. His own soon followed. He grabbed my hips and spun me round and I grabbed hold of the tree trunk, then took a couple of steps back, the air cold on my backside.

I caught my breath in anticipation, then cried out with the force of his entry and quickly bit my lip to stop any more noise escaping me. It was fast, furious and very, very good, yet I was relieved when it was over.

I straightened up and buttoned my jeans, still with my back to Mark.

'I love my wife,' he said. 'In nearly twenty year, I've never cheated on Kathy, never! And now this. I can't help meself. I don't know what the hell this is, but it has to stop. Whatever you're doing to me, it has to stop!' He turned and walked away.

Tears rolled down my face and I stared after him open-mouthed. I wasn't doing anything to him. *He* was the one doing this to me. He was the one who had started it, who kept starting it. I loved Dave. I did. I did not love Mark – I didn't even fancy him! Yet this kept happening. And I didn't know how to stop it.

I emerged from the trees and threw stones into the reservoir for the beasts to jump after. I sat on the shore to watch the dogs swim, and tried to make sense of the mess my life had become.

Once my tears had dried and I thought I could argue the flush in my cheeks and red-rimmed eyes were due to the fresh air, I went home to Dave, none the wiser about anything.

Chapter 29 - Jennet

4th August 1777

The rain had stopped. After two solid weeks of water, the sun at last showed itself. I threw my shawl around my shoulders, picked up my basket and set off. I needed feverfew, foxglove and a number of other plants that grew in the lush meadows down the hill.

I did not want to ruin my day, so I turned left at the Gate Inn to avoid the village and followed Street Lane towards the mill. I would turn off at the bridge and follow the river downstream towards Hanging Wood. With any luck I would meet no one.

I turned the last bend in the lane and stopped in surprise at the sight of a lake. The River Washburn were in flood. I waded through on to the hump of Street Bridge to get a better view, and gaped at the sight in front of me.

I could not make out the millpond, it were part of the river now. The mill and Mill House were awash, and I smirked when I saw both Robert Ramsgills bailing water.

The grain started the grind by being hoisted up to the top of the mill, then made its way through the grinding stones until it reached the ground floor as flour. I could only imagine the mess in there.

Little Rob paused in his work and stretched his back. He spotted me watching from the bridge and shook his fist in my direction. My smile grew broader and I waved at him. He said something to his father and pointed at me. The more diminutive Big Robert stopped what he were doing to glare, then turned away and waded back into the mill.

I laughed out loud and turned to see downstream, then leaned on the parapet to get a better look. A flock of sheep were trapped by water, and the small hillock of land they had gathered on were shrinking by the minute. The whole village seemed to be on the river bank, Richard Ramsgill at their head, trying to get them on to dry land.

I peered closer and realised they were his wethers and tups – the most prized of his flock – put to graze on the lushest, most nutritious grass by the river before market.

I waded back through the water pooled over the edge of the bridge, skirts held high, and made my way down to join my neighbours.

As I got closer, I realised the sheep were all clean and closely shorn. My suspicions were right – they had deliberately excluded me from the washing and clipping this year. I gritted my teeth against a sob and took a deep breath. I would not let them get to me.

I had clipped my girls myself – not the neatest job, but I knew I would not be able to sell their wool anyroad, not when Richard Ramsgill were the only wool merchant for miles around. I would need to card and spin it for my own use – I had to be self-sufficient now.

But they were my neighbours and customers, and to live out here on the moors, we had to help each other. Maybe if I lent a hand now, some of these folk would also see themselves right to helping me some time?

'What's happening?'

Susan Gill turned to me. 'They got trapped by flood, the men are trying to get them to swim over.'

I watched the fast flowing water a moment. I knew sheep could swim, but I did not think they could swim well enough to get over that without being swept away, and said so.

Martha Grange turned to me. 'We don't need thee ill wishing us! Thee's done enough! This is thy fault – thine! Thee cursed this village and thee cursed Richard Ramsgill

– and now look, his best tups and wethers are drowning!'

I backed away in alarm, both at her outburst and Mary's betrayal. She were the only one who knew. She *must* have gossiped. I had thought she were my friend, how could she tell the village about that day? How could she turn the worst day of my life into tittle-tattle?

'Thee did this!' Martha Grange had not finished. 'Thee cursed Ramsgill, and thee cursed this village, I heard thee!' she said again, her voice rising and everybody stopped what they were doing to stare.

What? I stopped moving and gaped at her in confusion.

'Thee were screaming blue bloody murder that day. I were coming up to see if I could help and I heard thee curse.' She dropped her voice a little. 'Aye, saw what thee did an'all. Them poor babbies.'

She spat at me. I realised everyone else were silent and staring. It had not been Mary Farmer who had spread gossip about me after all. It had never occurred to me that Martha Grange had seen me. I turned and ran home in shame.

Chapter 30 - Emma

29th September 2012

'Emma! Emma!'

'Wha . . . ?' I blinked in the bright light and glanced up at Dave. 'What's wrong? What is it?'

He sat on the sofa next to me and held his head in his hands.

'You really scared me, Em. This isn't normal, this is . . . I don't know what this is, but I'm scared.'

'Scared? Why?'

He stared at me. 'You have no idea, have you?'

I stared back, not wanting to admit I didn't have a clue what he was talking about.

He sighed. 'I woke up and you weren't there – again. You were sitting in here – the office – in the dark, writing.'

'In the dark?' I looked at him, did he mean it or was he teasing me?

'Yes, Emma, in the dark.' His face was haggard – he was serious.

'But that's not the worst of it.' He paused, took a breath. 'When I put the light on, you didn't notice. Em, your eyes . . .'

'What? What about my eyes?' I was starting to panic now.

'They were rolled right back – only the whites were showing. Emma, you were writing in the dark – blind!'

We stared at each other, then our eyes dropped to the notebook in my lap. The writing was not only legible, but neat and straight, although it didn't quite look like my handwriting. There were fewer ink blots on the page now as well, although I noticed my fingers were still covered in ink from the quill.

We stared at each other again and tears rolled down my cheeks. Dave opened his arms and I fell into his embrace. He held on to me, hard, as I sobbed, then led me back to the bedroom.

A few hours later, I woke to my husband depositing a steaming cup of coffee on the bedside table. I smiled at him and wrapped my arms around his neck when he leaned over to kiss me.

'That's better,' he said. 'I think you got more than three hours sleep for once!'

'I actually feel like I've slept,' I said. 'I'd forgotten what that was like.'

'You needed the rest – you're working far too hard. Just take it easy this morning, hey?'

I nodded. 'What about you, are you coming back to bed?' I asked, peering up at him from under my lashes.

'Ah, I'd love to,' he replied, then glanced towards the front of the house, 'but young Alex is outside, digging a garden for us – it wouldn't be right. Anyway, I need to go to Harrogate – I've some important papers that need to go to the post, and we need a supermarket shop too – there's barely any food in the house.'

I nodded, dropping my arms from around his neck and accepting the reprimand. I realised Dave had a point, I *had* neglected things lately.

'We need to be more careful – it's isolated here, the nearest shop's miles away; we need to make sure we have plenty in. Gas is getting low too, I've rung and ordered more cylinders.'

'Sorry, I've just been—'

'Busy,' he finished for me. I dropped my eyes, guilty. He had been driving to Edinburgh almost weekly for meetings and site visits. He'd driven nearly two hundred miles home the day before, and now he was getting into the car again to drive the fifteen miles to Harrogate to stock up the fridge.

I'd spent my time writing. Oh, and fucking the neighbour – can't forget that.

I reached over and burnt my lips sipping the hot coffee. I could not look at him.

'I'll leave the front door open so Alex can come in and get himself a drink.'

'Ok.'

He gave me a peck on my forehead and left.

I waited ten minutes and went to the window to make sure his car had gone. Alex was outside the front door digging the first flowerbed, and I watched him a moment, his young muscles bulging under his tight T-shirt. I sighed, just what I needed: another bloody Ramsgill.

I turned away from the window and got into the shower, trying to drench the past month and all its implications away.

It didn't work, I still felt terrible: tired, stressed and guilty. I went into the office to escape my world and write.

'Have you got a minute?'

I jumped and dropped the quill on the carpet, splattering ink everywhere.

'Mark, you scared me!'

'Sorry, the door was open.'

'What do you want?' I hadn't forgotten the last time I'd seen him, the way he'd treated me and what he'd said.

'To apologise. I made out it was all your fault and it's not, I just . . . I just don't understand what's happening.'

'No, me neither.' I shook my head, tears flooding my eyes once again.

He hesitated, then crossed to the sofa and put his arm around me. I stiffened, then leaned into his familiar body.

Chapter 35 - Jennet

18th October 1777

Marjory Wainwright were pregnant! Already! I had counted on at least another six months' supply of flour, but that had gone now. I were happy for her, really – there were sure to be someone else who needed a remedy, a potion, or a curse – I were being asked for more and more of them now. *They* could pay me in flour – and hay; the beasts would need extra food soon. It seemed Mam had been right, and Peg Lofthouse's preparations weren't worth the walk to Padside. Despite everything, I still had customers. They may be desperate to risk knocking on my door, but that boded well for me. They would pay whatever I asked.

Shouting outside had me rushing to the door.

'What's going on here?' There were a dozen people in my yard. 'Watch my plants!' They were standing on the herbs.

'There she is, the witch! Get her!'

I gasped in fear. Had someone called me a witch? I tried to shut the door so I could bar it against them, but I were too slow.

Thomas Ramsgill were the first man through, and he grabbed my arm.

'It's the stocks for thee, lass, come on. There's no point resisting. Put on thy coat.'

I calmed a little. When I had heard the word witch, I had pictured a gallows.

'The stocks, why? What for?'

'Marjory Wainwright's cooking pot.'

'What about it?'

'Thee stole it.'

'No! It were given in fair payment, she wanted children, I helped her, she's pregnant. The pot were payment for my remedy!'

'Well, she says thee stole it, and as she's respectable married lady, and thee . . .' he tailed off, a look of disgust on his face. I gritted my teeth and stared back at him.

'Not pregnant for long, though, were she?' somebody shouted. I thought it were Digger Blackstock.

'What?'

'Aye, lost babby – thy herbs weren't up to much were they?'

'What? She's lost babby?' I asked, horrified. Poor Marjory.

'Did thee curse her, too?'

'Has thee cursed whole village? Thy babby didn't live so no bugger else's will?'

Thomas Ramsgill pulled me through the door, and I could see them all now. People who used to be friends. Martha Grange, Susan Gill. Now they cheered and spat and hated.

Tears filled my eyes. *How could they do this to me?*

We had reached the lane, and I were still shouting, 'I didn't, I ain't, I didn't!' Nobody listened. Nobody cared. Then I remembered the corn dolly. *Did Marjory Wainwright make it?*

Past the junction – the lane Richard Ramsgill took to go home. And there he were, standing to one side, watching with Peter Stockdale. At least he weren't one of the mob.

'Richard! Richard, help me, please, I ain't done nowt!'

He stared at his boots and said nowt. I fell silent and looked at Peter. He turned away, a pained expression on his face. What more were there to say? Who to say it to?

We reached Low Green and I glanced up the lane to the church. No help there, neither.

Digger lifted the top bar of the stocks, and Thomas Ramsgill held my wrists in the half circle gaps carved into the lower plank of wood. The top came down and were secured.

I stared up at William Smith as he worked the metal links, but he would not meet my eyes. I had known him since I were a child, sneaking down to the smithy to watch him work his forge, sparks and fire flying. Now he were locking me up.

He stepped away, and I looked up at them; my wrists shackled by a plank of wood. I were bent nearly double and my back were aching already.

How long will they leave me here? Even with Pa's coat, I were chilled. To be stood here all night, unmoving, would be unbearable.

'Please, I ain't done owt, please!' I begged them, then dropped my head, it hurt to crane my neck to see them.

The crowd laughed and cheered. Nobody believed me.

Then they silenced, and I glanced up again, hopeful.

'Marjory! Please – I helped thee, I helped thee get with child, thee knows I did. I did nowt to harm thy babby, nowt! Please help me.'

She stared at me for a moment, then spat. It landed below my eye, but with my hands in the stocks, I could not wipe it away.

Then Elizabeth Ramsgill stepped forward and added her own spittle to Marjory's.

More women followed their example, and the rest of them laughed and clapped as if a band of mummers had trekked across the moors to entertain us.

Tears rolled down my face, *how had things come to this?*

They got bored after an hour or two. I mean, who would not? I only stood there, bent over, hands imprisoned.

After Marjory spat, I did not speak another word. There were no point. I heard their cheers, their laughter, their fun, but I did not listen. I did not react. Instead, I pictured myself on the moors, running free.

It were dark now and had been for some time. The crowd were long gone. The odd person scurried past; some stared, some looked away, but none stopped.

I were thirsty, hungry and cold. My wrists stung from the restriction and the wood – I were sure I had splinters – and my back had gone from ache to agony.

Thomas Ramsgill and William Smith were long gone, and I had realised some time ago that they really were going to leave me here all night.

'There she is! There's the witch, I told thee!'

I lifted my head, *now what?*

Three figures approached out of the gloom: Little Rob Ramsgill, Billy Gill and Johnny Ward.

'Go home, boys, there's nowt for thee here.'

They laughed and spat whilst crossing their fingers. I realised they were drunk. I jumped and squealed when a hand smacked my backside.

'Get out of here, boys! Thee don't want to do this!' I were scared now, and knew my fear were clear in my voice, but I had to keep trying. With my hands tied, my voice were my only defence.

'Go home, go home now!'

They laughed. 'Or what, thee'll curse us?'

'Damn right I will, if any of thee touches me, he'll lose his hand within a year!'

They laughed again, nervously now – they believed the stories. I could use that.

'Thee's calling me witch – watch out I don't grow fangs and howl at the moon! If thee don't leave now, thee'll be getting a visit from wolves first night I'm free! Who'll be first? Thee, Johnny Ward? Or thee, Billy Gill. What about thee, Little Rob?'

I realised I could not see Little Rob Ramsgill, only the other two, and grimaced as once again they spat.

'Thee don't scare me. Thee's no witch, only a trollop who opened her legs for me uncle.'

The words came from behind me and I looked round, moving away from the voice as much as possible. Bent over, in skirts, I knew how vulnerable I were.

I could not get away though, I could only move my feet half a yard or so, and I gasped when cold air hit my thighs and buttocks.

'Little Rob, stop that at once!'

I glanced up again at the new voice. A voice I knew well. Richard.

'Get away from here, all of thee!'

The two other boys ran, but I knew from Little Rob's groping hand that he were not going anywhere.

'What's wrong, Uncle Richard? Thee don't want to share?'

'Thee cheeky little runt!'

I heard the sound of flesh striking flesh, then a body tumbled to the ground. The hand had gone from between my legs and my skirt were pulled back down to cover me. Footsteps ran off.

Chapter 36 - Emma

21st October 2012

I woke, sweating and gasping, my heart pounding. The nightmares were back. Now that I was awake, I calmed and thought about my dream; I'd dreamed of Jennet throwing her dead babies on to the fire – except that I was Jennet. It had been my own lost baby I had cremated.

I shuddered and wiped tears from my face, then listened to Dave pottering about downstairs. I was worried. He'd been very quiet since we'd bumped into Mark earlier, and he hadn't wanted to come up to bed when I came up, which wasn't like him at all. *Does he suspect?*

My life was a mess. We had been here less than three months. Where had all the laughter and excitement gone? How could everything fall apart so quickly? Now look – my new book had taken over to the point it was worrying *me* now; I'd been having an affair I didn't want; and now I was pregnant, with no idea who the father was.

Then a thought hit me – what if I wasn't the mother? If this was Mark's baby, then it wasn't me who had slept with him – it was Jennet.

Yes! That explained so much. Jennet had got inside me – that was obvious from the way I was writing. The words weren't coming from me, they were coming *through* me. Jennet's words – not mine. I had no idea of what was coming next until it was written. It was all Jennet – she'd taken me over. It was she who was drawn to Mark – a direct descendant of Richard Ramsgill. *She* was this baby's mother, not me. It was *her* book and *her* baby!

I realised I had sat up in bed. It seemed preposterous, but somehow I knew it was true. I cupped my belly with my hands. This baby wasn't mine and Dave's. It was Jennet and Mark's – Richard's.

Now I was scared. *What the hell am I going to do? And how on earth will I make Dave understand?*

I jumped as thunder crashed overhead. I got out of bed and went to the office. I had to finish her story – it was the only way to get her out of my head and life. I had to write her out – to exorcise her.

Dave walked into the office. I glanced up at him and he stared at me for a moment. I realised he'd been drinking.

'Is there anything I need to know?'

'What?' *Shit.*

'About the baby. Is there anything I need to know?'

I stared at him.

'Why aren't you saying anything?' he shouted.

'Dave . . .'

'What? What? It's *his,* isn't it? I saw the way he paled when I mentioned the baby. Are you fucking Mark?'

I flinched. 'It's Jennet's.'

'What?'

'The baby, it's Jennet's. I think she's possessing me and the baby's hers, not mine.'

There was silence for a moment while he processed that.

'And who else's?'

I didn't say anything, just watched him, stricken.

'I knew it,' he muttered and sat on the edge of the desk, his head in his hands.

He lifted his head and looked at me. I flinched at the pain I saw there – pain that I had caused. And the tears started.

'Dave, I'm so sorry, I really am. It's not what you think, it wasn't me, it was Jennet.'

He stared at me in disbelief. I had no option but to keep

trying. No matter how ludicrous it sounded, it was the truth.

'I don't love him, I never did – I don't even fancy him! I love you, and he loves Kathy. It was like we had no choice, it was a compulsion. It was Jennet! She's inside me, and he's a direct descendant of the man she loved. It wasn't me, Dave, honestly, it was *Jennet!*'

My river of words stopped.

His face was like thunder, he looked like he'd been physically struck. 'You bitch. You *fucking* bitch! For a year you've refused to even try and I've waited. I'd wait as long as I had to until you were ready, and now you're knocked up by the fucking neighbour! What is it, you think you only lose *my* babies? You want to try it with someone else's sperm?'

I flinched away from his words.

'Is it still going on?'

I shook my head. 'She's got what she wanted, she's leaving us alone now.'

'You're sick, you really are.' His voice rose, along with his temper, and red flushed his cheeks. 'Your actions are your own, not those of a woman who's been dead over two hundred years! What kind of idiot do you think I am? I don't believe in all that ghost crap! You need a doctor, Emma, a psychiatrist!'

'No, Dave, listen. What about when you found me writing in the dark, with my eyes like that? How do you explain that? And the handwriting wasn't mine – it was Jennet's! That's why I've been writing so much – it's her, using me, *forcing* me to tell her story!'

'Emma—'

'No, listen! When I found that inkpot as a kid I think it must have connected me to her, then I came to live here, so close to Mark.' Dave's face flushed darker at the mention of his name. *'Listen!* He's descended from Richard Ramsgill! She's strong, Dave, so strong, she's taking over.'

He stared at me, fists clenched, and I thought for a moment he would hit me. He took a few deep breaths and got control over himself. The emotion left him and he stared at me coldly. That was worse than his anger; he'd switched himself off from me.

'I'm away to Edinburgh again on Wednesday, for two weeks. Until then I'll be sleeping in the spare room. Please, Emma, while I'm away, see the doctor. Please.'

'And when you get back?'

'I don't know, Jennet, I don't know.'

I stared at him in horror.

'Emma. I meant Emma.' He left the room.

Chapter 37 - Jennet

19th October 1777

'Thee's safe now, Jennet, he's gone.'

'Let me out, please,' I sobbed, tears pouring down my face. 'Please get me out of here, I want to go home. I don't deserve this, I don't.'

'I can't let thee out. Our Thom'll do that at dawn. But I'll stay with thee, make sure them lads don't come back. Why don't thee kneel down? Thee'll be more comfortable.'

I cried harder. *Why wouldn't he release me?*

'I can't, me knees . . .' I managed through my sobs. I had knelt earlier to ease my back, and my knees were red raw.

Richard Ramsgill took off his coat and folded it, then placed it on the ground in front of me.

I glanced at him in surprise at his kindness, then sank down on to my knees. I sighed as my back straightened, and arched – stretching my muscles. There were a loud crack and Richard Ramsgill jumped.

'What were that?'

'My back. It's easier now, thanks to thee.' I knew it were only a matter of time before my new position became too painful, but I would take the relief while I had it.

Kneeling in front of the stocks, my hands trapped and bloody from splinters, I leaned my head against the wood and closed my eyes.

'It's a rum do, lass.'

I glanced up at him. 'Eh?' What were he talking about?

'This past year has been Hell.'

'Past year and a half,' I said.

'Eh? Oh, aye,' Richard Ramsgill said. 'I suppose things ain't been easy for thee, neither.'

I lifted my head and stared at him. *Were he serious?*

'Elizabeth has made life Hell,' he carried on. 'Aye, got Pa onside an'all, she has, whole ruddy family's been punishing me.'

Did he really expect *me* to feel sorry for *him?*

'Alice's death really knocked me, thee knows lass,' he carried on.

'Mm, were a bit upset, mesen,' I said.

'Aye, that thee were,' he replied, having missed the bitterness in my voice. 'Thee knows that time with thee were happiest in a long time, Jennet. I miss thee sometimes.'

Tears dripped down my face, but he did not notice. 'Then why—?'

He glanced up at me then back at the ground. He shrugged. 'It were madness. Thee were just a lass . . .'

'That didn't seem to bother thee at start.'

He jumped, surprised at the venom in my voice.

'Aye, well . . . ' He paused, looked down again, then rose, walked over to the stocks and squatted in front of them so I could see him easily. He reached out and stroked my face, then wiped the tears from my cheeks.

'Thee were beautiful, lass, and so sad, me heart just . . . melted. I should've been stronger, I knows that, but I couldn't help mesen.'

'I loved you, Richard,' I whispered.

'Aye, lass. I loved thee too, but it were impossible.'

'Why?'

He stood and threw his arms out, indicating the village. 'Thee knows what Thores-Cross is like – folk talk. Eventually, too much talk fell into Elizabeth's hearing and she's canny – too canny.'

'What does thee mean?'

'She never said owt to me, went to me Pa and me

brothers first. They beat crap out of me, and threatened to take farm off me, wool business an'all.'

'I thought they were thine?'

He shook his head. 'It all belongs to Pa. Won't be mine till he's passed.'

Now I began to understand.

'So thee abandoned me. I were grieving and alone, and thee abandoned me!'

'I had no choice, lass.'

'Then you knocked me to the ground, kicked me and called me whore – told me to kill our child!'

Finally, he looked ashamed. 'I had no choice,' he repeated. 'I'd a lost everything.'

'I *did* lose everything – look at me!'

He looked – his eyes locked on mine.

'This is what's become of me! Due to thy cowardice and weakness! Mam died and Pa followed her. Then thee abandoned me and . . .' I could not finish. Sobs wracked my body.

'I told thee to get rid of child!' he said. 'It would'a been all right had thee got rid of child! No bugger would'a known. Instead . . .'

'I tried!' I screamed. 'I tried – it didn't work!'

He sat down again. 'Oh, lass . . . I'm sorry. I thought thee'd carried on with pregnancy to spite me.'

I shook my head, then rested it on the stocks. I could barely look at him. I had destroyed my life for this man, and he thought I had set out to destroy his.

He nodded in understanding, but said nowt more. He stared at the road in thought and did not raise his head till dawn.

'Richard! What the bloody hell is thee doing here?'

'None of thy business, our Thom. Now let her out, thee's made thy point, she's had an Hellish night.'

'Where does Elizabeth think thee is?'

'I neither know nor care. Get a move on, the poor lass is crippled.'

Thomas Ramsgill glared at his brother, then motioned to Will Smith to free the locks.

He lifted the wooden bar up and gently took my numb hands out of their grooves. I glanced up at him and he smiled. I did not return it.

I straightened slowly and winced. It hurt, but I were not going to give these men the satisfaction of crying out.

'Come on, lass, let's get thee home.' I looked at Mary Farmer, grateful to see her. A friendly face.

She put her arm around my waist and I rubbed at my wrists; then stopped and studied them in surprise at the sharp pain. Dozens of needle-prick splinters were embedded in my skin.

'We'll sort that out at home, lass, come on.'

Mary urged me on with her arm, and we struggled up the hill. I could not straighten up and my legs were weak, but eventually we reached my front door and I fell into the house. Mary half carried me up the stairs to my bed, then fetched up warm ale, a bucket of warm water, cloths and some of my comfrey salve. She sat on the floor next to my mattress and started pulling splinters out of my wrists.

She barely said a word to me; an occurrence I found more frightening than a night in the stocks.

Chapter 38 - Emma

20th December 2012

'Emma Moorcroft?'

I stood and followed a nurse from the waiting area into an examination room.

'Hop up there and loosen your clothes, love, the midwife'll be here in a minute.'

I unfastened my jeans and shirt and got on to the small bed. The nurse bustled about me, pulling at my shirt. 'She needs to get to your belly, love.'

I laughed, nervous.

'Is your husband not with you?'

'No, he's away on business.' I didn't tell her we had barely spoken for the past two months and I had no idea whether our marriage would survive.

'Morning.' Another woman came in and walked to the machine next to the bed.

'Any problems?' She picked up a plastic bottle.

I laughed. Yes, I had problems.

'With the pregnancy, I mean,' she added, squinting at me, and the nurse gave my hand a squeeze.

Yes, the baby isn't mine and it's parents are over two hundred years old. I didn't say it, just shook my head.

She nodded. 'This will feel a bit cold.' She squirted my belly with gel, and I flinched despite the warning.

She picked up the ultrasound wand and placed the head on my belly, squishing the gel around.

She paused, moved it, paused, moved, paused again.

'Is everything all right?' I asked, suddenly concerned. If

there was something wrong, what would Jennet do next?

'Don't worry, I'm just trying to get a clear picture,' she said. I glanced up at the nurse who gave me a reassuring smile.

The midwife pressed a button and a rhythmic sound filled the room.

'The heartbeat?' I asked.

'Yes – good and strong,' the midwife said, then moved the wand. The sound faded and grew loud again. She met my eyes for a moment. 'And that's the second.'

'The second?' I felt cold.

'Congratulations, you're having twins.'

'Twins,' I repeated.

'Do they run in the family?' the nurse asked.

Numb, I shook my head. There were no twins in my family or Dave's. Only Mark Ramsgill's.

'A bit of a shock, isn't it? Don't worry, you're not alone, identical twins are completely random and can be born to anyone – it's only fraternal twins that tend to run in families, and even that isn't set in stone – and they are more common in women your age.'

'Which are these?' I asked the midwife.

'Fraternal – there are two amniotic sacs.'

I nodded.

'Are you all right?' the midwife asked. 'It can be a bit frightening. We do have people here if you want to talk to someone?'

I shook my head. I wanted to go home. *What will I say to Dave?* No matter what these women said, he would see it as proof that these were Mark's babies. I knew it proved they were Jennet's. My blood turned cold at the thought. I was sure now that I carried Jennet's babies. I still would not have a child of my own.

Then another thought struck me, *what will Jennet do? Will she try to claim them?* I held my belly as tightly as I could, terrified. She couldn't have them. I would not lose these babies too.

*

I poured hot water on to the camomile teabag and stared at the phone. Maybe I just wouldn't call him.

The phone rang and I jumped.

'How did it go?'

'Hello, Dave, how are you?'

Silence, then, 'Fine. How did it go?'

'Ok. No problems. It's a boy.' I stared at the wall; I hadn't realised I had decided to lie. *Will this save my marriage, or imperil it further?*

'I see,' said Dave. 'And is everything all right with it?'

'Yes.' A pause. 'When are you coming home?'

'I'm not sure.'

'Will you be back for Christmas?'

'No. I'll stay with Ben.' His brother. I gripped the phone hard, trying not to panic. 'The roads'll be heaving, and I need to be back in Edinburgh early in the New Year. I might as well stay here,' he continued.

'I see.' Alice and the girls were supposed to be coming for our first Christmas in our new home. *What will I tell them?* My breath hitched in my throat.

'Oh, don't cry, Emma!'

I held my breath, trying to get my sobs under control, at least until we finished the phone call.

'I'll pass Ben and Julie your regards, shall I?'

'Yes.' My voice sounded strangled.

'Ok then, I'll call again soon.'

'Love you, Dave.' The phone went dead. I stared at it, put it back on its cradle, picked up my mug and hurled it at the wall.

Chapter 39 - Jennet

16th November 1777

I opened my eyes and shivered. Despite sleeping in woollens under sheepskin, I were frozen. I did not need to see the snow piled up at the window to know it had been a heavy fall. The wind whistling round the house and through the chimney had kept me wakeful most of the night.

I sighed. I were torn. I did not want to leave the bed – I knew however cold I were now, it would be nowt compared to the temperature downstairs.

Yet I enjoyed the crispness of a new snowfall, and then there were the Farmers to think about. They were getting old and John were running low on his remedy for his aches and pains. The cold made it so much worse for him, until he could barely walk. And Mary were getting frail an'all. I had made up a tonic for her, too, to help her through the winter chills – I just had not expected it to snow this heavily, this soon.

I threw the covers off and dressed, then went downstairs to stoke up the fire. The Farmers were the closest thing I had to family, and the only people in the world I could call friends. I remembered the kindness they had shown me when Mam and Pa had died – I had to go to them.

I grunted as I pulled my leg out of another thigh-high drift and planted it down, then paused to get my breath.

The moors were beautiful. Rolling hills of sparkling, unblemished white. Well, nearly unblemished. Those new dry stone walls were creeping closer and closer; black lines snaking through the snow like poisoned blood running through veins.

I pulled the coat away from my neck for a moment, sighing in the blast of cold air. Trudging uphill through this snow were hard work, and I were sweating. Well, the top half of me were anyroad. My legs – despite being wrapped tightly with sheepskin under my skirts – were numb.

I started at a sudden movement to my right and gasped. An owl! It flew past me on silent wings and soared over the moor. It were rare to see them in daylight, but snow this deep made finding food difficult – for everyone.

I scanned the hillsides again, thinking of the beasts, but couldn't spot any sheep against the white backdrop.

I had fodder for them at the house, but even if I knew where they were, I could not get it to them; they were on their own unless they made their way home. I knew they were hardy and bred to survive the winters up here, but I worried about how many would be left come spring – especially of the youngest.

That reminded me of another problem, and I stared at the walls again. When the tups were released in November to service the ewes they would roam free and I could expect a new generation to replace those lost. But what about next year when the lower moors were crisscrossed with these walls?

The tups' owners would keep them close, penned in with their own flock of ewes – and no doubt get a higher birth rate, but what about the rest of us? What about me? Where were I going to get a tup from? The best I could hope for were a shepherd with a very ill wife or child who would have my ewes tupped in return for my remedies.

I sighed again. That were next year's problem – a long way off.

I pulled my coat tight again and glanced up at the

Farmers' house. I enjoyed the crisp, clean coldness of the winter air, but the smoke from their chimney looked heaven-sent.

'Ey up, lass! What were thee thinking, coming out in this?' Mary Farmer greeted me. I smiled at her as she stood aside to let me in, then bustled about getting a third stool up close to the fire.

I sat down, grateful.

'I brought John's remedy, and a little something to strengthen thee up, an'all.'

'Ah lass, thee's a good 'un at heart thee is,' Mary said. 'We could have managed till snow's gone, thee knows.'

'Could thee? This won't go overnight, Mary. I couldn't rest easy, knowing John would be in pain. I worry about thee both.'

Mary looked away and John Farmer held his hand out for the herbs. He rarely said much. He left the talking to Mary.

'Here, have some posset to warm theesen up,' Mary said, ladling some into a jug from the large pot hanging above the fire.

'Thank thee,' I said, taking it then wrapping my hands around it. 'And thee knows how I love moors, Mary, in all seasons. It were worth it, just to see them like this.'

'Thee's a rum 'un, lass,' John said, and I shrugged. He nodded and lapsed back into silence.

'Aye, he's right. It ain't normal, Jennet. Most folks are worried sick at this time of year – over food, how sheep are faring and plenty more besides. Thee be careful who thee says owt like that to – thee knows what folk round here are like!'

I laughed. 'Mary, who does thee think I talk to? Who does thee think in this village wants to pass time of day with me? Apart from two of thee, that is.'

'Aye, well, just goes to show. They're already against thee

over that Ramsgill business, if anyone hears thee going on about how wonderful it is out there like this, they'll likely blame thee for snow an'all. Take care, lass, is all I'm saying.'

I nodded and sipped my posset. She were right. I were bewildered by how people I had known my whole life had turned against me. I had been fifteen, newly orphaned and barely a woman – I had known nowt of such things beyond a ram tupping a ewe. He were a middle aged man – a family man – who knew it all. Yet he were respected, and I were shunned.

'There's already rumours,' Mary continued.

'Rumours?'

'Barguests and the like.'

'Bah,' John said, staring into the flames.

'Barguests?'

'Aye, a great wolf's been seen on't moor above Gate Inn.'

'The moor above Gate Inn?' I repeated.

'Aye lass.'

'Thee means, near my farm.'

'Aye lass.'

I stared into the fire mesen. That were all I ruddy needed.

Chapter 40 – Jennet

23rd November 1777

I paused with my foot on the familiar worn step. I thought about my quiet farmhouse and the last time I had spoken to anyone but the Farmers – it had been months ago.

I needed people. I needed to give them a chance as much as they needed to give me a chance.

I took a deep breath then pushed open the church door and slipped inside. It were dark after the sunshine outside and I took a moment for my eyes to get used to the gloom. Rows of villagers turned their heads to stare at me. I glared at them then looked to the front of the church and the curate. He cleared his throat and continued with the service. I sat down on one of the pews at the back.

I stared around me at the disdain and disapproval etched on my neighbours' faces, and wondered what I had been thinking. They did not want me here. Well, bugger the lot of them. This were my church too, and I would not slink off. I stared back at the faces turned towards me, and one by one they looked away. I caught Mary Farmer's eye and she nodded at me.

Everyone stood for the first hymn, and I joined them. I had forgotten how much I enjoyed singing. One voice stood out above all the others; a voice I had always enjoyed hearing; a lovely deep tone that carried the words and tune like no other, and uplifted everyone in the building.

I watched him sing and gasped when he looked up and met my eyes. Peter Stockdale winked then turned back to the front, and I were glad of the gloomy church. No one could see my blush.

Service and sermon over, the good folk of Thores-Cross filed out into the crisp November snow. I smiled as eye after eye were averted from me. I would not let them see how much they hurt me.

I got to my feet and followed them out – I could not stay here all day. No one spoke to me or acknowledged me, not even the curate. As I passed him in the doorway, he stared straight ahead and ignored my greeting.

I moved directly in front of him – he did not shift his gaze, but stared straight through me and I grunted with laughter. 'Love thy neighbour, Curate,' I said. 'Love thy neighbour.'

I jumped as my arm were taken and relaxed when I realised it were Mary Farmer. She led me out into the sunshine, and John stood at my other shoulder.

'It's good to see thee here, lass,' Mary said. 'It's good for village to see thee at church an'all.'

'Aye,' agreed John.

I shrugged. 'Had nowt else to do today.'

Mary narrowed her eyes, but I needed my bravado – I could not show weakness in front of all these people. She said nowt and we walked down the yew-lined path.

We slowed before we reached the group blocking the way. Billy Gill, Johnny Ward and my old friend Little Rob Ramsgill were deep in conversation, and it seemed half the village were listening in.

'Aye, that's the third this week!' Billy Gill said. 'Pa went out with his gun, saw a great black dog, he said, but I were watching out window and I reckon it were a wolf!'

'Never!' Johnny Ward said.

'And it's killed three of thy sheep so far?' Little Rob Ramsgill asked.

'Aye. And Old Man Lister from Padside reckons it's had half a dozen of his an'all!'

'Grandpa and me uncles have lost a few too,' Little Rob said.

'A wolf!' Johnny exclaimed. He sounded excited.

Little Rob glanced up and saw me. 'No, not a wolf,' he said. 'A barguest. It's her.' He pointed at me. 'It's that witch! She told us she'd do it, don't thee remember? She said she'd turn into a wolf and come after us!'

Billy Gill and Johnny Ward looked embarrassed. I were stunned. I could not find any words and were aware of everyone staring at me.

'Everyone knows witches can turn themselves into animals!' Little Rob continued. 'She's the one killing the sheep! Have any of hers had their throats ripped out? No! *Her* sheep ain't been touched!'

Billy Gill glanced at me and paled. I opened my mouth to say something, but no words would come. Mary were equally silent and I stared at her in surprise. She were never backward in speaking her mind, but now she stared at the boys, her mouth hanging open.

'Oh, stuff thy nonsense!'

I glanced at Peter Stockdale, my eyes wide in surprise. I had not expected him of all people to speak up for me.

'There's no such thing as barguests, thee's letting thy fancies run away with thee!'

'Aye,' John Farmer agreed.

'There's been wolves on this moor since time began, and only reason Jennet's flock ain't been affected is because it's so small – she hardly has any sheep! Now come on, out the way, thee's blocking path.'

The boys moved to the side, and the Farmers and I followed Peter out of the churchyard.

I wondered if he saw the spitting and crossed fingers pointed at me. Whatever were going on, and despite Peter's words, folk believed Little Rob Ramsgill.

Chapter 41 - Emma

10th January 2013

'Are you ready?'

I glanced at Dave in surprise. It was the first full sentence or unsolicited comment he'd offered me since he'd arrived back from Scotland three days ago.

'You want to come with me?' I had an appointment at the doctors with a mental health assessor.

He stared out of the window at the light covering of snow. 'Whatever else is going on, Emma, you're four months pregnant and the roads are bad.'

'It's nothing the Discovery can't handle.'

'Even so, they're narrow country roads. I'll drive you.'

I narrowed my eyes, wondering if he wanted to make sure I actually went to the appointment.

'Emma Moorcroft?'

I looked up at the sound of my name, glanced at Dave, then hauled myself to my feet and followed the woman to a door. Dave stayed where he was and didn't say a word.

Inside, she introduced herself as Vicky Baxter and gave me a questionnaire to fill out. I looked at the questions that tried to gauge my mood and behaviour, and answered them as best I could. How could I explain what was happening to me with multiple choice answers?

Then the real questions started. 'How are you sleeping?'

I shrugged. 'I'm not, really. I can't stop writing, and I can't get to sleep.'

'You're a writer?'

I nodded.

'What's stopping you getting to sleep? Planning your book or worrying about it?'

'I'm not aware of the time, and can't tear myself away from writing. It's almost as if my character is taking me over.' It was the closest I would come to admitting to her that Jennet had possessed me.

Vicky nodded and made some notes.

'So, you're working hard?'

'Every waking minute,' I replied.

'It sounds obsessive.'

'I can't stop thinking about the book, or bear to be away from it.'

'And is it affecting your marriage?

I laughed, though without mirth. 'You could say that.'

There was a pause, while she made some notes. 'You've recently moved up to Thruscross?'

'Yes.'

'How do you like it there?'

'Very much. I used to go the old sailing club when I was a child. I love it there, it's my favourite place in the world.'

'It's very isolated.'

'I prefer to think of it as quiet.'

Vicky smiled. 'Do you have any children?'

My face fell and I shook my head. Tears pricked my eyes and I blinked furiously. Vicky said nothing, but pushed over a box of tissues and waited for me to continue.

'We started trying a couple of years after we got married, but . . .' My breath caught in my throat in a loud sob and I lost my battle with tears. I reached forward without looking at Vicky and took a handful of tissues. I pressed them to my eyes, then blew my nose. 'I . . . we . . .' I broke off again with another sob.

'It's ok, take your time,' Vicky said.

I nodded and fought to regain control of myself. I took a deep breath, then tried again. 'I had a miscarriage, at twenty three weeks.'

'I'm sorry,' Vicky said. 'That's terrible, and very difficult to get over.'

I nodded, tears falling freely again. 'It was just over a year ago, but it still feels like yesterday. Dave's been wanting to try again for ages, but I wasn't ready, I can't bear to lose another baby.'

Vicky nodded. 'And you're . . . at seventeen weeks now?'

'Yes.'

'With twins?'

'This is confidential isn't it?'

'Yes, as I said before, this is completely confidential unless I thought you were at risk of harming yourself or somebody else.'

I sighed. 'Yes, I'm expecting twins.'

'It sounds as if you're struggling with the idea of that.'

I stared at her, tears still falling. 'My husband may not be the father.'

She nodded, but made no comment.

'I had an affair. With our neighbour.'

She nodded again. 'Do you blame your husband for the miscarriage?'

I shook my head violently. 'No, no, of course not, it was just one of those things. If it's anyone's fault, it's mine. My body failed my baby.' I broke down again.

Vicky waited for me to calm. 'What did the doctor say?'

I sniffed and blew my nose. 'That it happens more often than people realise. He reckoned that there was nothing wrong with me, that it was food poisoning, but how can it not be my fault? I ate whatever it was killed my baby! And now with all the writing and not sleeping, I messed up my pills,' I said and stared at her, defiant. I did not want to talk about the miscarriage. She nodded and I carried on. 'Mark is a descendant of one of the characters in the book. It was like a compulsion. I didn't want to, but couldn't stop it.'

'He forced you?'

'No! No, he didn't want to either. *Jennet* forced us.'

'Jennet?'

'My character.' I stared at the floor. I had said more than I had meant to. 'I know it sounds crazy, but that's what it was like.'

She nodded again, and scribbled some notes.

'So, am I mad?' I attempted a laugh. 'Do I have that multiple personality disorder or something?'

She smiled. 'We don't use the word mad any more, and dissociative identity disorder, as it's called these days, is extremely rare. It's difficult to diagnose and to treat, and many psychiatrists don't believe it even exists. To be honest, you're describing obsession rather than dissociation, and it sounds like you've had a very stressful year, what with the move so soon after the miscarriage. You're grieving, and it's lonely up there as well. I don't think we need to worry about obscure disorders, but focus on you and your needs. Is the man you came with your husband?'

I nodded.

'Has your doctor prescribed any anti-depressants?'

'No, she didn't want to while I'm pregnant.'

Vicky Baxter nodded again. 'I think we should organise some counselling for you. CBT – Cognitive Behavioural Therapy – could help you recognise your altered feelings and behaviours and help you find ways of coping with your work/life balance. I also think some joint counselling with your husband would help as well. You can work through your grief together, as well as find a way to deal with this pregnancy. Do you think he would be amenable to that?'

I shrugged. 'I can ask him.'

She nodded. 'We would do the CBT here, over the course of three months, but for the couples and grief counselling there's a local service which would be more suitable—'

'No!'

She stared at me in surprise.

'I . . . I'm sorry, it's just that, well, the neighbour's wife . . . works for them.'

'I see, that's out then. I'll have a chat with my supervisor and see if we can offer the joint counselling here as well.'

'Thank you.'

'How was it?' Dave asked as we turned out of the car park.

'She thinks it's the stress of the move and the isolation.'

He said nothing.

'I'll start a course of counselling – they'll write with my first appointment.'

'Hmph. What good will talking do? It's gone too far for that.'

'She says there'll be tools to help me find a better "work/life balance".' I mimed speech marks in the air. 'She also wants us to do some joint counselling.'

'No.'

'Dave . . .'

'What's the point? Either that,' he jabbed his finger at my belly, 'is mine, or it isn't. Talking won't sort it.'

'Dave, it's either *ours* or it's Jennet's. Please, don't let her destroy us!'

I screamed as he hit the brakes and I was thrown forward against the seatbelt.

'Stop it!' he shouted and slammed his fists on the steering wheel. 'Just stop it! Stop saying it's Jennet's! Jennet doesn't exist! She's a figment of your imagination!'

I stayed quiet. Dave rarely lost his temper, and I'd learned to wait the storm out when he did. After a few moments, he took a deep breath and let out the clutch. We drove home in silence.

Chapter 42 - Jennet

25th November 1777

I had spent the day on the moors, gathering rosehips and nuts. It were where I felt safest; my only company the sheep, plus shrews and mice, and the buzzards, owls and hawks that hunted them. No people and plenty of warning of any approach.

I loved it up here. The biting wind fresh and clean in my face; blowing all my worries – and the hate of the village – away.

But it were time to go home. I had more than I could carry with ease and I were cold, thirsty and hungry.

I set off towards my house and saw the Farmers' place – I would stop off there; say hello. It had been over a week since I had spoken to somebody; Mary Farmer would help put off the loneliness of my empty house. Just for a little while.

'Ey up, lass, how's thee?' Mary greeted.

'I'm well, Mary, how's thee?'

'Ah well, can't complain. Come on in, lass, have a sit by the fire, thee looks nithered. I'll get thee some warm ale.'

I pulled a stool closer to the fire and hunched over, holding my hands out to the heat.

'There thee is, lass,' Mary said, holding out a jug of steaming, spiced liquid. I took it and held it between both hands, letting the warm jug finish what the fire had started and bring feeling back into my fingers.

'It'll be a hard winter, lass, will thee be able to fend well enough? I fret about thee, sometimes, alone in that house.'

'I'll be right enough, Mary. The moors give me most of what I need, thee knows that.'

'Aye, well. Much of grain's rotted in field this year, we've had that much rain over summer. Folks won't part with it, not for herbs, not this winter.'

'Oh they will, Mary, the bastards will.'

She flinched at my words.

'If they don't, I'll threaten another bad harvest next year. I'm sure they already think I'm to blame for this one, the bastards!'

Mary frowned and sipped her ale.

'Thee'll never guess who came to see me last week, Mary.'

She glanced up at me – I could not read her eyes. 'Who?'

'Marjory Wainwright!'

'Marjory Wainwright? She never did! Don't tell me she were after thy help making another babby – not after last time!'

'No.' I laughed bitterly. 'Not that, she were after a curse to hex that Lizzie Thistlethwaite. Apparently Bert's been carrying on with her behind Marjory's back.'

'Oh lass, I hope thee sent her packing.'

I studied my ale and drank.

'Lass, are thy wits that addled? Thee's been in't stocks once, and thee's believed to have had curses come true – don't forget them sheep of Ramsgill's that drowned, and mill flooded not long after Big Robert Ramsgill refused to grind your grain!'

I fidgeted on my chair, but Mary had not finished and wagged her finger at me.

'They all blame thee for that – and for Marjory losing her babby. Then there's that wolf they're all convinced is thee. Thee must take better care, lass!'

I met her eye, scared. I had only been thinking about what I could do to them; not what they could do to me.

'Richard Ramsgill had a right do with Thomas over stocks – he won't lock me in them again, Mary!'

'Oh lass, how can thee be so trusting, after all that's happened? Believe me, they can – and would – do a Damn sight worse!'

I flinched, then stared at her. I finished my ale as John walked in, stamping mud from his boots, and Mary jumped up.

'John, look at mess thee's made! Get them boots off!'

He glared at her, made to answer, then spotted me. 'Oh, how do, Jennet.'

'Evening, John. I'm just on my way.'

'Thee don't need to leave yet, lass, stay.'

'No. Thank thee, but I need to get back. I'll be salving sheep starting tomorrow and I want to get some herbs sorted for a tonic for them.'

'Salving? That should'a been done last month, lass!'

'I know, I'm a bit behind, but it still needs doing.'

'Aye, well, all right then, but mind how thee goes.'

I would have to examine each ewe carefully to make sure she were healthy enough to survive the winter, while I rubbed the Stockholm tar and tallow mixture (along with my own medicinal additives) into their fleeces to proof them against water and protect them from scab and lice. The new walls were getting closer, and it might be the last time my beasts would be found by a wandering tup. I had to make the most of it – the lambs that resulted may be the last ones I would see from my girls.

I gave Mary a hug, then picked up my baskets and set off down the hill.

I breathed the fragrant air deeply. I had a great bowl of herbs steeping and the steam filled my home. They had to stay a good two hours, then I would drain them ready to mix in with the salve in the morning.

I sighed and poked the fire, then sat at the table, head in

my hands. It had been a hard year, in all sorts of ways. Mary's warning ran round my head; things would only get tougher. It were not fair. Why did they treat me so?

I got up with new resolve, and fetched Mam's inkpot – there were still some ink left. And a few sheets of Pa's precious paper. I needed to tell my story. I needed folks to know my side of things.

I sharpened a goose wing feather and dipped the nib into the inkpot, then paused to think. I would likely not be able to get more ink or paper; I would have to make my words count.

I bent over the page and started to write.

Chapter 43 - Emma

14th January 2013

I put the quill down and flexed my fingers. I'd been writing for hours and had cramp. I needed a break.

I put the kettle on and stared out of the window. The reservoir was a dark grey dotted with white horses and surrounded by thick white snow. I shivered; it looked cold, forbidding and unwelcoming, and I was starting to hate it here. My dream home, built in my favourite place in the world – everything I had once loved, I now hated.

Dave was still giving me the silent treatment. But at least he was home, and the snow would keep him here for the time being.

I hadn't seen much of Mark, although I had been spending time with Kathy – she wouldn't leave me alone now she knew I was pregnant. She had no idea I was carrying twins or that they were Ramsgills.

I shivered; the unwelcome hold Mark had on me seemed to have dulled. It was as if Jennet had what she wanted – babies – and had no further need of Mark.

Dave was walking up the hill to the house, dogs jumping in the snow around him. When he was home – which seemed to be as little as possible – he walked for hours. I wiped away a stray tear; he avoided me as much as possible – not hard in a house this large.

I held a hand up in a wave, knowing the dim table light behind me meant he would be able to see me. He bent and threw a snowball for the beasts. I knew he had deliberately ignored me. I couldn't find a laugh for the dogs as, bewildered, they snapped at snow in their search for the snowball.

I gritted my teeth; enough was enough. Yes, I'd cocked up – literally – but it wasn't my fault. This was all down to Jennet. I turned and walked downstairs to the kitchen. He *would* stop avoiding me.

'Good walk?'

'Aye.' He didn't look at me.

'Where did you go?'

'Moors.'

'Dave, please . . .'

He briefly met my eye. *'Please? Please what? Please –* there's no doubt over the father of your baby? Please – my wife didn't fuck the neighbour while I was away working? Please – my wife isn't mad and doesn't think the mother of the child she's carrying is a ghost?' He threw his coat on to a chair and finally faced me, fists clenched at his side.

I took a deep breath. 'I know things have been difficult—'

'Bah!'

'—but you can't deny something weird is going on. You've seen how I've been writing – have you ever known me work like this before? You know about the nightmares, and you were the one who saw me writing in the dark – I had no idea. I've not been myself. Can you not open your mind just a little bit and accept something we can't explain is going on? Or are you arrogant enough to believe that the human race knows absolutely everything, and can explain it all with the science we know? Is there not even a tiny bit of doubt in your mind?'

I took another deep breath. 'I've told you how sorry I am. I've told you I never even fancied him, and can't understand why this happened. You've seen how Jennet's story has taken me over – why can't you see that it's even more than that – that *she's* taken me over? It's like . . . like I'm her pen or something. *I'm* not writing her story or living my life – *she* is!'

His lips remained pressed closed.

'I've done what you asked, been to the doctor and had the assessment. I'll go to counselling when the appointments come through. I know I've hurt you and I wish with every fibre of my being that I hadn't. But what's happened has hurt me too – I didn't make these choices, they were made for me by something evil and vindictive. My body was taken from me!'

I sat down at the table and put my head in my hands. 'God, I need to get away from here – from her.'

'That's not a bad idea.'

I glanced up at Dave, hardly daring to hope.

'I can't deny you've been different since we moved in. I'm not sure I can believe it's Jennet, but I want to . . .' he tailed off. 'I really do, it would mean you're still the Emma I married. It's just so . . . preposterous.'

I stared down at the table again. 'I don't want this to break us, Dave. I love you, I want to fix this, but I don't know how.'

I looked up at him, and finally he met my eyes.

'Please, let's go away somewhere – a last minute booking. A week away and leave the book here, have a complete break. Please, can we try and save our marriage?'

He watched me for a couple of minutes; I didn't look away. Then he nodded, and I felt my body crumple as the tension left my muscles.

'All right, I can't deny this place is getting to me. We'll find a last minute deal somewhere warm, and talk. It doesn't matter where we go, but I do want to see who you are away from Thruscross.'

He wasn't smiling, but I was. I got up, crossed the kitchen and hugged him. His body was tense, and his arms stayed by his sides, but he didn't push me away. We had a chance.

Chapter 44 - Emma

29th January 2013

'Cheers.'

'Cheers.' We clinked glasses and I grinned at my husband. After a tense couple of days wondering if our flight would be cancelled due to the weather, we had made it to the relatively balmy Algarve. We'd had a lovely week here, and it was our last night.

We hadn't talked – not properly – but we were speaking. We were even sharing a room. Ok, so it was a twin rather than a double, but it was an improvement on separate rooms.

We'd played golf every day. Well, Dave had played golf; I had walked and hit lots of little balls in directions I hadn't meant to.

'I believe you.'

'What?' I glanced up at him, scarcely daring to accept what I thought I'd heard.

'I believe you, about Jennet.'

'Oh, Dave.' Tears welled up in my eyes.

'You've been different here – the old Emma. You're sleeping again. I thought you'd be itching to fill the hotel stationery with Jennet, but I've not seen you glance at it once. You're a different person, you're the Emma I used to know.' He leaned towards me and took my hand.

'I feel different, I really do, she can't—'

'Let me speak, Emma,' he said, and I shut my mouth. 'If it was psychological, the problem would have come with us and it hasn't. Therefore, the logical explanation is some kind of haunting.' He smiled wryly at the paradox.

I thanked the waiter when he put a plate piled high with fresh clams in front of me, and returned Dave's smile with relief. Finally, he got it. I took a sip of wine from the one glass I allowed myself with dinner.

'It's been awful, Dave. She's so strong, she took me over completely! I can't tell you what it means to me that you finally understand.'

He stared at my belly and frowned. 'I can't say I do understand. How can a ghost make you sleep with another man? Why is her love for Ramsgill stronger than your love for me?'

I sat back, stunned, then said, 'She doesn't love Ramsgill. It's a different motivation altogether, and I don't fully understand it yet. But please don't doubt my love for you, Dave.'

He nodded, then ate. I tucked into my own food. The clams were delicious. I had chosen them every night and would miss them once we were back home.

'So what do we do?'

I was disappointed that Dave hadn't said anything about loving me back, but maybe that was expecting too much.

'I don't know, Dave. All our money is tied up in your project, and that house and land – it won't be easy to move.'

'No, and in this housing market, we'll be hard pressed to find a buyer.'

'Even if we did move, the problem would still be there, and another family would suffer.'

'What are you suggesting?'

I took a deep breath. 'I finish her story – write her out. Maybe once what happened to her is known, she can rest in peace.'

'And what about Mark?'

'She's got what she wanted from Mark, he's not a problem any more – he didn't want to be with me any more than I wanted to be with him.'

He stared down at his plate. 'What if the baby's his?'

'I don't know. What if it isn't?'

He raised his eyes and looked at me. I needed all my willpower to meet his gaze. I was trapped in my lie about twins. We were still in trouble.

We flew home the following day. The easy atmosphere between us grew more and more strained as we approached Thruscross, and as soon as we entered the house I went to the office and started writing.

Chapter 45 - Jennet

7th December 1777

I threw a handful of scraps to the chickens and glanced up at a noise. I stared at the new wall that were slowly creeping up the lane toward my house, but heard nowt else. I threw more scraps, but kept looking at that wall. It would soon be right round the house; enclosing me; cutting me off from the moorland I loved. Soon, there would be no such thing as open space.

I bent to pick up a rare winter egg, then went back to the house.

I opened the door, stepped across the threshold and fell forward from a violent push. I heard the door slam and the locking bar fall into place and I pushed myself up; only to feel a boot in my back, kicking me down.

'Stay there, witch, on the floor where thee belongs!' It were Robert Ramsgill's voice – the young one. I heard laughter – at least two more.

I tried to speak, but Little Rob Ramsgill's boot were still on my back, and my face were pressed into the flags; only a garbled sound came out of my mouth.

'She can't get air!' Billy Gill.

'Aye, turn her over, Rob, we're not here to kill her.' That were Johnny Ward speaking, it were the same three who had threatened me in the stocks.

I took a deep breath as I were rolled over.

'Billy Gill, what does thee think thee's doing? What'll thy mam and pa have to say about this?'

He stared at the floor, then at Rob Ramsgill, who kicked me.

'Nowt to do with thee, witch! Does thee think anyone in't village cares what happens to thee?' He kicked me again, spat, then bent and ripped my dress down the front, exposing me to the three boys. All three laughed and the other two crept closer to get a better look. Little Rob planted his boot on my belly to stop me scrabbling away.

'Don't do this, boys, thee don't want to do this,' I begged, but Little Rob only laughed.

'Who's first?' he asked.

'Don't thee dare!' I screamed at them. 'I curse any part of thee that touches me to rot and fall away!'

'Come on boys, don't be shy!' Little Rob laughed again. 'They're just words; no potions or owt like that, she's just trying to scare us. Who's up for it?'

The other two stared at the floor as I continued to scream curses at them. I tried to get away, but Little Rob put more pressure on my belly – he stood with enough force to keep me pinned in position.

'No? Blithering cowards! Hold her down, then.'

The two boys grabbed a shoulder each. Under other circumstances, I might have laughed to see them both spit on the floor as a charm against witchcraft, before they pulled their sleeves down so their skin did not touch mine.

'Billy, Johnny, please . . .' I tried again; but neither boy would meet my eyes. Their stares were fixed on my exposed breasts.

I looked back up at Little Rob; he were untying his breeches.

'Thee won't get away with this, Rob Ramsgill—' The rest of my threat were knocked away by his kick to my mouth. My head snapped to the side; blood pooled on the stone.

My legs were pulled roughly apart and a new weight settled on me.

I struggled hard, but fingers dug into my shoulders and Little Rob's weight kept my lower body still. I screamed at a sharp pain between my legs, then again and again. It were hard to believe this were the same act I had enjoyed with Richard.

I shut my eyes and kept my head turned to the side. I gritted my teeth against more screams. I were not a party to this, so I would play no part. I tried to blank out what were happening, and welcomed the darkness that spread through my mind.

'Is she dead? Has thee killed her?'

I opened my eyes, saw the boys and sat up. They pulled away from me, startled. I covered myself as best I could with the remnants of my dress, and pushed my way backwards across the floor, away from them.

'I curse thee, Little Rob Ramsgill! And thee Billy Gill and Johnny Ward! None of thee will forget this day, all thy lives will be lost because of it!'

I lifted a shaking finger at Little Rob. 'Thee! Thee'll be first to die. Thee won't see year end, I promise thee that!'

'Remember that wolf, Little Rob!' Billy Gill squealed.

'It means nowt, they're just words,' Little Rob shouted at them, but his two friends had backed away. They were at the door, freeing the locking bar.

Little Rob glanced at me, then his friends. If he did not move quickly, he would be alone with me. I saw fear flare in his eyes, and he stepped away, spat once more, then turned and ran after the other two boys.

Chapter 46 - Jennet

8th December 1777

There were a banging at the door. I flinched and huddled under Pa's coat in fear. *Is it them? Are they back?*

'Jennet! Jennet! Is thee well? Jennet!'

My body shook with sobs. It were Mary Farmer.

'Jennet! Why's door barred? What's up? Let me in!'

I pulled the coat around me and pushed myself up from the floor where I had spent the night huddled in front of the fire, though it had now burned out. I had not been able to face going outside for more peat. I kept my eyes firmly on the door and did not look at the room. I pulled up the locking bar and unlatched the door. Mary Farmer burst in.

'What is it, lass? What's wrong?'

I checked there were no one else outside, then shut and barred the door again.

'What the heck's happened, Jennet?' Mary Farmer stared at me and my swollen mouth.

I glanced around the room, but kept my face still. After the boys had gone, I had burned the remnants of my dress, then washed and washed and washed, before wrapping myself in the coat – the familiar smells soothing me. But I could not tell Mary Farmer any of that.

'John saw there were no smoke at thy chimney, we thought something had happened. What's gone on?' She reached her hand out to my face, and I flinched away from her. The coat fell open and her face paled.

'Them marks! Thy wrists, thy shoulders! What's happened, Jennet, tell me!'

I covered myself again and shook my head. Mary sighed and shook her head. She hunted around my cooking area.

'Why's thee got no peat in, lass? There's no water, neither! Unbar the door, and I'll be off to well. Get theesen dressed, and get that fire going – I'll put on some posset and we'll talk.'

I did not move, but that did not stop Mary Farmer. She picked up a couple of buckets and let herself out. I barred the door behind her, then went upstairs to find some clothes.

Mary took one look at me when she returned. I wore the thickest, most shapeless woollens I had over Pa's hobnailed boots. She said nowt.

She stared at the fire. It were still dark and cold.

'I couldn't go out there,' I said, my voice sounding small and childlike even to my own ears.

She sighed and went back out, returning with a scuttle full of peat from my precious supplies in the turf-house. The fire soon blazed, then glowed with heat. She added water to a pot, along with some mutton bones I had left over and a handful of herbs. I had no cream or eggs for posset. She hung the pot over the heat, then sat at the table. She stared at me, and I sat opposite.

'Is thee gonna tell me what happened, or do I have to guess?'

I hung my head and hugged myself.

'Did they hurt thee?'

I nodded.

'Did they . . . did they . . .' She did not know how to ask. I nodded again.

She blew out another sigh and sat back. 'Who were it, lass?'

I stared at the table. I could not tell her. If those names passed my lips it would bring it all back. I could not bear to form the sounds of their names in my mouth.

Mary Farmer sighed once more and got up. She stirred the soup, then poured liquid into two jugs.

'Here, drink this, then we're off up to Thomas Ramsgill's. If thee won't tell me, thee'll tell him.'

I stared at her in horror and shook my head.

'No use arguing with me, lass. Thomas Ramsgill's Constable. It's his job to keep peace. He did thee a disservice in October, locking thee in stocks like that. He can make up for it now.'

'No! Not Ramsgills! No!'

She looked at me a moment, then shrugged. 'Can't be helped, lass. Now drink down that soup, and we'll be off.'

As usual, there were no denying Mary Farmer when her mind were set, and we walked up the hill to Thores-Green; a collection of three or four farms set in the middle of the moor itself. Thomas Ramsgill's property were stone built, as they all were round here, with a long, sloping, slate roof. Mary walked straight up to the door and banged on it. I cringed behind her.

His eldest son, Neville, opened the door. His eyes widened when he saw me. I knew he knew. 'What's thee want?'

'Thy father, is he here?' Mary pushed past him and I followed. We stood in a small enclosed hall. Tapestries hung on the walls, and lanterns lit its entire length.

'Wait here,' Neville Ramsgill muttered, and disappeared through a doorway. A few moments later, Thomas Ramsgill appeared. He were shorter than his brother Richard, and fatter, but his features were similar and it were hard to look at him.

'We's here to report a rape, Constable,' Mary said, coming straight to the point. 'Jennet here were attacked in her own home last night. Look at her face!'

Thomas stared at me; his face betrayed no expression.

'It can't be allowed, Constable, rape's a serious matter, it needs dealing with.'

I winced every time she used the word.

'Tell him what happened, Jennet, go on.'

I glared at them both in horror, *would they really make me say it?*

'Go on, Jennet, tell him!' Mary squeezed my arm and I told a very short version of my story. Mary paled.

Thomas turned back to the doorway and spoke to whoever were inside. At the same time, Mary whispered to me, 'Thee should've told me it were Little Rob, afore we come.'

I glared at her. I had not wanted to come in the first place, nor had I wanted to tell anyone at all.

Thomas came back into the hall, followed by his wife Hannah, who hid behind her husband and refused to look at me. Richard and Elizabeth followed, then Big Robert Ramsgill and his wife Margaret. Neville smirked behind them.

I watched Richard, wondering if he would help me. He had heard his nephew threaten to rape me when I were in stocks, after all.

He did not look at me, and dread crept through my insides with icy fingers.

'So, had to have another Ramsgill did thee, Jennet?' Elizabeth sneered. 'What is it about men in this family thee finds so fascinating?'

'Elizabeth!' Richard tried to shush her, but she ignored him and spoke louder.

'There are no secrets here, not any more, we all know about Jennet. I wouldn't be surprised if she'd cursed them into it. We all know thee's a witch, Jennet. What did thee do, call on thy Devil lover? Have him trick the boys into lying with thee? Is thee that desperate for a man?'

'Elizabeth! Enough!' Richard grabbed her arm and pulled her back into the room. The door slammed shut, but did not shut out the sound of raised voices.

Mary Farmer put her arm around my shoulders, and I realised I were trembling. Not with fear as Mary seemed to think, but with rage.

'I'll talk to them,' Thomas Ramsgill said, backing away towards the front door.

'What good'll that do?' Mary asked, but took Thomas' hint and, with a last glance at the door where Richard and Elizabeth were still shouting, led me out of the house.

She pulled me down the lane as if scared they were coming after us, then, with a glance back to make sure we were far enough away, said, 'Did thee see Hannah's face? She believes tales, and she has influence over Thomas. If Ramsgills add their weight to witch talk, thee's in big trouble, Jennet. What happened last night's just start.' She sighed, looked me in the eye, and I realised with a jolt she were crying.

'Whole village is already wary of thee – living alone in that house of thine. Then there's business with babbies and cursing. If Ramsgills are calling thee witch – and they'll do owt to protect one of their own – thee's not safe here. Is there anywhere thee can go? What about thy pa's family?'

I shook my head. There were nowhere – no one.

'I don't know anyone outside of this valley,' I said. 'And Pa never spoke about his family. All I know is that he's from Scotland.'

'Well, thee needs to think of summat, lass. Thee can't stay here.'

I shook my head. 'This is my home,' I hissed. 'They've taken everything else from me, they won't take that as well!' I were shouting now. 'I won't let them! I won't! I'll see them all dead first – and I'll start with Little Rob Ramsgill!'

I glanced up, saw Thomas watching us, and ran down the hill, cheeks streaming with water, back to the safety of my house. I hated the Ramsgills, hated the village, hated them all, but I would not run away. I would not.

Chapter 47 - Jennet

27th December 1777

I stared at the moors, then shifted my attention back to the village and the lane – something had moved.

There! A bonnet bobbing up from behind the new wall that hid the lane from view.

She walked nearer the entrance to my farm, but I still couldn't make out who it were. I gritted my teeth in frustration, then relaxed when she paused at the new gate, glanced at the house, then back to the village, Mary Farmer. I had last seen her that time at Thomas Ramsgill's. I caught my breath in anticipation. She carried on walking.

No! No! Before I knew it, my fists were in my hair and pulling my scalp backwards and forwards. 'No!' Now the word had voice.

Mary Farmer turned back, opened the gate and walked to the house. There were about fifty yards between window and lane. I were sure she could not have heard me.

I flung the door open before she reached it. 'Mary!' I cried, and sank to the ground.

She reached the threshold and I clung to her, sobbing.

'Hush, lass, people will see, get inside.'

I let go and sat back, allowing Mary to enter, then stood to shut and bar the door behind her.

'By heck, lass, thee's let theesen go! When were last time thee washed?'

I looked down at myself. I wore the same shapeless clothes Mary had made me put on three weeks ago. I could not remember venturing out to go to the well. I shook my head.

'And what's this?' She held up a dish with some meat scraps.

'For cat,' I said, embarrassed.

'What?' She stared at me in amazement. 'Is thee telling me thee's *feeding* cat?'

I nodded. It let me stroke it now.

'Thee can't be feeding cat, lass. It's supposed to keep mice from oats!' She pointed at the grain stored at the opposite end of the room to the chimney. 'If it's fed, why would it bother to hunt?'

I nodded, I knew she were right.

'Has thee been like this all Christmas?' Her voice softened. 'We were worried when we heard nowt from thee, thought thee'd be up to see us.'

Mary sighed when I did not respond, went to the fire and peered into the pot that hung there. She tutted and went to the baskets she had put on the table and which I had barely noticed. Cream, spice, and honey went into my posset.

'Keep an eye on that, lass, while I go to well. Thee needs cleaning up, then we can set about house.' She looked around her in distaste. Blood and broken egg still stained the floor, and I had no holly, ivy or any other kind of greenery as decoration, never mind a yule log.

She stared at me, sighed, rested her gnarled hand on my shoulder a moment, then picked up a couple of my buckets, unbarred the door and left. I barricaded myself in again as soon as the door had closed behind her.

I stayed at the window until I could see her hunched form struggling with the weight of two buckets of water. Guilt pierced me and I opened the door.

I took two steps outside, and panic overwhelmed me. I looked round -- trying to see in every direction at once – searching for the source of my fear. I could see nowt and ran back inside. Only two steps, but I were gasping for breath. Mary followed and looked at me in confusion, but said nowt about my brief appearance and sudden dash back through the door. She thumped the buckets down and water sloshed on to the dirty stone floor.

'We'll get thee priddied up, then we'll see about getting more water for floor.' She stared at my look of panic, but did not shift her eyes until I dropped my gaze and nodded. 'Right then, get them rags off.'

Fingers trembling, I untied and discarded. The Mary Farmer of my youth were back – the one that were impossible to deny.

She rummaged until she found a couple of clean cloths, dipped them in one of the buckets, gave one to me and started to scrub my back with the other.

Slowly, I washed my face, chest, belly and legs, and Mary moved on to my arms.

I screamed at the sound of laughter from the open window, and scrabbled round to see young Robert Ramsgill leaning on the sill, pointing. 'Look at her, being washed like a babby! Where's thy curses now, witch?'

Mary shot through the door – faster than I thought her old legs could carry her.

'Little Rob Ramsgill, thee little shite! It's high time someone gave thee a beating – knock some sense into thee! Get back here thee little runt!'

'Get away with thee, thee awd carlin! Get back to thy babby!'

Mary came back in, barred the door, closed the window shutters and lit a candle.

'It's all right, lass, he's gone.' She picked up her cloth again, ignoring my trembling, but were much gentler as she wiped off the dirt that had stuck to my wet skin as I had lain curled up on the floor.

'Right, thee's done, now get theesen dressed. We'll go for some more water, then clean rest of house.'

'I can't! Mary, I can't go out there!'

'Nonsense, lass. Thee loves moors, we're only going to well, we'll stay out of way of village and folk – that little bugger is long gone. Thee'll feel better when thee gets back out into fresh air.'

I sighed and pulled on bodice, petticoats, and collar over my shift, then replaced my forehead cloth and coif, and finally pulled on Pa's hobnailed boots. I knew from experience there were no arguing with her in this mood. And she were right, I had missed the moors. There were no way in Hell I were going anywhere near folk though, whatever she said.

'Thee can't go out with thy hair like that, and a comb'll be no use. Where's thy carders?

I fetched the wooden paddles studded with nails normally used to untangle wool ready for spinning, and she dragged one through my hair. It hurt, but I did not scream; I remembered Mam doing this when I were a nipper, and enjoyed the memory despite the scrapes to my scalp.

'Thee needs to be seen, folk are talking about thee and way thee is now. They're afeared of thee and they have enough to fear already.'

I shrugged into Pa's coat.

'Winter, starvation, plague,' Mary carried on, oblivious to my silence. 'They'll get rid of owt else that scares them. They'll get rid of thee, lass, if thee don't take better care.'

I glanced at her and shook my head. She were just an old woman worrying too much.

'Mark me words, lass, thee needs to take better care!'

I nodded in the hope she would stop all her doom and gloom.

'Right then, where's rest of thy buckets?' she asked.

I looked at the corner of the room and she bustled over, found two more and tossed them at me, then picked up her two and led the way outside.

I hesitated on the stoop and looked around. There were nobody about. I took a deep breath and a small step, paused, then took another. Mary stood just ahead, waiting for me. I turned and shut the door, then faced her again and took another step. They were getting easier.

A breath of wind rustled my hair and I lifted my face to it, enjoying the peaty, heather smell of the moors.

'All right, lass?'

'Aye.' I walked slowly to join her. The wall had not yet surrounded the house and we could walk unimpeded up the hill.

Half an hour later we had four overflowing buckets of water and struggled back to the house. Mary had been right – this were what I had needed, and I felt like my old self again.

I were relieved to be home, though, and hurried to my door, then fell against it when something hard hit the back of my head. More stones rained around me and the water I had dropped. I cowered into a ball, screaming, and tried to protect my head with my arms. I were aware of Mary's shouts and male laughter, then Mary's arms around me.

'It's all right, lass, they're gone.'

'Who?' I mumbled, though I knew.

'Little Rob Ramsgill and his little gang of reprobates. Come on, let's get thee inside.' She opened the door and I crawled in. Mary barred the door behind us.

'Right, let's have a look at thee.' She tutted and got to work cleaning the blood from my hair and applying poultices.

An hour later, clean, tended and defeated, I crawled into bed, unable to face more of the day. Mary took her leave, promising to come back in the morning. I forced myself back downstairs to the door to bar it, checked the window shutters were secure, then back over the newly scrubbed floor to the stairs. I lay for some time shuddering and sobbing, and had never been more grateful for sleep.

Chapter 48 - Emma

8th February 2013

I dropped the quill and notebook, and buried my face in my hands. That poor girl. Tears flooded down my face as I thought of her attacked in her home, then terrified to go out – at a time when there was no running water or electricity. If Mary Farmer hadn't found her when she did, she would have died.

I wondered what had taken Mary so long to visit her, knowing what had happened. Why had she stayed away? Were the gossips of the village getting to her? Or was she scared of Jennet and her curses as well?

'Emma, what is it?' Dave had heard my sobs.

'Jennet,' I managed to say through a spasming throat. He said nothing, but sat beside me and held me until my sobs subsided.

Once I had calmed, he pulled away.

'This is getting beyond a joke, Emma. I know we agreed for you to write her out, but look at the state of you. You haven't slept since we got back from Portugal, and you look ill.

'I know the counselling starts in a couple of weeks, but what about going back to the doctor for some sleeping tablets?' he continued.

'I can't take sleeping tablets when I'm pregnant.'

'How do you know? There may be some herbal ones that are safe. Go and ask her.'

I said nothing.

'Emma, please! I'm really worried about you – you know

I'm away back to Edinburgh next week – I need to know you're sleeping, at least.'

I nodded. I'd give him anything at the moment – not many men would have stayed in this situation.

'Do you have to go?'

'Aye. I've to see some potential buyers at the site to show them what's what – I've already put it off twice, I can't do it again. I'll make it as short as I can, but I have to go.'

'Ok, I'll ring the surgery now.'

'Then we'll eat.'

I smiled, kissed him and picked up the phone.

'Do you fancy going out for supper?' Dave asked. 'We haven't been up to the Stone House for a while.'

'Oh yes, that's a good idea. It'll be nice to get out of the house for the evening.'

'Great – jump in the shower, we'll go as soon as you're ready.'

I grimaced, realising I hadn't washed for a few days. My routine was all over the place; I started writing as soon as I got up – some days I even forgot to get dressed until it was time to go to bed.

Half an hour later, I was back downstairs: clean, refreshed and looking forward to an evening out with my husband.

Dave held the front door open for me and I led the way to the car. Five minutes later, we pulled into the pub car park, then made our way inside.

'Kathy! Mark.'

They were sitting near the door, full plates in front of them.

'Evening,' Mark said.

'Oh, hello!' Kathy was much warmer. I smiled at them both, but Dave ignored Mark and only greeted Kathy.

'How are you? We haven't seen you for ages!' Kathy said. She glanced at Mark and Dave in confusion.

I carried on regardless. 'We're well thanks, Kathy, how are you? How are Alex and Hannah? Have they made their minds up yet?'

'Yes, thank goodness – they've both put Leeds as their first choice.'

'That's great!' I stopped, not knowing what else to say.

'Well, better get to the bar, good to see you,' Dave said into the silence, and we escaped. I glanced back while Dave was ordering our drinks, and saw Kathy hunched over the table, questioning Mark.

'Here you go, Emma.' Dave passed me a glass of red wine, and sipped his pint of bitter. 'Do you know what you want?'

I studied the menu chalked above the bar and smiled, remembering our dinner here with Alice and the girls and how we had laughed. It seemed a long time ago now.

'Shepherd's pie,' I replied. Dave ordered, beef and ale for him. He paid, then we sat down – at a table as far away from the Ramsgills as we could find.

'Dessert?' Dave asked. 'Treacle sponge or bread and butter pudding.'

I pulled a face. 'No, they're too heavy, I'm already stuffed. I'll just have coffee, please – decaf.'

'You'll be lucky.' Dave laughed, and went to the bar.

I waited until he was back, then got up to go to the ladies.

On the way back out, I bumped into Mark. He must have been waiting for me in the narrow corridor.

'How are you?' he asked.

'Fine.'

'And the baby? He reached out to touch my belly, and I knocked his hand away, stepped back and crossed my arms over my chest.

'The baby's fine,' I said, looking over his shoulder. Had Dave seen him follow me?

'Is it . . . is it mine?' he asked. I glared at him.

'No, Mark, it's not yours. It's not mine either, come to that. It's Jennet's. It's Jennet's baby.' For some reason I did not want to tell him I was expecting twins.

'What? Oh, don't start all that again!'

'Start what? Think about it, you know it's true – neither of us wanted to do what we did – it was her! She's connected to me somehow, and you're a Ramsgill. This is Jennet and Richard's baby – not mine, and certainly not yours!'

'Mark?'

I glanced up and gasped. Kathy stood behind Mark – shock written over her face. Dave stood further back, hands in pockets, frowning.

Mark whipped round. 'Kathy, it's not what you think.' He stepped towards her – she backed away.

'How could you? Twenty years and you do this, you bastard!' she shouted, and I was aware of silence in the rest of the pub. 'And you! I thought you were my friend!'

Mark stepped towards her again, and she slapped his face. 'Get away from me, get away!' She turned and ran, barging past Dave, who stared at Mark. Mark didn't meet his eye.

'I'm sorry,' he muttered. 'So sorry.' He followed Kathy.

'Time to go?' Dave asked.

I nodded at his cold tone, and followed him through the pub and out to the car. Nobody spoke. Everybody stared. I wanted to go home and lose myself in writing. I couldn't deal with this. Couldn't think about poor Kathy. Couldn't look at Dave. I had to get rid of Jennet.

Chapter 49 - Jennet

4th January 1778

'Ey up, lass, summat's wrong.' John Farmer walked in, looking worried, and both myself and Mary glanced up at him.

'What is it, John?' Mary asked.

'Looks like fire. Lass, I think it's thy place.'

I jumped up and ran to the Farmers' door. Smoke rose from below. John Farmer were right – my house were on fire. I ran down the hill, heedless of anything but my home. Everything I had bar the sheep were under that roof. Everything I had left of Mam and Pa were in that house. I had to save it.

I ran over the last rise and stopped. The thatched turf-house, sheltering a couple of months' supply of peat, was well ablaze, and smoke poured out from the gaps in the window shutters of the house itself. A dozen people stood around, watching and doing nowt.

I hurried to the house, shouting at people to get buckets. I saw Richard Ramsgill and gave him a push to get him moving towards the smithy – William Smith always had buckets of water by his forge.

I shoved open the door and coughed. Burning peat had been strewn over the floor, and I watched the flames reach the wooden staircase, then the grain store, and take hold.

I grabbed the besom and started to push the burning peat outside. I screamed as a torrent of water hit me, then I were pushed out of the house mesen.

I fought against my attacker, trying to get back inside.

All Mam's things were in there, her journal, my herbs, Pa's paper, Richard Ramsgill's gifts. I had to put the fire out.

'Thy skirts lass, thy skirts!' John Farmer shouted in my ear, and I realised he were my captor. I glanced down – the hem of my gown were charred and smoking. The water he had thrown had saved me from being horribly burned.

I let him drag me away to Mary, who held on to me while he went to refill his buckets.

Richard and Thomas Ramsgill, Robert Grange and William Smith arrived carrying full buckets, which were thrown through my front door.

'It'll be well, lass, it'll be well,' Mary soothed. 'See, it's started to rain, it'll soon be out.'

'Somebody did this, somebody set fire to my house!'

I saw Little Rob watching, not making any attempt to help or join the line of people between well and burning house, and pointed at him.

'Thee! This were thee!'

He turned to me and laughed. 'Serves thee right, witch! Thee should burn with it!'

I screeched and jumped at him. 'Thee'll regret this, Little Rob! Thee and thine, thee'll rue this day!'

'Aye, thee's said that afore! Weren't going to see year end, were I? But here I is. Thy curses mean nowt, witch!'

'Lass, hush now, come away!' Mary Farmer dragged me off. She may be old, but a lifetime of tending sheep on the moors, wrapping fleeces, carding and spinning wool had kept her strong. I collapsed in a heap and raised my face to the sky, feeling utterly hopeless.

The rain fell harder and washed my tears away.

'See, it's nearly out! Thee were lucky, lass, thy house'll be saved!'

I looked back at my home. The turf-house were still smoking, but there were only water pouring out of the front door now, not smoke.

'See, I told thee! A witch! She called the rain down, did thee see that?'

'Shut up, Little Rob!' Richard Ramsgill clouted him. 'Thee had better not have had anything to do with this!'

'Or what, Richard?' Big Robert Ramsgill, asked. 'Is thee accusing my son of summat?'

'Care, Richard,' Thomas warned.

Richard shook his head and fetched more water. He did not look at me.

The buckets were being emptied on to the remains of the turf-house now, and I shook Mary off to go back inside. I stared at the ruins of my home.

Everywhere were black with soot and running with water. There were no staircase and the boards above me were charred. I had nowhere to sleep, nowhere to sit, nowhere to eat. It were all gone.

'Walls are sound, lass, don't despair. Thee'll stay with us till we can get this cleaned up.'

I leaned my head on Mary's shoulder and sobbed. I had lost everything.

Chapter 50 – Emma

12th February 2013

'Emma!'

I jumped, splattering ink over my notebook and clothes.

'Alice! What are you doing here?'

'I haven't seen you for ages – we've hardly spoken since you cancelled Christmas, I was worried.'

'Oh.' I realised she was right. We normally spoke two or three times a week and met up for lunch regularly. I'd been neglecting *her*, too.

'I've been banging on the front door for ten minutes, didn't you hear me?'

I shook my head. 'How did you get in?'

'The kitchen door was open. You need to be more careful, Em, especially when Dave's in Scotland. Anybody could have walked in.'

'Yes, you're right. Hang on, how do you know where Dave is?'

'I rang him, I was frantic. I've been trying to talk to you for weeks – you've not taken any of my calls.'

'I'm sorry, Al, I've been writing non-stop. I don't have a phone in here.' I waved my arm around the office to demonstrate.

'I've left loads of messages, Em. On your landline *and* your mobile, you've not returned a single one.'

'I'm sorry, Alice, I guess I *have* been a bit lax lately.' I felt terrible. How could I have been so swept up in my life that I'd forgotten my family? It was Jennet's fault. I ground my teeth together. I hated her.

'Em? You ok?'

I nodded, tears pricking my eyes. 'I'm glad you came, Al. It's good to see you.'

'Mm, it's been a while. Come on, leave that, put the kettle on and we can catch up.'

'Great idea.' I threw the notebook and quill on to the table – by now it was more ink than bare wood – and stood.

'Em!'

I looked down at my belly, and cupped my hands around it. I grimaced. 'I've got a lot to tell you.'

'You're not kidding.' Her voice was cold. She looked furious.

We walked downstairs to the kitchen in silence. I could feel Alice's eyes burning a hole in my back. So that was everybody. Jennet had hurt everybody in my life: my husband, my sister, Kathy. No doubt my nieces would be upset too. The sooner she was gone, the better.

'Why didn't you tell me? It was hell trying to explain to the girls that you'd lost the baby and they wouldn't have a baby cousin after all! We've all been walking on eggshells around you, but don't you think we've been grieving too? It would have been wonderful to share this with you and support you! And what about Dave? He's been doing his best to look after you, who's been looking after him? I'll tell you who, nobody!'

I stared at my coffee in silence and led the way to the sofas in the lounge.

Alice sighed. 'So when did you decide to start trying again?'

'We didn't.'

'Oh! It was an accident?'

'You could say that.' I made a strange laughing noise – more like a cackle, really. 'Al, the baby . . . it's not Dave's.'

She stared at me, her mouth hanging open.

'It's not mine, either.' I made that strange cackle again, then lost my battle with tears.

'What do you mean? Of course it's yours! And what about Dave? If it's not his, whose is it?'

I held my hands over my face and fought to regain control of myself. Eventually I faced Alice and took a deep breath. 'Since the miscarriage, I've hardly been able to write.'

'What about the baby, Emma? Who's the father?'

'I'm coming to that, please listen, Al.'

She closed her mouth and sat back, arms folded, and raised her eyebrows at me.

'I hoped that would change when we moved in here, but you know what they say, careful what you wish for.' Alice's expression did not alter. I carried on.

'It started with dreams – nightmares – and I kept hearing church bells.'

'Em!' Alice knew as well as I did that the church had been flattened before the reservoir had been filled.

'No, listen Alice, please.' I filled my lungs again. 'Then we went for dinner to Mark and Kathy's – they live in the haunted house.' Alice didn't react. 'They told us about Jennet, apparently she used to live there in the 1770s.'

'And?'

'She was supposed to be a witch, and hearing the bells means she's back.' I held my hand up to forestall Alice's tut. 'She's been making me write her story – I've been in a frenzy writing it. It turns out she was in love with Mark's ancestor, and she made us have an affair.'

'Oh Em, as excuses go, that's pathetic!'

'No, it's true! It's like she's possessed me, Alice. *I* didn't sleep with Mark, *Jennet* did. She's got into me somehow, my body isn't my own – it hasn't been since we moved here.'

'That's ridiculous, Emma.'

'I know how it sounds, but it's true. Just ask Dave – he

walked in on me writing back in September. I was writing in the dark and he said my eyes were rolled up to the whites. I had no idea, Alice, none at all!'

'What were you writing or was it just scribbles?'

'It was Jennet. I was writing Jennet. It wasn't scribbles, it was legible, but it wasn't my handwriting.'

'Has anything else happened?'

I laughed, but with no humour. 'Isn't that enough?'

'Have you talked to the doctor?'

I cackled again. 'That's what Dave said. Yes, I've been to the doctor's, I've seen a counsellor, but they can't help. I need to get rid of Jennet.'

Alice leaned forward and put her mug on the coffee table. 'But . . . things like this just don't happen!'

'Yes, Alice, they do.'

'But why? How?'

'You remember that day at the haunted house when I found the inkpot?'

'So it's my fault for daring you?'

'No, of course not. It's Jennet's fault. It's her inkpot.'

Alice thought a moment. 'Do you still have it?'

I nodded.

'Then get rid of it.'

'It's not that simple, Alice. I'm using it. I need to write Jennet out.'

'But assuming what you're telling me is true, if she's getting to you through the inkpot, get rid of it.'

'No!'

We stared at each other, both of us startled by the vehemence of my refusal.

Chapter 51 - Jennet

8th January 1778

I looked down the valley at the reds, pinks and oranges splashed across the sky ahead of the sun as it woke. If I just kept my eyes on that beauty, maybe I could forget everything that had happened.

I sighed, even that beautiful sky were a harbinger of more storms to come. I turned to look at my ruined house and walked towards it.

The turf-house and its contents were destroyed. The wooden shutters were damaged and my front door were nowt but a few hanging pieces of wood. Those could be repaired. Mary and John Farmer would help feed my sheep over the coming winter, but at least the sheep themselves had been well away from the danger.

I walked inside. This were what I could not replace. Everything of Mam and Pa's had gone up in flames. All the furniture were destroyed. I would need a ladder to get upstairs, and my home stank of charred wood and burnt fleece. Everything were filthy black – covered in soot and ash.

The Christmas celebrations, such as they had been, were finally over, and there were nowt for it but to start. I grabbed a piece of wood from by my feet – a table leg – and dragged it outside. Then another and another. The fourth and the tabletop itself had disintegrated.

I used a rake to scrape the smaller debris out of the door into a pile in what had been my garden – now trampled into mud by my neighbours.

Three hours later, the ruins of my possessions were cleared – I had not had much to start with. Now I had nowt but stone walls and a few sheep. I had managed to salvage the iron- and stoneware, though it would all need a good scrub, but my wooden implements and fabric were beyond salvage – at least downstairs; I would have no idea what the situation were above my head until I could find some ladders.

'How do, lass.'

I turned quickly. Peter Stockdale had arrived with Matthew Hornwright and a cart loaded with stone to extend the enclosure wall. Nobody from the village were here to help me after my house had burnt down, but men were here to wall me in. I nodded to Peter.

'Sorry for thy troubles, lass.'

I stared at him and he stared at the ground, embarrassed. Matthew jumped off the cart beside him, stared at me, then turned to Peter.

'Got no time for thee to be courting, Stockdale! Give us an hand with this stone!'

Peter Stockdale winked at me and turned to heft stone from the cart to the ground. I took Mary's besom (mine had burned) to sweep the floor clear. Then all I had to do were scrub the soot from the walls, rinse off the floor, pull some new heather to thatch the turf-house – at least it were the right season for it – then cut peat to fill it. Oh, and find some new furniture and a ladder from somewhere – and some grain, of course, to feed me till the next harvest in August.

One thing at a time. I picked up my buckets and went back outside to fill them from the well.

I turned to the front wall – with two windows and the front door, it were the most awkward and I wanted to get it out of the way. Every stone had to be scrubbed. Soot had got into every crack and join, and the stone were rough-cut to begin with. At this rate, it would take weeks if not months to get every wall clean.

I started with the window – now little more than an empty hole in the stone. I worked my way round from the top, down each side, then the ledge.

I jumped when something fell and bent to pick it up. My thumb rubbed at the soot and ash caking it – it were Mam's inkpot. I dumped it in the bucket and scrubbed the rest of the soot off, then put it in my pocket. At least I had salvaged something that were special to me, although it were not of much use. I had nowt to write on or with.

I picked up Mary's scrubbing brush and attacked the window ledge again.

Arm, shoulders and back aching, I finally allowed myself a rest. I watched Peter Stockdale and Matthew Hornwright pick up stones, examine them and discard them for others. They were making a right palaver of building that ruddy wall.

I sat on the filthy floor, my back against the filthy wall, and stared at the remains of my home. I took out the inkpot again, turned it round and round in my hands. My story needed to be told. Just because *I* could no longer write it, did not mean that somebody *else* could not.

I looked around for something sharp, but could not see anything. I went outside to my pile of ruined belongings, and found a knife. I went back in and cleaned it as best I could, then drew it hard and fast across the pad of my thumb. Blood dripped into the inkpot. I sucked my thumb, then went back outside and examined the ruins of my herb garden.

'Can thee salvage anything, lass?'

I glanced up with a start, then shook my head. 'No idea. I'll have to wait for spring, see what sprouts.'

'Shame,' Peter Stockdale said. 'Crying shame it is, lass.'

I nodded, then spotted what I were searching for, bent

and snapped a sprig of rosemary off the bush lying in the mud. Back inside, out of sight, I pushed the rosemary into the inkpot and held it tightly in both hands next to my heart. I whispered the most powerful words I knew; begging, no, *demanding* that somebody tell my story, wishing and praying with my deepest soul that what were happening to me would someday be known.

I put it back in my pocket, rinsed off the wall and window alcove I had scrubbed, then went back outside carrying the empty buckets.

When I got close to the new wall, I stumbled and dropped them.

'By heck, lass, is thee well? Thee should be resting after all this, not working theesen hard like thee's doing!'

I smiled up at Peter Stockdale. He had always been decent to me, although I had not seen much of him after Richard.

'Here, rest theesen. I'll fill them for thee.'

I thanked him, then stepped over to Matthew Hornwright, who barely glanced up at me.

'It looks so strong! How does it stay up without mortar or anything?'

Matthew straightened up, stretched his back and looked admiringly at the length of wall.

'It's all in't stones, lass. See? Pick right shape and fit it in snug like.'

I peered closer. 'Oh, it looks like *two* walls!'

'Aye.' He seemed friendlier now that he were talking about walling. 'See, thee's building a double wall, fitting stones together close and angled in towards each other. Then thee fills in space in't middle with smaller pieces, top it with a nice solid capstone and wall'll still be standing one, two hundred year from now.'

'No! Two hundred year?' I could not wait that long, but I did not believe him. I were sure it would fall down long before then with the winter storms up here. And no matter how well he chose his stones, there were nowt holding them together!

'Does thee want me to take them inside for thee, lass?'

'Aye, that'd be grand,' I answered Peter and, as he bent to pick up the brimming buckets again, I added, 'But what am I going to do once thee's finished wall? It'll cut me off from well!'

Peter glanced behind him at the well and frowned. 'By heck, thee's right, lass.' He looked at Matthew, then back at me. 'Don't fret, we'll build thee a stile so thee can climb over, ain't that right, Horny?'

Matthew Hornwright frowned at him and Peter waved his hand in Matthew's general direction. 'Oh, stop thy mithering, this here lass has had enough trouble to be going on with. We can't cut her off from her water an'all. We'll stick some flat stones in, so they jut out.'

Matthew's brows drew together as he thought over the idea, then he turned and walked to the cart, presumably to choose some appropriate stones. Peter winked at me and bent again to pick up my buckets and take them to the house. I turned, took the inkpot out of my pocket and shoved it hard into the gap in the middle of the wall. Just another piece of rubble, unremarkable, hidden – until the right person came along: my storyteller.

I hurried after Peter Stockdale and thanked him, even putting my hand on his arm in the wave of relief and hope I felt knowing that my story would be told.

He ducked his head, but not before I saw the blush that stained his cheeks. I stared after him in wonder. After everything that had happened, Peter Stockdale had blushed at my touch. I put my hands to my face and were surprised to feel tears – but, for the first time in a long time, they were not tears of despair.

Chapter 52 - Emma

18th February 2013

I ran; my four legs just long enough to lift me free of the heather with each bound. As a cub it had been hard work, running through this stuff; more like a series of jumps than a run.

I reached the stream and drank deeply, then lifted my head. I'd heard something. I sniffed the air. Yes, I had not been mistaken. An animal – a young one, and alone. I took off in its direction; I were hungry.

The lamb had been easy prey. I lay beside the carcass and licked blood from my muzzle. It had been a while since I had eaten so well – the villagers had started to protect their flocks by setting traps outside the new walls; some of them even patrolled with guns.

I glanced up at the tree I lay under, and a shiver rippled my body. It weren't natural: a single big oak alone in the barren moor. It were a freak of nature, and I normally avoided the place. It stank of death and were just – wrong.

I got to my feet and trotted off. I would not have approached the death tree if it hadn't been for the promise of a meal and now I'd eaten my fill, I did not wish to linger. I headed in the direction of the village – not to cause trouble, or even to enter it, but to keep an eye on it and what they were up to. They were my enemy; I needed to know what they were doing.

The wind changed and brought a strange scent. I lifted my snout to it and sniffed deeply. I did not understand. The village normally brought smells of peat-smoke, rotten meat and human waste, but this breeze smelled clean, even fresh. A bit peaty, yes, but there were none of the disgusting elements that usually signalled the humans.

Perplexed, I carried on, speeding up a little. By the smell of things I did not need to take as much caution.

I crested the brow of the hill and stopped in surprise. The village were gone – a vast lake of water were in its place; the humans were drowned. I bared my teeth, then lifted my muzzle to the moon and howled my delight. The moors were mine.

I woke in a sweat. It had been ages since the last nightmare – they'd disappeared once I'd started writing Jennet's story. Although this hadn't been a nightmare as such, not like those early ones. Still, it had disturbed me. I reached over to Dave, but my hand met empty bedding. He may have admitted what was happening, but he couldn't bring himself to return to our bed yet.

I sighed and put my hands to my belly as tears tickled my ears. I prayed with all my heart that these babies were mine and Dave's and not Jennet's, but somehow I knew the babies were the reason for the dream. I groaned when I realised that meant I'd have another four months of them.

I swung my legs out of bed and stood, then walked to the window. Why was the wolf so happy to see the reservoir? Why was it so happy that the village had drowned? I shivered, moved to put on my robe, and went to the office. I would not sleep any more tonight. I may as well get on with Jennet's story. I wanted it finished and this waking nightmare to end.

Chapter 53 – Jennet

16th January 1778

Someone banged on the door and I dropped my scrubbing brush with a little cry. I got up from the floor I were scouring and peered through the window. I could only see the tail end of what appeared to be a ladder.

Puzzled, I walked to the door as whoever it was banged again, and jumped when my name was called, 'Jennet? Is thee there, lass?'

Peter Stockdale! I hurried to unbar the door, then flung it open.

'How do,' I said. 'What's thee doing here?'

'Well, that's a fine welcome, that is, seeing as I've missed church to bring thee this,' he said, lifting the ladder slightly.

'But, but, where'd thee get it?'

'Made it,' he said. 'Now, is thee gonna invite me in so we can see if it'll reach?'

'Oh, aye, sorry,' I stammered, standing aside.

'By heck, lass, thee's done a grand job here!' He looked around at the clean walls and the clean patch on the floor.

'Haven't started in there, yet,' I said, indicating the grain store. I were trying to make this room right again first.

'Well, I can give thee an hand with that – and turf-house an'all,' Peter said, 'but first, does thee want to take a gander upstairs – see what damage there is up there?'

'Aye,' I said. 'That'd be grand.'

He stretched and pulled a few bits of wood away that I had not been able to reach, and propped the ladder where the staircase had been. He climbed up.

'Stand back, lass,' he called, and more bits of stair joined the wood on the floor.

'Right, reckon it's safe for thee to come up,' he called down, and I made my way up the ladder. It were slow progress – I had to pull my skirts away before stepping on each rung – but before long I were stood upstairs again – the first time since the fire.

'Reckon floorboards are sound, lass,' Peter said. 'Thee were lucky.'

I glared at him – *lucky*? He did not notice. I walked into my room and Peter followed. I threw open the shutters for light and looked around.

Peter seemed embarrassed to see the bed and stayed in the doorway, refusing to meet my eyes.

'I thought thee were here to help?' I asked, all innocence.

'Aye, but,' he gestured at the room, 'it ain't seemly to be in here alone with thee!'

'Nonsense,' I said cheerfully. 'Everything's saturated with smoke – it needs to go outside and air. How am I gonna get it down ladder on me own?'

He nodded, but his face were still beetroot red. I stepped towards him.

'Peter, thee's only one bar Farmers who's offered me any aid, and I knows thee's an honourable man.' He glanced up at me and finally met my eye. 'Let's be honest, me own reputation can't get much worse – or is it thine thee's fretting about?'

He laughed and shook his head.

'Right then, will thee help me get mattress downstairs? I can wash cover, but it'll need repacking with heather and straw.' That were it for the soft feathers. 'Clothes ain't too bad — at least lid were down on't chest — but they'll all need washing, then room'll need scrubbing.'

'It's easy enough to get mattress down.' He had found his voice again. He picked it up, crossed to the window, and heaved it out into the garden below, followed by the brocades that had covered it. I laughed.

'See, I wouldn't have been able to do that!'

'Aye, reckon thee could do with a man around place!'

I glanced at him – his cheeks were flaming red again.

'Will thee help me haul buckets of water up? If I can get this room ready, I can move back in – give Mary and John their storeroom back.' I had been living with the Farmers since the fire, sleeping on a pile of old fleeces in a room full of them waiting to be carded and spun.

'Aye. If thee wants, I can go pull some heather for thee an'all – both for mattress, and for turf-house roof – I'll help thee rebuild that if thee wants.'

'That'd be grand, Peter, I don't know how to thank thee.'

He turned beetroot again, and I smiled.

'There's no rush though – I've no peat to put in it. No grain, neither, come to that.' I sat on my clothing chest and put my head in my hands.

'What am I going to do? It's seven months before harvest – Mary and John don't have enough spare to feed me till then. Most of my herbs are ruined too – if they're not burnt, they're mucky with smoke and useless, I can't even *earn* me bread!'

'Hush.' He crossed to the chest and put a clumsy arm around my shoulders. He squatted in front of me and lifted my chin up with his fingers.

'Will Smith has been going round village, telling everyone how badly they've treated thee, and it's time to make amends. Whole village'll each donate a couple sheaves of oats – there'll be enough to get thee through winter.'

'What? Why would they do that? They all hate me!'

'No – well, aye, some do.' My eyes dropped, and he lifted my head back up before he continued. 'But most see things've gone too far. Anyroad, they'll all need smithy at some time or other; they won't risk angering Will.'

'Oh, Peter!' I threw my arms around him. He laughed and pulled back.

'Richard Ramsgill's promised to feed thy sheep through winter an'all.'

'What? Richard?'

'Aye. Must feel guilty for summat.'

'Aye, well, his nephew tried to burn me house down – never mind all that other stuff.'

'He's treated thee bad, lass, right bad.'

I grimaced, then froze as his lips touched mine. I relaxed and held him closer as his tongue pushed against my top lip.

'Jennet!'

We broke apart and giggled at the interruption.

'Up here, Mary, I'll be right down!' I called.

Peter grinned at me, gathered an armful of clothing out of the chest, and we walked to the ladder.

Chapter 54 - Jennet

29th January 1778

The fire blazed and posset bubbled, lending a sweet spiced smell to the house, and I sat at the new table Peter Stockdale had made for me. It almost felt like home again.

Admittedly, the shelves were a little bare, but I had managed to salvage a few items – stoneware and the like. Mary Farmer had done wonders to fill the gaps; raiding her own kitchen for spare items and bullying others into doing the same.

There were still a lot missing; a lot to replace, but I had made a good start.

I had been living here again for a week and whilst I still did not like leaving the house, Peter Stockdale and Matthew Hornwright, true to their word, had incorporated steps into the wall that now stretched far beyond my farm and I could easily get over it to the well and the moors beyond.

I went to the window and stared at the wall. Mam's inkpot were there – I knew the exact spot – safe and sound. My gaze lifted and I watched the valley: sun shining on moors and glinting on the river below; hawk swooping to the catch; rabbits chasing each other in front of the house. I smiled; I had my home, and now a new friend in Peter – I had a future. And if that rabbit would run a little to the left and find my snare on its way back to its burrow, I would have a rabbit for the pot tonight.

My smile grew broader as I spied Peter hurrying up the lane. I knew he were coming here – he had visited me near every day since that first time; had made all my new furniture with his own hands and actually seemed to enjoy my company. I certainly enjoyed his.

He turned through the gate in the wall and hurried up the path to my front door. I opened the door in welcome before he reached it.

'Has thee heard news?' he gasped, and I realised he were out of breath. I frowned and shook my head.

'Little Rob Ramsgill – he's dead!'

I raised my eyebrows in surprise.

'Fool were showing off to them mates of his at Beckfoot Bridge, walking parapet, and he fell.'

'Drowned?' I asked.

'Broke his neck.'

I clapped my hands together and laughed. 'Serves little bugger right!'

Peter stared at me in horror. 'Jennet, did thee hear me? He's barely more than a child and he's broke his neck. I ken he did wrong by thee, but thee can't be rejoicing in his death!'

'I ruddy well can, Peter! That little bugger taunted me, raped me, and I'm sure it were him who nearly burned me house down. Thee's damn right I'm rejoicing in his death! I feel like celebrating. I've some elderberry wine of Mary's here somewhere, would thee like a taste?'

'Nay I ruddy well wouldn't! I'll not celebrate the death of a lad, no matter what he's done!' He stopped and stared at me. 'They say thee cursed him, is it true?'

I met his eyes and stared back. 'He cursed hissen.'

'This is thy doing!' He stepped back a pace. 'He were just a lad! A bit wild, aye, but a lad – he could've made a good man!'

'He would never have made a good man!' I snapped. 'He were cruel, ruthless and had no conscience – just like rest of Ramsgills. And he'd have grown to be worst of them! I didn't kill him, but aye, I cursed him, and aye, I'm glad he's dead. There'll be nay sympathy for a dead Ramsgill in this house!'

He backed away again. 'It's right, what they're saying about thee – thee's evil! A witch! I's been consorting with Devil – I'm as Damned as thee is!'

He turned, ran through the door and dashed back down the hill. I watched him go, then something caught my eye. I smirked – rabbit for dinner.

Chapter 55 - Emma

20th February 2013

The hammering on the door eventually got through, and I glanced up from my notebook. *Who could that be? Where's Dave?* I looked at the door to the spare room, then remembered: Scotland.

I sighed, pulled my robe tighter around me, and went to answer the door. Whoever it was, they were pretty insistent; it sounded like they were kicking it down. 'Oh God, please don't let it be Mark,' I said to the ceiling, took a deep breath and opened it. 'Kathy!' I said in surprise.

She looked me up and down. 'It's eleven o'clock,' she said, then laughed, full of scorn. 'Nearly lunchtime. Or were you expecting my husband?'

'Er no, no, of course not.' I was bewildered. 'I've been writing since the early hours – lost track of time. What are you doing here?'

'I think it's time we talked, don't you?'

I nodded and moved to one side. She strode into my home, looked around, then led the way to the kitchen. I shut the door, full of trepidation. This would not be pleasant. I took another deep breath – I seemed to be doing that a lot these days – and followed her to the kitchen.

I didn't look at her, but went straight to the kettle, filled it and switched it on. 'Coffee?'

'Yes.' No please. I got out mugs, coffee and milk. I knew I was avoiding the start of the conversation, and was aware that she knew it too. I could almost hear her smirk.

Coffee made, I turned. I couldn't put it off any longer. I put hers in front of her, then sat.

'You don't have to sit so far away, I'm not going to bite.'

'Why not?' I asked, finally meeting her eyes. 'I would.'

Kathy sighed. 'I'm furious, yes, and part of me wants to throw this coffee in your face.' I flinched. 'But I won't,' she continued. 'I've known there was something wrong with this place since we did up Wolf Farm and moved in.'

I sipped my coffee and nodded. 'There's something very wrong – it's driving me insane. *She's* driving me insane.'

'Jennet,' Kathy stated.

I nodded again. 'Please believe me, Kathy. I love Dave, and Mark loves you – dearly. What happened . . . well, it was madness. It was Jennet. She made us do it somehow. She's taking over.'

'I know.'

I stared at her. 'How can you be so accepting? Dave's seen . . . well he's seen some pretty weird shit happen to me, and he's struggling to believe it. You've seen none of it.'

'I've seen plenty. I've seen the changes in Mark – strange changes. It's like in a certain light he has muttonchops – you know, those thick whiskers all down the side of his face, and there's a smell sometimes – sheep and whisky.' She shivered.

I stared at her, open mouthed. I knew Jennet had possessed *me*: it hadn't occurred to me that Richard Ramsgill was here, too.

Kathy glanced up and smiled, 'Anyway, I'll only believe my husband has cheated on me after twenty years of marriage if it's the only possibility left.'

I gave a small nod and stared at my coffee. I drank. It was getting cold. 'So, you know about these things – what do we do?'

She raised her eyebrows. 'I don't think *anybody* knows about these things – not really.'

I nodded, she was probably right.

'I've been doing some research,' Kathy continued, 'ever since I realised something – someone – was here who should be resting, and basically, all the books – the more credible ones, anyway – all say you need to give the spirits what they want. Then they'll leave.'

'I know, I need to finish her story,' I said. 'I've been saying that to Dave for weeks.'

'Yes. Finish her story,' Kathy repeated. 'And pray it's enough.'

'Why wouldn't it be enough?'

'She's been taking her revenge on Ramsgills for over two hundred years, she's got a taste for it now. She might want more than just her story known.'

I finished my coffee in silence. I hadn't thought of that. I didn't want to think about it.

Kathy stood and delved into her bag. 'I've brought you Old Ma Ramsgill's journal back, it might help.'

I took it, 'Thanks.'

Kathy gripped my wrists, hard. 'You'd better get this story told right. This is one hell of a vengeful and powerful being we're dealing with. I've read that – all of it.' She nodded at the book. 'And I'm terrified for my family.'

I stared at her, shocked by her intensity, but just as frightened.

'The Ramsgills are cursed – the evidence is all in there. You need to lift the curse – do what she wants and maybe she'll spare my children. Yours too.' She glanced at my belly. 'If it is a Ramsgill.'

'The story is what she wants, Kathy,' I tried to reassure her. 'She's in my head when I'm writing – so much so, it's like she's writing it herself. It's nearly finished. She'll be gone soon.'

'I hope so, Emma, I really hope so.' She let go of my wrists and picked up her coat. 'Don't let me take any more of your time. I'll let myself out. You get back to work. But eat something first, you've lost weight. She won't thank you if you lose that baby – she might just make another one.'

I stared after her, staggered by that idea, then obediently opened the fridge.

Chapter 56 - Jennet

30th January 1778

'Ey up, Jennet, how's thee faring?' Mary greeted me when I opened the door to her and the foggy moors afternoon.

'Mary! Has thee heard? That little bastard Robert Ramsgill's dead!'

'Aye, lass, I've heard.' Mary sat at my new table with a sigh.

'Ain't it grand? Happen there is a god after all!'

'Jennet, thee can't go round saying things like that! How many times have I told thee to take care of thy mouth?'

'Oh, who am I going to say it to? Thee's only one that speaks to me!'

'Peter Stockdale.'

'What? Oh him, he won't say nowt.'

'Aye, lass, he will. He were at church this morn, telling all who'd listen that thee rejoiced when thee heard.'

I were stunned into silence. I had thought he liked me, now he were spreading gossip?

'Well, that means nowt. No bugger could blame me, not after he raped me and burned this house.'

Mary sighed. 'Folk'll believe what they want to believe. Little Rob Ramsgill were a *Ramsgill* – no one can afford to speak ill of the Ramsgills round here, no matter what they might think. And thee, well . . . a fallen woman, turned mad, who turns herself into a wolf at night and curses innocent village folk.'

'But . . .'

'But nowt! I've told thee over and over to take better care! Folk are easily afeared and now they're afeared of thee!'

'But . . .' I tried to interrupt the sermon again, but she had not finished.

'I don't like the way they're talking, lass, I really don't. I'm afeared myself.'

'Thee's frit of me too?'

'Not *of* thee! *For* thee! By heck, lass, thee can be dense sometimes!'

I said nowt. I had no idea what words to use.

'That young man of thine went straight from here to Richard Ramsgill yestern – thee knew he'd been defying Ramsgill to aid thee, don't thee?'

I nodded, smiling to myself. I had loved that he had gone against Richard's wishes.

'Well, Ramsgill didn't want to know at first, sent him on his way.'

I smiled again.

'Will thee stop grinning, lass! This is serious! Stockdale had whole church up in arms this morning – including Ramsgills, all of 'em. Nobody can talk about owt else.'

I stopped smiling and stared at her.

'Aye, and they're there still, talking and crying. No one's left the place, only me, and I don't like it, lass, I really don't like it.'

Something caught my eye and I got up and walked to the window.

'They've left now,' I said.

'Eh?'

In answer I nodded at the window and Mary joined me.

'By heck,' she said.

It looked like the whole village had come; Ramsgills leading the way, looking grim – even Richard.

The villagers behind carried lit torches in the fog, and the sound of their voices singing about Christ chilled me. I spotted the curate up in the front, leading the hymn. I gritted my teeth.

I glanced round. There were no way out by the front door – if I ran that way, they'd soon be on me. I barred the door instead, then the window, and looked for something to use as a weapon.

I threw a handful of dried rosemary on to the fire for protection and uttered a quick prayer, then picked up the poker and turned to face the room.

Chapter 57 - Jennet

The door rattled. 'Open up!'

'Thomas Ramsgill,' Mary said to me. I nodded; I knew his voice well enough to recognise it.

'Jennet Scot, open this door, or we'll break it down!'

I did not move.

'Lass, the window!' Mary pointed. Smoke curled around the wooden shutter.

'No!' I screamed. I dropped the poker, grabbed a bucket half full of water, and threw it at the wood of both front windows. I picked up the full bucket and soaked the door, then poured water at the base in case they tried to shove a burning stick through the gap at the bottom.

'What's thee saying, lass?'

I glanced up and gritted my teeth. I had been praying to Mam to protect me and turn the villagers away, but had not realised I had been speaking aloud. Even Mary might mistake my words for a curse. '*The Lord's Prayer*,' I said. I could tell she did not believe me.

The door shuddered. Mary grabbed my arm, and I almost screamed. They were trying to break it down. Another hymn started up outside as whoever it were threw himself against the door again.

I shook Mary off, and hurried over to the few herbs I had been able to salvage from the garden, and which hung from the chimney breast – it were the best place for them to dry out, which increased their potency. I made my selection and threw them in the pestle and mortar as the door shuddered again.

Muttering an incantation as I ground – bugger what Mary thought now – I walked over to the door, then scattered the mixture at the wood.

'What's thee doing, lass?' Mary had backed away from the door – and me.

'It's a protection spell – 'twill help door stand firm,' I replied, too scared to lie now, then screamed as the shutters of both windows crashed open. Two men hoisted themselves through the gaps before I could react further – Peter Stockdale and Matthew Hornwright.

Peter grabbed my arm and I stared at him in astonishment.

'What's thee doing?'

'Stopping thee before thee hurts any bugger else.'

'Peter, I ain't hurt nobody!'

Matthew unbarred the door then threw it wide open and Peter said, 'Tell it to them!'

I tried to pull away from him, but he did not loosen his grip. I threw the rest of the herbs into his face and he swore, then slapped me.

'Thee'll regret this day, Peter Stockdale! Thee'll rue the day thee betrayed me, thee mark me words!'

He slapped me again and shook me, and I realised he were afraid. I laughed.

'Jennet, no! Thee's only making things worse!'

I stared at Mary. 'There is no worse than this!' I told her, then turned my attention back to Peter, but other arms grabbed me and my hands were pulled roughly together and bound.

I screeched and tried to pull myself free, but could not break the bonds.

'Calm down, Jennet. This'll go easier for thee if thee's calm,' Richard Ramsgill said.

I turned to face him and his brothers.

'How is this going to go easier for me?' I asked, nodding at the door. Dusk were falling and all I could see were flame from the torches; all I could hear were voices raised in the praise of Jesus as my neighbours surrounded my house and watched my humiliation and fear.

Richard Ramsgill did not answer, but looked away.

Thomas grabbed my arm and pulled me through the door.

'Thomas Ramsgill! What's thee doing? Where's thee taking her? She's done nowt!' Mary shouted.

'The moors,' Thomas replied, not looking at either Mary or myself. 'She cursed young Rob to his death. We've had enough. She loves the moors so much, we're taking her to them.'

I felt cold inside and planted my feet on the ground. I would not help them by walking. Thomas pulled me and I fell. I cursed, unable to break my fall.

'She's going to turn into a wolf!' someone cried.

'Stop her! Stop her curses and witchcraft! Don't let her go now!'

I recognised the voices and shouted the names out, grinning at the terrified screams.

I were pulled to my feet, still spitting names of people I had once counted as friends – Susan Gill, Marjory Wainwright, the Granges, the Smiths, Fullers, Weavers – until a slap stunned me into silence. I stared into Richard's face and shook my head, trying to tell him that I had done nowt, but his expression were cold. He did not care.

Chapter 58 - Jennet

Richard and Thomas dragged me to the lane and heaved me on to a waiting cart.

'Walk on,' the driver said to the horse, and I froze in panic. That were Digger's voice. They had me on the back of the gravedigger's cart.

I scrabbled to sit up as the cart jerked forward. 'Stop! I ain't done nowt! I didn't do it!'

Nobody answered; just carried on singing:
'Praise God, from Whom all blessings flow;
Praise Him, all creatures here below;
Praise Him above, ye heav'nly host;
Praise Father, Son, and Holy Ghost.'

'Richard, Thomas, please! He had an accident, that's all! I didn't hurt him! I didn't do owt!'

'Liar!' Margaret Ramsgill shouted and pushed her way to the cart. 'You killed him, Witch, with your curses and ill wishing!' She spat at me. 'You killed my baby!'

'Come on, Margaret, don't fret theesen. She'll pay for what she did to our Rob.' Big Robert Ramsgill took his wife by the shoulders, glanced up and threw his own spittle in my direction.

They walked beside the cart in grim silence, Rob's sister Jayne between them, and would not look at me further. I glanced at Big Robert as he tried to keep up; he stared straight ahead. There were no point trying to convince him of my innocence. My eyes drifted to Jayne. She stared at me, her gaze unwavering and full of hate. If anyone were a witch here, it were her.

'Curate! Curate! Thee's a Christian man – thee can't let them do this!'

He glared at me and raised his finger to point. 'Thee let Devil in, lass, only the Lord can help thee now.'

'I didn't!' I screeched. *Why would they not listen? How can I make them see?* I grabbed the side of the cart as best I could as we turned on to the path over the moors to try and stop myself being thrown around with its jolting. I spotted Peter in the gloom, carrying a torch and singing at the top of his beautiful voice. I had used to love hearing him sing at church; now he were singing for my destruction.

Then I glimpsed another figure trying to push through the crowd.

'Mary! Mary help me! Please, Mary!'

The look she gave me were so worried, so despairing, that my voice dried up. I watched her catch up to Big Robert Ramsgill and plead with him. He shook her off so violently she nearly fell. I bowed my head and let the tears fall. 'Mam, help me,' I whispered.

The cart jerked to a halt, and I glanced up. It were full dark now, but I knew these moors so well, I could see exactly where we were by the flickering light of a hundred torches. There were only one place on't moors with a single oak tree amongst heather. Hanging Moor.

Thomas and Richard climbed on to the cart and pulled me to my feet.

'Stop this, please stop! She's nowt but a young lass! Don't do this!'

I tried to smile at Mary, my sole defender in this mob.

'Aye, young she may be, but she's dangerous, and we're all in danger if she lives.'

I glared at Peter Stockdale.

'Aye,' a chorus of voices rang out.

'She's not dangerous, thee daft beggars!' Mary were

angry now. 'She's had an hard life, losing her pa and mam the way she did. If anyone's dangerous, it's him!' She pointed at Richard Ramsgill. 'Taking advantage of a young lass in trouble, it's shameful.'

'She bewitched me, caused me to come to her,' Richard protested with an anxious look at Elizabeth.

'Oh ballocks! She did nowt of sort! She came to thy notice, thee fancied a bit of what she had, then thee threw her down when she fell into trouble for it. Thee's only Devil here!'

'Enough!' Thomas roared.

'Not nearly enough!' Mary shouted back. 'And what about rest of thee? Standing by like good Christian neighbours? Watching it all, gossiping and shunning poor lass! That's Devil's work an'all, not Lord's!'

'How dare thee! She barely came to church, holed hersen up in that house and roamed moors alone every night! She cursed hersen by letting in Devil and brought a curse down on whole valley!'

'Aye! She cursed Ramsgill and his flock drowned!'

'Of course she cursed Ramsgill!' Mary shouted back. 'Who amongst thee wouldn't have? He'd got her with child, threw her over and her babbies died! We all curse in grief – she weren't to blame for them sheep drowning!'

'Babbies?' Richard asked.

'Aye, babbies – twins – born dead, no thanks to thee!'

'So that's why she gave hersen to Devil – revenge!'

'No!' Mary screamed in frustration.

'Shut thy mouth, thee awd carlin! She killed my brother! Why's thee defending her?' The mob cheered Jayne.

'Come on, Missus, there's nowt to be done here.' John Farmer put his arm around her shoulders and tried to pull her away. He did not look at me. I understood he had to protect his wife. In this mood, the villagers would likely turn on Mary too.

'Enough of this! We all know facts,' Thomas shouted and everyone else silenced.

'Her curses have been heard and come to pass. We know she turns hersen into a wolf to worry our sheep – it only appeared after she'd lost child.'

'Children,' I said, quietly. He ignored me.

'And I myself heard her curse Little Rob, God rest his soul. There's no doubt in my mind she's a witch.'

'Witch! Witch! Witch!' the crowd of my neighbours and one-time friends chanted. I had no hope.

'Aye! That's right! Witch!' I screamed. Nowt could save me now, but I could hurt them as much as I could before they killed me. 'And how many of thee's drunk my potions? Whispered my spells? How can thee be sure they were to heal, or for love? Which of thee men can be sure thy woman ain't snuck a "love potion" in thy ale?' I glanced round at them, in triumph. 'Everyone here's cursed by my hands!'

Richard and Thomas dragged me further back on the bed of the cart so that I were closer to the tree. I looked up at the branch above me, then at Richard as he let me go. I pulled against Thomas, but he had me in a firm grip. Richard bent and picked up a coil of rope.

'And the Ramsgills carry the heaviest curse of all.' I spat the words out. 'All of thee bar one will be dead within a year.'

Richard threw one end of the rope over the branch.

'Only one son of Richard's will live.'

'Shut up, shut her up!' someone, Elizabeth I think, screamed from the crowd.

'Every generation, only one son will live, to carry on Ramsgill loss.'

Big Robert grabbed the other end of the rope and Peter Stockdale helped him secure it around the tree trunk.

'The Ramsgill name will bring nowt but death and grief!'

'Shut up!' Richard slapped me.

I glared at him, then at the rest of the villagers. They stood in horrified silence.

'This whole valley will suffer!' I could hear my voice, shrill and panic-stricken, but I did not care – it were my only weapon, once again. 'I call down a plague on thee – on to thy flocks and on to thy families! I call floods to sweep away thy homes, I call–' I gagged when a noose were shoved over my head and pulled tight against my neck.

'Thee'll regret this.' I did not know if anyone could hear me. Richard tested the knot, then spat in my face.

'Thee were not worth all this trouble, Devil's whore! Burn in Hell!'

The Ramsgills jumped down from the cart and left me standing alone. Hands bound before me; neck bound to the tree.

'Curse thee all–' The cart jolted beneath my feet and were gone. The rope jerked tight against my neck and I could no longer breathe. I kicked out, searching for somewhere to prop my feet, but found nowt but air.

I could feel the rope biting into my flesh, the tiny bit of air I could get into my throat rasping against it. My head swelled like moss put to soak. Surely my skull would burst through my skin. My eyes met Jayne's and she looked away from my gaze. No matter now, she would be joining me soon – one way or another.

Something grabbed my leg and pulled, increasing the pressure on my throat. Mary. She could only do one thing for me now, and hurry this up.

I gasped, but could not take in any air. I tried to scream, but could make no sound. Darkness closed in – a total darkness now, no torches to light my way. I succumbed to it, my last thought a promise to bring my curses to pass. I would destroy this valley. I would destroy the Ramsgills.

Chapter 59 - Emma

24th February 2013

I threw the notebook and quill on to the table in horror. No wonder Jennet was filled with enough hate to sustain her for two hundred and thirty years. I stared out of the window at the reservoir that covered the homes of the people who had hanged her, and shivered. Then had another thought, could I verify if her other curses had come to pass?

Old Ma Ramsgill's journal was on the desk and I fetched it, then sat down again. I had been writing so much that I hadn't read it when Mark first showed it to me; only glanced at the family tree, then taken it back as an excuse to see him – finding Kathy instead.

Half an hour later, I had my answer and I sat back and stared at Jennet's notebook. In 1780, after their sheep had been devastated by sheep scab, half the village, and all the Ramsgill's bar Richard's son, had died of typhus. It had taken her two years, but Jennet had killed them with her curse.

I put my hand on my belly. *What if these babies are Ramsgills? Will they die young? Or live to know nothing but loss?* An image of Alex and Hannah Ramsgill flashed into my mind. *What of them?* I picked up the notebook and crossed to the desk and computer. I needed to type up the manuscript as quickly as possible. *What if writing her story isn't enough?* I needed to get the book out there so people could read it.

*

Exhausted, I picked up the phone.

'Kathy? It's done.'

'Jennet's book?'

'Yes.'

'Thank God.' She blew out a big sigh into the phone and I winced. 'Can I read it?'

'Yes of course, I'll print a copy off. Would you mind popping down, though? I'm so exhausted I'm not sure I can make it to your house, even in the car.'

Kathy was full of concern. 'You all right? You sound, well . . .' she tailed off.

'Just tired. I've been up all night typing the manuscript up.'

'Well, now that it's done, life should get back to normal.'

'God, I hope so.' I tried and failed to stifle a yawn.

'I'll have to send Mark down. I'm up to my elbows in bread dough. If I leave it now, it'll be ruined.'

'Oh, ok,' I said, feeling awkward. I didn't want to see Mark, especially not with Dave away. But if Kathy trusted us . . .

'Are you sure?' Kathy asked.

'Yes, yes, it's fine,' I said. 'Thank you.'

'What for?'

'Well, you know.' Silence again.

'Yes. Let's hope this is it now and she can rest in peace.'

'Amen to that!' I said, put the phone down, then pushed myself up to go upstairs and start the printer going again.

*

The doorbell rang as I was on my way back down, and I opened it to Mark.

'Hi.'

'Hi.'

'Come through, there's a copy on the kitchen table.'

'Have you printed it off already?'

'Yes, this is the first copy. Take it, I'm printing another off for myself.'

I staggered and grabbed the table.

'Emma! Are you all right? Let me help you.' Mark grabbed my arm then put an arm around my waist and led me to a chair. 'Sit down. What's wrong?'

'I'm ok, just tired. I've been up all night typing, and, come to think of it, I don't think I've eaten anything since yesterday lunch.'

'Bloody hell, Emma, you're pregnant for God's sake!'

'I bloody well know that!' I screamed, and he took a step back. 'Sorry, Mark. I'm not myself at the moment.' I managed a small laugh.

'No, neither of us have been that for some time.'

'Kathy told me, about seeing Richard Ramsgill in you.'

I waited until he made the coffees and sat down. 'Do you think it's over now?'

He sighed. 'I don't know, Emma, I really don't.' He glanced at my belly.

'They could be Dave's.'

'They?'

I nodded.

He took a deep breath, then said, 'Hope so, for all our sakes.'

I sipped my coffee.

'So what happens now?' Mark asked.

'What do you mean?'

'With that.' He nodded at the pile of A4 pages. 'It's not a book yet is it?'

'No, not quite. Normally I'd send it to my agent, but that way it would take nearly a year before it's published.'

'That's too long!'

'I know. I'll go over it tomorrow when I've had a rest, make any corrections—'

'Corrections? Careful Emma, don't provoke Jennet by changing her story!'

I put my hand to my head and rubbed my forehead. 'No, you're right, I won't change anything, just format it.'

'Aye, ok. Then what?'

'I'll upload it to Amazon and Smashwords. It'll be published within the week.'

He sighed, 'That sounds grand. Can you not do it any quicker?'

'Not really, they have to review it and then it takes a day or two to go live, but it'll be out there as soon as possible, I give you my word.'

He nodded and looked relieved.

'My agent and publisher aren't going to be happy, but to be honest, I'm more scared of Jennet.'

'You'll sort them – tell them you had a nervous breakdown, or somebody stole the manuscript or something. Do you have to publish it under your own name?'

I stared at him, 'No, of course I don't!' I laughed. 'It's not my book, anyway, it didn't come from me, it came *through* me – from Jennet. I'll publish it under her name.'

I grabbed a pen, crossed out my name and scribbled *Jennet Scot* on the title page.

'There you are then.' He gulped his coffee. 'What'll you do with the money?'

'Spoken like a true Yorkshireman!' I was starting to cheer up. 'I'll put the book on for free or as cheaply as I can, at least at first – try and get as many copies out there as possible. Then, I don't know, we can always find a charity to donate any proceeds to. Maybe that counselling service Kathy's part of? Something that would help people today who are in a similar situation to Jennet then.'

'I suppose so.'

'I can't make money from this, Mark. None of us can. We can't exploit her – it might be enough to bring her back!'

He opened his mouth, presumably to argue, but was stopped by a deep rumbling noise.

'What the hell was that?' I screamed, panicking.

Mark's face turned white and he jumped up and ran to the door shouting, 'Kathy!'

Chapter 60 - Emma

'What is it? What was that noise?' I hurried after Mark and stopped in the open front doorway. Thick black smoke poured out of the Ramsgills' house. Mark was running towards the house, then he climbed the wall into the field.

I dashed back inside to the phone and called 999.

'Fire engine and ambulance! Wolf Farm has exploded! They're inside! Hurry!'

By the time I had answered all the operator's questions and made it back outside, Mark had reached the high wall surrounding his house and was trying to climb it. I shook my head. It was too high – it had been built to keep people out.

I grabbed the keys to the Discovery, jumped in and roared up the lane. I turned in a big arc at the road so I was facing the entrance to Wolf Farm, then floored the accelerator. I screamed at the impact with the gate, but made it through, slammed on the brakes and pulled the car to one side so the fire engine would be able to get in.

I got out of the car and screamed, 'Mark!' He had managed to get over the wall and was at the front door, fumbling with his keys.

'Stop, Mark! You can't! Wait for the fire brigade!'

'Kathy!' he screamed again. 'Alex, Hannah!'

I had been moving towards him to try and prevent him running inside, but stopped. His wife and kids were in there; he would not stay out here. At last, he got the door open. Thick smoke poured out into the fresh air and he ran in. I stared at the house in disbelief, not knowing what to do.

*

'Emma! Are you all right? What's happening?'

I turned and fell into Dave's arms. I spotted his car abandoned down the road, and realised he'd just arrived home.

'Oh Dave,' I sobbed. 'The house exploded! Mark ran up here and has gone in – they're all in there!'

'What you mean, Mark ran up here? Where was he?'

'At our place – picking up the manuscript.'

'Is that all he was doing?'

'Yes! Kathy was baking or something and couldn't come herself, she sent Mark to get the book.'

'It's finished?'

'Yes.'

'And then the house exploded?'

I nodded, mute, and we stared at the house for a moment. There was no sign of life.

'Oh, thank God.' Sirens and flashing blue lights heralded a fire engine, which pulled to a stop in front of the house. Firefighters swarmed from it pulling hoses and ladders from the machine, and one crossed to us. He held his arm out in a shepherding gesture. 'Please move back from the house.'

We took a couple of steps and stopped when he added. 'Can you tell me what happened?'

'It just exploded!' I said, still in shock.

'How long ago?'

'Uh, I don't know, fifteen minutes? I rang 999 straight away.'

'Is anyone inside?'

'Yes – all of them.'

'Two adults, two teenagers,' Dave added.

I screamed as another explosion tore through the house, and was thrown to the ground. Dave landed on top of me and the firefighter alongside. Debris rained around us and the air was filled with noise and heat.

After a moment, Dave's weight lifted from me and I saw

his mouth moving. I couldn't hear him. His mouth moved again, and I squinted, trying to lipread, then nodded. Yes, I was ok.

We got to our feet and stared at the house. There was no roof, only flame – and jets of water from the fire engine. I screamed. They were still in there.

'You have to get them!' I shouted at the firefighter. I could just about hear my words now.

'We have to make sure it's safe first, I can't risk my crew in another explosion. And you need to move back.'

'But Kathy! The kids! Mark!'

'We'll get them as soon as we can.'

I struggled to hear, it felt as if I were listening underwater or had been standing by a speaker in a nightclub for hours, but realised what he was saying.

'No! No, you have to get them out!' I screamed, and stepped towards him.

'Emma,' Dave's arms were around me. 'Hush, he knows what he's doing. Are you all right? The baby?'

I sagged against him, then doubled up in a scream as a pain ripped through me. *Please no, not again!*

The ambulance is here, they'll get her to hospital,' the firefighter said. 'I need to go and talk to my crew.'

Dave half pushed, half carried me towards the ambulance, but the paramedics met us halfway with a gurney and I was bundled on to it. I screamed at them to help Kathy and the others.

'She's had a hell of a shock, she was knocked down by the explosion and she's five months pregnant.' I heard Dave tell the paramedics. 'She's had a miscarriage before, please, save her baby.'

I tried to correct him – they were Jennet's babies, *Jennet's*, but I felt a prick in my arm and everything went black.

Chapter 61 - Emma

3rd March 2013

I blinked my eyes open and looked around in bewilderment. I was in a white room, with horrible green and blue checked curtains round the bed. No, not a proper bed, one of those hospital trolley things.

'Emma! Oh thank God!' Dave leaned over and hugged me. I gripped hold of him – hard.

'What . . . what happened?'

'Do you remember anything?'

'I remember an explosion and Mark ran out to get Kathy.'

Dave nodded. 'There were two explosions at Wolf Farm – they think there was a leak from the gas cylinders. Apparently they kept them in a small alcove off the kitchen instead of outside like they're supposed to. You know what a stubborn bugger Mark— Anyway, all it would have taken was a spark . . . Mark ran in to try and get the family out—' He stopped speaking.

'Are they ok, Dave?'

He shook his head. 'They think Kathy and the kids were in the kitchen when the first tank blew, they didn't stand a chance.'

'And Mark?'

'They found him cradling Kathy's body. The second explosion . . . well . . .'

'Tell me.'

Dave looked at me, his expression concerned, and held my hand. 'They're saying at the Stone House that he was blown apart, Emma. I'm sorry.'

'No!' I gasped. 'But, but you said he was cradling Kathy?'

'Yes, his arms . . . were around her.'

I stared at him in confusion, then realised what he meant, 'Oh! Oh! Oh!' I covered my face with my hands in horror and Dave hugged me again, then pulled me close to his chest as I sobbed.

When I quietened, he eased me back on to the bed and said, 'Emma, there's something else.'

I raised my eyebrows at him.

'The baby . . .'

'The baby? Oh no! No, not again!' My arm dropped to my belly.

'We think the fall from the second explosion . . . I'm so sorry, Emma, the babies are gone.'

'Babies?' So he knew, then.

'Yes.' He took my hand. 'Twins.'

We stared at each other for a moment, then I nodded, feeling numb. I didn't know how to react. They hadn't been my babies, they were Jennet's, but my body had let them down – killed them. At twenty three weeks. Again. *Will I ever be able to give birth to a living child?*

'So she's taken them all. Writing her story wasn't enough. She killed *all* the Ramsgills.' I started to cry again. 'Those poor, doomed babies. None of this was their fault, and they didn't even get a chance to live. How bitter and twisted must she be that she'd kill her own babies too? When we thought we could break Jennet's curse, I never imagined that this would happen. The babies. Poor Kathy, Alex, Hannah, Mark . . .' I broke off in sobs.

'I know, I know,' Dave said, his voice soft. 'None of us guessed that this might happen. She's been hellbent on revenge for 250 years. I guess that's enough to turn anyone to such evil.' He held me and stroked my back and head until I calmed.

'I know there's not much point now, but . . .' He pulled away, reached down and handed me a plastic bag. I looked inside and pulled out a book, wiping moisture off my face.

It had a picture of Thruscross on the cover. '*Thores-Cross* by Jennet Scot,' I read aloud, then looked at him.

'You published it?'

He nodded. 'To be honest, after everything that's happened, I was terrified she'd come back for you. I'm not taking any chances.'

Tears pricked my eyes again and I hugged him. Then I pulled back. 'Is it over?'

'I don't know, Emma. I hope so, I really hope so.'

I nodded. That was all we could do. Hope and pray it was over. There was nothing left for her to take. The Ramsgills were gone. Wolf Farm was gone. Her story was published.

I picked up the book again. 'Hang on a minute, it takes days to get a proper book, how long have I been here?'

'Just over a week.' I glanced at Dave in surprise. 'You had to have an operation because of the babies, and then you wouldn't wake up.' He nodded at the book. 'It was all I could think of to do. It's a bit rough, you might want to redo it properly later, but I did my best.'

I nodded. 'You did well – it worked, thank you.' I leaned forward to wrap my arms around him and held him tightly, fighting tears. He had saved my life.

After a couple of minutes, I sat back and ran my hands over my belly once more. The babies had been Jennet's and Richard Ramsgill's. They had never been mine, yet I still felt their loss. Damn Jennet for making me go through this again.

'Emma?'

I looked up at Dave.

'I was starting to believe I could finally be a mother, that it would actually happen.'

He smiled. 'You still can be. The doctors still say there's no reason you can't give birth. We can try for a baby if you want to.' His voice sounded tentative, as if he hardly dared to make the suggestion.

I regarded him a moment, then nodded. 'Yes,' I said.

'Jennet lived in fear and isolation, and look what it led to. It's time to live in hope.'

'Oh, Emma.' Tears ran down Dave's face and I hugged him as a nurse bustled into the room.

'Well now, look who's awake!'

Epilogue – Emma

9th June 2014

'Here we are – home!' Dave said as he pulled the Discovery on to the drive. He twisted in his seat. 'Her first car ride. How is she?'

'Took it like a pro.' I grinned, then tickled our daughter's chin. 'Didn't you, Louise?' She was beautiful. Only three days old, she had Dave's blue eyes and my smile. I could hardly believe it, we were a family at last. I gazed into my husband's eyes and we grinned at each other.

He got out of the driver's seat and opened the back door. I loosened the seatbelt holding Louise's carrier, and Dave picked it up to lift her out of the car. I glanced past him at Mark and Kathy's house.

'It looks like a haunted house again,' I said.

Dave turned to stare at it. Derelict once more; no roof, no glass in the windows or doors in their frames, only the garden wall was still sound. 'But it isn't,' he said. 'No ghosts here, they're all at rest.'

'I hope so.'

Louise burped and I lifted her down from my shoulder.

'Was that good?'

She gave another small burp and I giggled at her, then stood and carried her over to the cot.

'Your first night at home, I hope it's a good one, darling,' I whispered, laid her down, then pulled her blanket up to her chin and froze.

I heard it again and ran, screaming for Dave. Louise

matched my screams with her own and I picked her back up, holding her close as I ran from the room.

'She's still here! Jennet! I heard the bells! Dave, she's still here, I heard them again! The church bells!'

Dave charged up the stairs and I ran into him in the office. 'She's not having Louise, Dave, she's not! I don't care what I have to do, Jennet is not taking Louise!'

He grabbed hold of me and held us tightly. 'Shh, Ems, shh. She's not here, she can't be.'

I stiffened in his arms. 'Did you hear that? Church bells! I'm telling you she's back!'

Dave said nothing.

'Dave! Did you hear them?'

He nodded slowly, and my blood ran cold. Part of me had hoped I'd imagined the sound.

I pulled away from him and looked into his eyes. He looked as scared as I felt.

'You didn't hear them before. If you can hear them now, then she's definitely coming for us!'

'Ems.'

'Dave, what are we going to do?'

'Ems!'

I stared at him, then realised. 'You *could* hear them before, couldn't you?'

He nodded.

'But you made out I was mad!'

'I'm sorry, Ems, I couldn't believe what I was hearing.'

I had already pulled out of his embrace; now I stood before the windows, watching the darkness. I turned to speak, then spotted something on the coffee table.

'The inkpot!'

'What?'

'Jennet's inkpot!' I rushed over and grabbed it, still holding Louise close. 'It's this thing! This is why she's still here!'

'Then we need to get rid of it.'

'No, we have to give it back to her. Bury it in the ruins of Wolf Farm.'

'No, somebody else might find it. We'll take it to the dam, throw it into the reservoir.'

I paused, then nodded. 'Yes, that's a better idea.'

The next morning, after breakfast, we put Louise into her baby carrier and strapped her into the backseat of the Discovery. I had the inkpot in my pocket. We drove across the dam to the car park and took Louise out, still strapped in her carrier, and walked down to the dam.

Halfway across, we stopped, and Dave put Louise down on to the pavement. We leaned over the parapet of the dam and stared at the reservoir.

It looked calm and beautiful; the wind rippled the surface and a flock of Canada Geese came in to land. I gave the inkpot to Dave – he had a stronger throwing arm.

'No, you have to do it, Em.'

I looked at him for a moment, then nodded. He was right. Jennet had come into our lives because of me, because I had found this inkpot twenty six years ago. I was the only one who could break the connection.

I took the inkpot back from him and looked at it one last time. Then I stepped back, leaned back and flung it as far as I could.

There was a small splash, and a few ripples spread across the water, then disappeared.

'Is that it? Do you think she's gone?' I asked Dave.

'Hope so.'

'It seems such an anti-climax.'

Dave smiled. 'What did you expect? Thunderbolts from the sky?'

'No, of course not, just . . . something. Something to tell us she's gone.'

Dave put his arm around me and stood in silence, watching the still waters of Thruscross. 'I think in this case, nothing is much better than something.'

I nodded and we turned to go home.

That evening, Dave came upstairs with me to put Louise to bed. I leaned down to put her in her cot, then paused.

'What is it?' Dave asked.

'Shh, I thought I heard something.' I stayed still and listened.

'What?'

'Nothing. It's nothing.' I smiled and glanced up at my husband. 'I can't hear anything.'

❧ THE END ❧

For more information on the full range of Karen Perkins' fiction, including links for the main retailer sites and details of her current writing projects, please go to Karen's website:
www.karenperkinsauthor.com/

If you would like to contact Karen and/or join Karen's mailing list to be kept updated with news, upcoming releases and special offers, please go to:
www.karenperkinsauthor.com/contact

Author's Note

Thruscross Reservoir does exist, and covers the drowned village of West End – one of a number of small hamlets that made up the parish of Thruscross. The sailing club also existed and I spent a very happy childhood there – even finding an old inkpot built into a tumbledown dry stone wall by the "haunted house". I was fascinated by it being in the wall, and knew at the time that one day I would write a story about how it came to be there – although I didn't expect it to take thirty years.

I have worked hard to be as accurate as possible with the landscape, village and way of life, and most of the farms and buildings I mention do (or did) exist – although I do admit to a little poetic licence on occasion. The residents, however, are wholly fictitious and in no way represent the real life inhabitants of the township of Thruscross and its hamlets – past or present.

My apologies to The Stone House Inn. I have enjoyed many delicious meals there over the years – and have always been offered a warm welcome along with a full and varied menu.

The lyrics, *'Praise God, from Whom all blessings flow . . .'* are taken from the hymn: *Awake, My Soul, And With The Sun* by Thomas Ken.

Acknowledgements

Many thanks to everyone who has helped me with their time, information and editorial skills; in particular Peter Mutanda, Lesley Taylor, Chris White, Christina Robinson, Glen Beale, Claire C Riley, my fellow authonomites and the writing group, as well as my friends and family for your constant and highly valued support and encouragement.

A massive thank you also to Cecelia Morgan, whose eye and quite simply amazing talent have created such a fantastic cover. I am so proud to be working with her, and so lucky that *Thores-Cross* carries her work.

About the Author – Karen Perkins

Karen Perkins is the international award-winning and bestselling author of six fiction titles in the Valkyrie Series of Caribbean pirate adventures and the Yorkshire Ghost Stories. All of her fiction has appeared at the top of bestseller lists on both sides of the Atlantic with over 200,000 downloads so far.

Her first Yorkshire Ghosts novel – *The Haunting of Thores-Cross* – is a silver medal winner for European Fiction in the 2015 Independent Publisher Book Awards, and *Dead Reckoning: A Caribbean Pirate Adventure* reached the top 50 in the UK Kindle chart as part of *The Hot Box* set that also included work by international bestselling thriller authors David Leadbeater, John Paul Davis and Steven Bannister.

See more about Karen Perkins, including contact details, on her website:
www.karenperkinsauthor.com

Karen is on Social Media:

Facebook:
www.facebook.com/karenperkinsauthor
www.facebook.com/Yorkshireghosts
www.facebook.com/ValkyrieSeries

Twitter:
@LionheartG

Fiction by Karen Perkins

<u>Yorkshire Ghost Stories</u>

Parliament of Rooks: Haunting Brontë Country
Knight of Betrayal: A Medieval Haunting
The Haunting of Thores-Cross

To find out more about the full range of books in the Yorkshire Ghost Series, including upcoming titles, please visit:
www.karenperkinsauthor.com/yorkshire-ghosts

<u>Valkyrie Series</u>

Look Sharpe!
Ill Wind
Dead Reckoning

To find out more about the full range of books in the Valkyrie Series, including upcoming titles, please visit:
www.karenperkinsauthor.com/valkyrie

Knight of Betrayal:

A Medieval Haunting

1170, Canterbury Cathedral.

Four knights break sanctuary to brutally murder
Archbishop Thomas Becket for their king, Henry II.

Running from their crime, the four knights - Hugh de
Morville, William de Tracy, Reginald FitzUrse and Richard
le Bret - flee north to Knaresborough Castle where
Morville is overlord. Initially celebrating ridding their king
of the pest that Becket had become, they find themselves
increasingly isolated as the Church and public opinion
turn against them.

2015, Knaresborough, North Yorkshire.

August is FEVA time - a celebration and festival of the
arts. The local amateur dramatic group has been accepted
to perform a play of their own creation: *Knight of
Betrayal,* based on the events leading up to Becket's
murder.

Taking the honour very seriously, they work very hard to
get into character - but are they channelling more than
just the characters of the knights they are portraying?

As the group of friends begins to disintegrate, concern
becomes certainty - this is one opening night that will
never be forgotten as life in the small Yorkshire market
town of Knaresborough tumbles into horror.

Read on for an excerpt from
Knight of Betrayal by Karen Perkins:

Knight of Betrayal

Chapter 1

Saltwood Castle

29th December 1170

'This is our chance. You heard the King's words,' Sir Reginald FitzUrse said. 'Becket has shamed him.'

'He called us all drones and traitors for allowing Becket to get away with it,' Sir William de Tracy said.

'Yes!' shouted FitzUrse, and slammed his fist against the table to emphasise the word. The four men sitting with him flinched at his exuberance. Sir Reginald FitzUrse, or The Bear as he liked to be called, resembled the ursine creatures he was named for in more ways than one. Large, hairy, loud and strong with a temper to beware of, his friends and vassals were afraid of him, although were eager to please him – even the mature yet impressionable Sir William de Tracy. Sir Hugh de Morville exchanged an exasperated glance with Sir Ranulf de Broc – the overlord of Saltwood Castle and the knights' host.

'No one has avenged me,' FitzUrse quoted their king, Henry Plantagenet of England, leaning forward now and staring at each man in turn. 'No one has avenged me,' he repeated.

'A clear plea,' Broc, FitzUrse's master in the King's household, agreed. 'King Henry raised Thomas Becket from a low-born clerk to Archbishop of Canterbury, for God's sake, and look how he has repaid him.'

Tracy nodded with enthusiasm. 'Yes! He excommunicated l'Évêque, Foliot and Salisbury, and for no good reason.'

Broc glanced at him in annoyance. 'As I was saying, two bishops and the Archbishop of York excommunicated and damned for eternity for crowning the Young King.'

'Well, his father, King Henry, still lives.' Morville tried to calm the rising tempers as Broc signalled to his steward to refill the jugs of fine Rhenish wine. 'It may be customary for a king to crown his successor before his own death in Normandy, but it is rare in England. Only King Stephen did it, and that was just to spite the Empress Matilda.'

'It is King Henry's prerogative!' FitzUrse slammed the table again, and Sir Richard le Brett – still a boy – steadied the now full flagon of Rhenish, then proceeded to empty it into goblets. Morville sighed as he watched Tracy down half in a single gulp.

'Yes,' Tracy slurred. 'It's nothing to do with Becket. It would not surprise me if Becket meant to depose the Young King and try for the crown himself.'

'Always was an ambitious bastard,' Brett agreed, then picked up a bone and noisily sucked the marrow from it.

'Are you sure we arrived on England's shores before Mandeville and Humez?'

'Yes, I have had my men patrolling the coasts to slow them down. They failed me when they allowed Becket to beach from France. They will not fail me again.'

'How can you be so sure?' FitzUrse asked, pointing a half-eaten pheasant leg at his host.

Broc laughed. 'Oh, I can be sure. One captain lost his

head – the rest all want to keep theirs.'

Morville drained his wine, once again regretting FitzUrse's choice of ally. The other men laughed, and Morville realised they were well into their cups. He poured more wine and drank again – in their cups may well be the only way they'd survive this day.

'So we shall beat them to Becket?' Tracy asked.

'We have to,' Broc said. 'If they arrest Becket, they shall receive all the accolades – the two of them already hold more castles and titles than the five of us put together. If we can take Becket to the King, he will surely be indebted to us and who knows what his favour may bring?'

'Then what are we waiting for?' FitzUrse roared, pushing himself to his feet. His fellow knights followed suit, throwing down the remains of the meat they'd been gnawing on and draining their goblets.

The men-at-arms seated in the hall below shoved as much meat in their mouths as possible before following their masters to the stables. Half an hour later the company of over a hundred armed men cantered through the imposing towers of the castle's gate and took the road to Canterbury.

While Broc garrisoned his men in the town, FitzUrse, Morville, Tracy and Brett – along with a small retinue of their most trusted vassals – clattered through the gatehouse to the Archbishop's Palace and dismounted in the courtyard.

Morville glanced at his companions, still concerned at the glazed eyes which the three-hour ride had done nothing to clear.

FitzUrse produced another wineskin which he passed to Tracy after taking a large slug himself. 'Are you ready for this?'

'We need to disarm,' Morville said before the other knights – still focused on the wine – could reply.

'Disarm? God's blood, Hugh, we are here on the King's business.'

'This is a house of God – the Archbishop will have mere monks, priests and clerks about him. No men-at-arms and no weapons. We shall not need arms to arrest him.'

'He is correct,' said Brett, 'we can kill him with our bare hands if necessary.'

'Richard!' Morville was horrified. 'We are not here to kill him, merely to arrest him and take him to King Henry to deal with as *he* sees fit.'

'If necessary, the boy said. If necessary,' FitzUrse jumped to his sycophant's defence.

'Why should it be necessary?' Morville asked.

'Thomas Becket stands against not only the Young King, but King Henry himself. He has just returned from exile. Look what he has done already, who knows what he would do when called to account? We must be ready for anything.'

'But we leave swords and mail here,' Morville insisted. Despite FitzUrse's bluster, as Baron of Burgh-on-the-Sands, Sir Hugh de Morville held the highest status amongst the four men.

FitzUrse hesitated, then succumbed to him. 'Very well, if it shall make you happy. Arms and mail stay here.'

Mauclerk, Morville's clerk, helped the knights out of their heavy hauberks and mail hoods and piled the armour, along with their long blades, under a nearby mulberry tree. 'They will be safe here with me,' he said.

FitzUrse glanced round the knights. William de Tracy in particular looked nervous and vulnerable without his arms or armour. Despite his thirty seven years, he appeared younger with a boyish clean-shaven face, copper curls and slim build. At this moment, if one ignored the lines of worry around his eyes, he appeared a child.

FitzUrse passed him the wine. 'Who are we?' he called.

'The King's men,' the other three chorused.

'*Who are we?*' FitzUrse shouted louder.

'*The King's men!*'

'*WHO ARE WE?*' Louder still.

'*THE KING'S MEN!*'

'Á Henry Plantagenet!' FitzUrse roared, and the others joined in, the wineskin forgotten and trampled on the cobblestones.

FitzUrse crossed to the door of the great hall and banged his clenched paw upon it. 'In the name of the King, open up!' Then again, and again, the other knights joining in the cry and the thumps on the door – even Morville was carried away now with the purpose of their mission.

'Thomas Becket, in the name of King Henry, permit entry or we shall break down this door!' Tracy yelled, then stumbled back at the sound of bolts being drawn.

Knight of Betrayal is available now

CPSIA information can be obtained
at www.ICGtesting.com
Printed in the USA
LVOW12s2236310517
536513LV00006B/400/P